# GNOME COMING

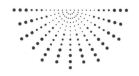

## WARD PARKER

MAD MANGROVE MEDIA

# GUARD GNOME

O nce again, the ghost woke Missy. Don Mateo of Grenada, 400 years dead, crashed into a chair in Missy's bedroom. He wasn't some clever type of ghost, like a poltergeist, that moved furniture mischievously.

No, he was just a dork. A very awkward, uncoordinated ghost who couldn't seem to find his way around the bedroom in the dark even though that's precisely what ghosts are supposed to be good at. Did other people with an ancient ghost in their house have the same problem?

One of her cats, she couldn't tell which, hissed.

"What is it?" Missy asked. "Why are you stumbling around my bedroom?"

"The gnome is missing," the ghost said in his heavy accent of archaic Spanish.

"What gnome?"

"The sentinel garden gnome in the front yard. The one we enchanted."

Missy groaned as she remembered. The gnome, made with

some heavy plastic-like material, was the stereotypical folklore character. It was about a foot tall and had a huge white beard, a pot belly, a pointy red hat that curved halfway, and an impish smirk. The previous owners of the house had left it behind in the garage. It would have stayed in there forever if Don Mateo hadn't suggested otherwise. She had never had the desire to decorate her front lawn with a garden gnome.

"What do you mean he's missing?" Missy asked. "Someone stole him?"

"No, I believe he left on his own accord."

Missy sat up in the bed, finally abandoning her hopes of going back to sleep. It was just before dawn and she had gone to bed only a couple of hours ago after her overnight shift of caring for her vampire home-health patients.

"How could he leave on his own accord?" she asked, irritated. "He's not even a he. He's an it, an inanimate object."

The spell they used was supposed to turn him into an alarm of sorts, not much more than a motion detector and sensor for magical intruders. All he was meant to do was make loud noises. Not run off somewhere.

They had tested the spell, and it had worked. Missy had left through the back door, went around the house, and approached it from the street. The gnome stood next to an areca palm beside the walkway to her front door (and boy was she embarrassed to have it there in full public view). It would detect anyone who trespassed while armed with magic, so she had conjured a weak protection spell around herself and strolled into the driveway.

The gnome began screeching. Loudly. It had a high-pitched, rodent-like voice, pretty much what you'd expect from a gnome. It babbled in an indecipherable language until Missy turned off the gnome's guarding spell. She then asked Don

Mateo to help her alter the spell so it only created audio in her head, not in public where her neighbors would hear it.

Apparently, the alteration did not go well.

"I admit we screwed up, to use the contemporary parlance," Don Mateo said.

"No, *you* screwed up. You're the one who directed me how to create the spell."

Don Mateo had written the spell instructions in the back pages of a grimoire centuries ago when he was alive. He was a wizard who fled Spain with the Spanish Inquisition at his heels. He had filled the addendum to the grimoire with a blend of European sorcery and the natural, earth magick practiced by the shaman of the native Timucuan people who had lived in north Florida when the colonizers arrived.

The grimoire was *The Book of Saint Cyprian*, which later belonged to Missy's father, a witch who died when she was an infant. Someone had stolen the book from her father, and it ended up with Bob McGuinn, the Arch-Mage of San Marcos. After Missy retrieved the book, on written instructions from her father, Bob had tried to steal it back. He even tortured Missy to get her to hand it over.

The spell, intended to turn the garden gnome into a guard gnome, was another line of defense in case Bob came back. Her other lines of defense were a protection spell over the house and your typical burglar alarm. She didn't have a dog, and her cats were worthless at protecting the house, so adding the gnome—no matter how kitschy it was—seemed like a good idea.

Until now.

Missy considered using various locator spells to find the gnome. But those took a lot of effort, more than was worth to find a corny lawn ornament.

As if he had read her thoughts (and she sorely hoped this ghost didn't have that ability), Don Mateo said, "We *have* to find it."

"Why? Maybe it will end up in the garden of someone who actually enjoys gnomes."

"You added magick to it, and, clearly, that magick malfunctioned. We have no idea what that gnome is capable of doing."

"We know it's capable of leaving my property," Missy said. "Maybe that's a good thing."

A distant siren pierced the pre-dawn silence.

"It is never a good thing to release magick unsupervised into the world."

"Well, it's very difficult to find an inanimate object with a spell."

"The gnome is no longer inanimate," Don Mateo said.

The siren was much louder now. In fact, it sounded as if it was in her neighborhood. Probably an older resident having a medical scare.

"Well, I suppose I can send out some tracer spells," Missy said. The tracers were tiny bursts of magick she broadcast in great numbers. They behaved like drones, flying at low altitude in search of an image she focused upon in her mind. If they made a match with the image, they pinged her with the general location. Usually it required additional magick, a more powerful locator spell directed at the tracer's location, to pinpoint the precise location of the search subject.

Flashing lights seeped through Missy's window blinds as the emergency vehicle directly passed her house.

"Oh my," Missy said.

"Perhaps the gnome didn't go far after all," said Don Mateo.

"Do you mind? I need to get dressed."

The ghost faded away. She still didn't feel very private

knowing his presence was near. But she got out of bed, took off what she called her old-lady pajamas, and threw on a T-shirt, surfer shorts, and flip-flops. They considered this *haute couture* in Florida.

A police car was parked, strobe lights flashing, down the street in front of Old Man Vansetti's house. A deep rumbling behind her came from a red Fire-Rescue ambulance and a fire truck driving down the street to park in front of the police car. Paramedics popped out. Something appeared to be wrong in Vansetti's front yard.

Normally, Missy wouldn't be nosy about her neighbors. But this morning she had a heavy, foreboding feeling. The old man lived alone, after all. She hurried toward the emergency scene. Old Man Vansetti's dog, Fifi, was barking furiously.

Missy arrived at the Vansetti front yard and realized the white Pomeranian was on a leash still attached to her owner's hand. The old man lay face up beneath his mango tree, next to the hand-lettered sign he planted each fruit-bearing season warning he would shoot mango thieves. His head was tilted back, and he was not moving. His face was blue.

A softball-size mango protruded from his mouth.

There are dozens of varieties of mangos, but none are small enough to fit in a human's mouth. And Mr. Vansetti's mangos were large. How this one fit into his mouth was a mystery.

"He ain't breathing," one of the paramedics kneeling beside him said. "No pulse either."

"We have to get the mango out of his mouth anyway," his female partner said, "to show we at least tried."

While they busied themselves trying to pry the fruit from Vansetti's mouth, Fifi continued barking at the emergency team.

"Can someone take this dog out of here?" the first paramedic asked.

The police officer, a young, skinny rookie, struggled to keep a straight face while he pried the leash from Vansetti's hand and led the dog a short distance away. Fifi kept barking.

"You think he was staring up at the tree with his mouth open and the fruit fell and landed in his mouth?" the cop asked.

"Nah," said the male paramedic, a serious type with a buzz cut. "I think he fell face down and landed on the mango, then rolled over while he was being asphyxiated."

"Both theories are far-fetched," the female paramedic said. "What are the odds a mango would go right into his mouth?"

"My theory is the best one. It took a lot of force to get this thing rammed so far in his mouth. He must have fallen on it," her partner said.

"Maybe someone else rammed it in there," the cop said.

"Either we use the jaws of life, or we'll have to make incisions to get this mango out," the female paramedic said.

"Now the question is, who would choke a guy to death with a mango?" the rookie cop pondered.

None of them had noticed Missy hovering there. Something caught her eye across the lawn, beyond the lights from the emergency crew.

Two garden gnomes stood side-by-side in the middle of a flower bed, silhouetted by the faint rays of the rising sun. One of them she recognized as always being in this garden—a chubby gnome holding a tiny shovel.

The other gnome was hers. Its eyes appeared to twinkle in the reflected light.

What was it doing here, trying to make friends? Did it have anything to do with the mango incident? And how was she going to take it out of here? She couldn't simply pick it up and leave while the cop was here. Was she supposed to explain that it had run away from home?

When the lawnmower-like roar of the jaws of life splintered the night and the work of mango extraction turned ugly, Missy left the scene. Fortunately, Vansetti's immediate neighbor, a retired widow, agreed to take care of Fifi.

Missy waited at home until the police and fire-rescue teams drove away and the last of the curious neighbors departed. Then she strolled back down the street to Old Man Vansetti's house. No additional police vehicles had arrived and there was no crime-scene tape, so they must have judged the death to be an accident and not murder-by-mango.

The sun was bright in the sky by this time and Missy walked across the front yard to the flower beds, sweating already. She picked up her gnome and brought it home. She didn't sense any trace of magick in the gnome. It was simply a tacky decorative object that had somehow behaved like a naughty child and run away.

A dreadful question lingered in her mind: Did the gnome have anything to do with Old Man Vansetti's death? It should have been a preposterous question, but not when magick and Missy were involved. She hoped the gnome being on the accident scene was a coincidence. After all, how could a poly-resin figurine, barely over a foot tall, murder a man by jamming a mango in his mouth with enough force to asphyxiate him?

She considered the possibility that Vansetti saw the gnome crossing his lawn and was gaping in astonishment when the mango dropped from the tree into his mouth.

Yeah, too ridiculous. Although the police seemed to accept the accidental death thesis, it was too much of a stretch for her. The mango had to have been forced into the old man's mouth not by gravity but by the physical effort of an individual, by black magic, or by a combination of the two.

She arrived home and placed the gnome in the garage, in the same corner behind a bag of mulch where it had always been.

Don Mateo would have to help her fix whatever had gone wrong with the sentinel spell they had used on it. But first she needed to shower and get dressed for real.

When she returned to the garage forty minutes later, the gnome was gone.

"Don Mateo!" She shouted. "Get your phantasmic butt in here!"

Summoning a ghost without using a spell was difficult. What are you going to do to it if it doesn't obey you—kill it? No, ghosts are way beyond worrying about any live person's approval. It was their afterlife and they would do as they pleased. In fact, very few would bother to talk to a person as much as Don Mateo did.

"Come on, be a good ghost. Please?"

He was a no-show. She went back inside and as she passed through the laundry room, she entered a cloud of Renaissance-era cologne and ripe body odor.

"Thank you for coming," she said to the empty air.

"I was enjoying some eternal rest," said his voice behind her.

She turned around. The ghost was sitting on her dryer. His apparition was faint, as if he was sleepy.

"The gnome was at a neighbor's house, standing next to his own garden gnome. The neighbor was dead, asphyxiated by a mango. I brought my gnome home, put it in the garage, and now it's missing again."

"Egads! What are you going to do about it?" Don Mateo asked.

"What am *I* going to do about it? This sentinel spell is *your* spell from *your* grimoire."

"When I was alive, I used that spell only twice. Once was on a bronze figurine sitting on a table outside my quarters to prevent my spell books from being stolen. It turned out that no one wanted to steal my spell books. They stole the figurine instead."

"Because your spells don't work," Missy said.

"The second time was with a statue of Saint Francis, that stood outside of the building that housed my quarters, to warn me if the Inquisition was coming. And it worked perfectly."

"You escaped?"

"Exactly."

"Why do I sense there's something else to this story?" Missy asked.

"Well, the Inquisition had not been coming for me. They were coming for someone else in the building. But when they saw the statue had been enchanted, and my neighbor mentioned that I was a wizard, the Inquisition came after me. And I had to leave the country."

"I see."

"The point I was trying to make," Don Mateo said, "was the spell never misfired before. I suspect someone else's magic is involved. You said your neighbor has a gnome? You had better see if that gnome is still there."

"Why?"

"Why was your gnome visiting with it?"

Missy bolted out the door and jogged the few houses down to the late Old Man Vansetti's house.

Vansetti's gnome was gone.

Missy reported this to Don Mateo.

"Just as I suspected," he said. "Whatever strange turn the

sentinel spell took in your gnome, has now been passed to your neighbor's gnome."

"Do you think his gnome killed him, rather than mine?"

"I would wager you are correct. The morphed version of the spell can spread to another host like a disease. If this spreads to other garden gnomes, I'm afraid you living people have a bit of a problem on your hands."

"Wait, it's not only our—"

The ghost of Don Mateo disappeared. Ghosts could do that —run away when things got difficult.

## 2

## HUNTING PARTY

On Tuesdays they played bridge. On Thursdays they turned into wolves and ate possums. Those were just two of the regularly scheduled events of the Werewolf Women's Club of Jellyfish Beach. Josie Denton was their president. The lycanthrope retirees were always busy with fundraisers, road beautifications, fashion shows, and, of course, potluck lunches.

They were an earnest group of women that numbered around two dozen depending on whether the snowbirds were in Florida or up north. The club's mission was to have some fun, do some good, and kill some prey.

Attacking humans was forbidden, though. At Josie's age, there was little pleasure in that anymore. What she still enjoyed was loping through the woods in wolf form at speeds her aging human body could never approach. She savored her heightened sense of smell and the complex pattern of odors the forest and its creatures created.

Every week she looked forward to this evening of bonding

with her fellow she-wolves. There was nothing finer than howling at the moon, hunting as a pack, cornering their prey, and tearing it to shreds.

Possums tasted much better than raccoons. Rabbits were a rare delicacy. Every so often they'd take down a deer, but at their age the women didn't want such a heavy meal. Sometimes they quarreled over that and it was up to Josie, as the alpha of the pack, to decide whether to pursue any deer they scented.

Josie sat in the front seat of the community's shuttle bus as it rolled through Jellyfish Beach toward their hunting grounds. When the women were younger, they would have shifted into wolf form at their beachfront condos and run the eight miles to the undeveloped land west of town. But today, in their sixties, seventies, and eighties, they rode in comfort, gossiping the entire way. Once they entered the woods, they would shift.

"Oh. My. Lord." Thelma Lou said, staring into her smartphone. She was two rows behind Josie. "The Unger tract has been sold to a developer!"

The Unger tract was their destination. The large parcel of land lay in what used to be an agricultural region. In recent years, the sprawling suburban developments spread west of Jellyfish Beach like a contagion, driving up land prices and turning vegetable fields into communities of cookie-cutter homes with gated entrances and elaborate fountains.

Aside from some fields of tomatoes in the north of the property, the Unger tract was dozens of acres of virgin forest— native slash pines, palmettos, and scrub oak. It teemed with wildlife. Josie knew nothing about the Unger family except that they lived elsewhere in the state and they apparently didn't know that elderly werewolves trespassed on their land.

Hearing that the land had been sold to a developer put an

icy grip on Josie's heart. At her age, she didn't like anything at all gripping her heart.

"Where did you read that?" she asked Thelma Lou.

"*The Jellyfish Beach Journal.* They keep sending me these news alerts on my phone. I don't know how to shut them off."

"What's going to happen to the land?" Mary Beth, sitting across the aisle from Josie, asked.

Everyone already knew the answer: Developers don't buy land to make nature preserves.

Thelma Lou studied the article on her phone. "Oh, my gosh. Four hundred single-family homes, two hundred condos, and retail," she said. "Our land is being destroyed."

"It's not our land," Mary Beth said. She was a smart aleck know-it-all from Kentucky.

A tear rolled down Josie's cheek. "We can't let this happen. We have to stop it somehow. Does the article say if the county approved the plans?"

"Um, let's see. . ." Thelma Lou scrolled down her screen. "The county commission is voting next week to change the zoning and approve the deal. They had a public hearing last week." She shot a disapproving look at Josie. "Why were we not at that hearing?"

"I didn't know anything about it," Josie said. How would she know?

Clucks of disapproval came from the rear of the bus.

"If we lived out there, we might have seen if they posted notices. Who goes out there except on Thursday nights?"

No one answered. The energy on the bus was dark as everyone contemplated losing their cherished hunting ground.

"We could start going to the state forest that's only an hour away," Josie offered meekly.

The clucks of disapproval were louder this time.

Though Josie was the alpha of the club, her seat of power was wobbly. Women at this stage of life were difficult to push around, and the same applied when they shifted to wolf form. The only thing these werewolves had in common, aside from their wolf instincts, was the fact they had all been infected with lycanthropy by being bitten by other werewolves in their past. None had become werewolves by being cursed or using sorcery. None of them were evil. An evil werewolf would never join their women's club, anyway.

Josie stood up in the aisle just behind the driver. The petite, eighty-seven-year-old was hardly an imposing figure, but her voice was loud enough to set off car alarms.

"Ladies, listen up," she commanded. "Tonight, we will hunt as planned. Tomorrow we will begin protesting against the development."

"Why don't we just kill the developer?" Tanya asked.

"I'm not even going to dignify that with a response," Josie said.

Tanya growled and looked out the window.

THEY WERE FAR west of Jellyfish Beach now. The shuttle bus passed occasional walled subdivisions, but the landscape was mostly flat vegetable fields and irrigation ditches that glimmered in the moonlight. At last, thick trees appeared on the horizon.

The bus turned left into a dirt parking lot and parked behind an abandoned building out of view of the road. Just beyond a small overgrown field, the forest began.

The signs were disturbing. A big, white sign mounted on four-by-fours proclaimed, "Coming soon: Fox Landing. Luxury homes by Loopi Communities." Josie knew there were only a couple of families of foxes living here, and the werewolves left them alone. Soon, Fox Landing would be devoid of foxes.

Small, hand-lettered signs on sticks dotted the edge of the road vowing, "Stop the sprawl," "No more homes," and "Don't ruin our neighborhood."

"Ignore the signs, ladies," Josie said as she stood at the front of the bus. "Remember, tonight we hunt. Tomorrow, we protest."

The bus driver, a resident of Seaweed Manor named Kevin, exited the bus and walked a discreet distance away. He was also a werewolf, but wouldn't be shifting tonight.

Inside the bus, the Werewolf Women's Club disrobed, carefully folded their clothes, and placed them on their seats. While shifting during a full moon was involuntary, most werewolves can shift at other stages of the moon. All it takes is intense concentration until an ancient switch is flipped inside their brains.

And then they began their transformation.

First came the growls spreading throughout the bus. Some growls were painful ones. Changing into a wolf-like creature required enormous musculoskeletal changes and it could hurt, especially if you were older and suffered from arthritis. They say ibuprofen helps when shifting.

The first sign of transformation is the sprouting of coarse fur all over your body, except for your palms and the soles of your feet. Your canine teeth grow longer, and both your upper and lower jaws push outwards, a condition known as maxillary and mandibular prognathism. Your fingers extend in length, and long, sharp nails protrude from beneath your normal nails until your hands become deadly claws. But you keep your opposable thumbs, so your hands still work like hands.

Your upper body grows in size and strength while your arms extend slightly in length, allowing you to run on all fours if desired. Though you could stroll about as a biped if you wanted. Alas, you don't grow a tail, so you can't run in circles chasing it for amusement.

While the ladies were shifting, Kevin patrolled the immediate area to make sure no one else was around. He stuck his head in the open door and gestured for the werewolves to exit.

Josie reached the dirt parking lot first and stood, human-like, a short distance away until all the she-wolves gathered around her. They looked strong and magnificent, unlike their frail human bodies. Of course, their dark-brown fur was heavily streaked with gray and white. And many refused to remove their cherished earrings.

Tanya whined as she examined her forepaws and saw that her manicure from the previous day had been ruined by the sprouting of wolf claws. Josie barked authoritatively to get the pack's attention. With a transformed mouth and tongue, human speech was possible but very difficult.

Josie yipped sharply, dropped onto all fours, and trotted toward the forest, her pack close behind. Once they were inside, they stopped and raised their heads, drinking in the scents.

The forest in this part of Florida was not one of massive trees forming a canopy above. Spindly slash pines stood the tallest and the low, wide saw palmettos provided plenty of cover for game. In the wet, marshy parts of the tract, cypress trees grew. The only drawback, in Josie's opinion, were the ticks that ended up in her fur.

Electricity sparked through the pack. They had all picked up the scent of possums foraging in the underbrush a couple hundred yards away. The pack took off, Josie in the lead, loping across the sandy ground, adroitly leaping between the saw palmettos, sniffing the air to pinpoint their prey's movements. There were three possums—plump, mature ones.

This was what they lived for: the thrill of the chase and feet pounding across the forest floor. No one needed to make a meal of the possums. In fact, Josie had dined on a chicken pot pie for dinner earlier. It was the unleashing of their wolf-hybrid instincts that gave each member of the pack satisfaction. These instincts cannot be denied.

Some of Josie's werewolf neighbors at Seaweed Manor were partly in denial of their morphed genes that resulted from the virus that had infected them when they were turned into werewolves. These folks tried to pretend they were normal retirees until the one night a month their genes forced them to shift into their true selves. But Josie knew that to be happy, you had to embrace your truth.

Tanya, to the right of the pack, barked an alert: One of the possums had scrambled up a nearby pine. She and a few members of the pack circled the base of the trunk, guarding it. Eventually, they would use their human-like hands to climb the tree. Josie and the rest of the pack raced onward through the trees.

A second possum scrambled up a tree ahead and a cluster of the women werewolves stopped running and paced anxiously below it. Josie, Thelma Lou, and Mary Beth continued their pursuit of the third possum. The ground was slightly higher, and the underbrush was thicker. Josie plunged through a beautyberry shrub and her legs became entangled in the branches.

Mary Beth reached her and tilted her head questioningly. Josie barked for her to continue the pursuit. Mary Beth raced onward, Thelma Lou just behind her. Josie shook herself free of the shrub and tried to catch up.

The gunshot shattered the night. Mary Beth, leaping over a saw palmetto, yelped and jerked in midair, landing on her back.

Josie whined and rushed to her pack member. Mary Beth lay in a patch of ferns, convulsing, her coat drenched in blood.

Her neck arched backwards in agony, her elongated, muzzle-like mouth opened, and her lips stretched tight against her fangs.

Mary Beth was dying.

Instantly, her fur dropped off her body as she transformed back to her default human form. The change was much more rapid than a normal shifting. In less than a minute, Mary Beth lay naked among the blood-spattered ferns. An aged, feeble grandmother with liver spots on her skin. No longer a magnificent beast.

She abruptly went still. And was gone.

Josie arched her back and howled. Her agonized cry echoed through the slash pines.

Thelma Lou approached, whining.

"Who did this?" she asked, her words difficult to understand in her non-human mouth. "A hunter?"

"A regular bullet wouldn't have killed her," Josie said, "though some say if one strikes a werewolf directly in the heart it will kill. The wound is in her back. I don't know where the bullet traveled inside her body."

"I don't believe that," Thelma Lou said. "It has to be a silver bullet."

Josie's head swiveled, trying to catch the scent of their attacker.

"Then we're being targeted by a hunter of werewolves," she said.

3

CRYING WOLF

The rest of the pack converged in the forest around the fallen body of Mary Beth.

"Let me get her clothes from the van," Tanya said. "We can't leave her naked like this."

"No," Josie said. "We can't dress her. We have to leave her as she is, because this is a crime scene. We can cover her with a blanket, though. Please call 911 when you shift back."

Tanya trotted back to the van and the other she-wolves whined and nuzzled each other in grief, pacing the forest floor nervously. They would have to return to the van and shift soon before the police arrived.

Josie ran in the direction from which the shot was fired. She doubted the shooter would be around, but she wanted to pick up a scent. She searched toward the southwest but didn't feel confident about it. She also had no idea how far away the shooter had been.

She slowed her pace, moving her head from left to right, sniffing deeply. The forest held a rich tapestry of scents telling the stories of flora and fauna, rainfall and drought, birth and death, plenitude and hunger. Often during their hunts, one species or other would be in reproductive mode while others were dormant. She knew these woods well, but there was always more to learn.

A non-natural scent caught her attention. The harsh smell of rubber. There was no road or path nearby, so she doubted the scent came from an illegal trash dump. The rubber was on an item worn or carried by a human. Probably the shooter. No one else would be in the thick of the woods with no trail nearby.

The human in her compelled her to search visually as well, having better eyes than a true wolf.

That's when she saw the broken twigs and a spot on the ground where leaves and pine needles were scuffed aside. She planted her nose there and sniffed, but all she got was the acrid rubber scent. It blocked everything else.

So who would shoot at them? An errant shot from a poacher made the most sense, but why would a silver bullet have been used? She couldn't think of anyone who would want to kill werewolves, let alone believe in them.

Unless it was one of the few rogue cops who did believe in werewolves.

She wondered if anyone else knew that werewolves hunted here each week, such as someone who lived nearby. Or, even, the developer. She suspected a territorial individual who wanted to rid the place of werewolves.

A distant warning bark came from the north of the property where the parking lot was. She needed to return, shift back to human, and get dressed before the authorities arrived. She raced through the trees.

When she reached the spot where Mary Beth had been

killed, some ladies had returned there in human form. Kevin knelt beside Mary Beth's body and sobbed violently.

"No, no, no." He moaned with grief.

Kevin was a stocky widower with a bald head (which strangely remained bald when he shifted) and a hairy chest that spoke of an abundance of testosterone. He and Mary Beth had regularly flirted, but Josie never thought much about it. Wouldn't you know it, there was more going on in Kevin's heart than she had realized.

Tanya placed her hand softly on Kevin's shoulder and squeezed. He didn't seem to notice and kept crying, bringing tears to the rest of the group. Josie whimpered, then loped back to the van. Fortunately, no first responders had arrived at the parking lot yet, so she safely entered the van and induced herself to shift.

Shifting back to human was a little less painful than shifting to wolf. Maybe that's why werewolves are so vicious—they're cranky.

Another misconception about werewolves is that their fur shrinks back into their bodies when they shift to human. No, hair doesn't grow backwards. It sheds. And when you shed your entire coat, except for the hair on your scalp, it creates a monumental mess. Normally Kevin, or whoever was doing the driving for part-time wages, swept and vacuumed the van after the ladies dressed. But Kevin was too distraught tonight.

As Josie pulled on her palm-tree print jogging suit, she looked at the piles of wolf hair covering the floor of the van. This would be hard to explain to a cop, she thought.

And at that moment, the flashing lights of emergency vehicles arrived. It was the Crab County Fire Department and sheriff's deputies. The property was outside the Jellyfish Beach city limits, so it was odd that one detective identified himself as working for the city police department.

Detective Affird wasn't a charm machine.

"Aren't you ladies too old to be going on nature field trips this time of night?" he asked while the crime-scene technicians trooped into the woods to examine Mary Beth's body.

"We're not too old to do anything," Josie replied.

"Trespassing is a crime no matter what age you are."

Josie had almost forgotten about the trespassing part. On such a large piece of natural land, it was hard to remember that someone owned it, especially when there was no longer any sign of human activity.

"I see you live at Seaweed Manor," Affird said, pointing to the large logo on the van.

"You observed correctly, detective."

He smirked. "You have some rough characters living there."

The realization struck Josie. This might be the cop who executed a werewolf drug dealer in Building A. If so, he might be here tonight because he suspected that she and the Women's Club were werewolves.

"Yes, we have some unsavory characters there, due to the unfortunately low prices of some of the condos. Most of the residents are fine, upstanding people, such as the members of our Women's Club," she said, straightening her posture with pride. "We perform many acts of philanthropy for the community."

"Be that as it may, do you know of any reason someone would shoot one of your members?"

"I'm assuming it was a hunter, a poacher."

"The victim's name is Godfrey?" he asked.

"Mary Beth Godfrey, yes."

"Had she made any enemies?"

"Not that I know of. Certainly not anyone who would shoot her to death." Mary Beth didn't have a lot of fans in Seaweed Manor. But a seventy-five-year-old widow is not someone you'd feel the need to shoot. Unless life insurance or a will tempted you.

"Where was Ms. Godfrey in the hierarchy of your community?" the detective asked.

Lord, he was asking pointed questions, Josie thought. He was barely hiding the fact he knew about werewolves.

"I don't know what you mean," Josie said. "We're all very easygoing at Seaweed Manor. We don't have a hierarchy."

People who think they know about werewolves imagine they all live together in packs dominated by alpha males. Maybe criminals, biker clubs, and cultists do. But most werewolves are more human than wolf. They have to hold down jobs, raise families, go to church. Then they retire to Florida. Being a werewolf is more of a hobby, like the Werewolf Women's Club.

Josie was the president of the club, and if you want to call her the alpha, go right ahead. But senior women don't get pushed around by anyone and they were hardly subservient to Josie. And at Seaweed Manor, Harry Roarke was the president of the HOA and an informal leader of the community. But he didn't act much like an alpha.

In fact, at Seaweed Manor, the women were the dominant ones. Partly because they were in greater numbers, due to their longer life expectancy. And partly because of feeling liberated after a lifetime of being slaves to child raising, old-fashioned husbands, and discrimination at the workplace. There were plenty of men who still tried to behave like alphas, but they were weak and defanged at their ages. It was their wives and the single women who now called the shots.

If Detective Affird was floating the theory that Mary Beth

was murdered in a contest for domination, he was barking up the wrong tree.

TWO DETECTIVES from the sheriff's department took statements from all the club members, while Affird listened in. The detectives repeatedly asked the women if they were involved with any of the groups protesting the plans to develop the land.

"We didn't even know about the development until I read an article about it in the news," Thelma Lou told them.

Of course, only twenty yards away at the edge of the road were the dozens of hand-painted signs decrying the planned development. The problem was, the club had never bothered to come up with a common excuse to explain why they were out here at night, at least not since Josie first joined.

After each woman was interviewed, they allowed her to get back on the shuttle bus. Each admitted to her friends she had used a different lie when questioned.

Josie had said they were coming home from a late church event and some of the ladies desperately needed a bathroom break. She couldn't explain why Mary Beth had gone so far into the woods to pee and why she was naked. Thelma Lou told the detectives the women wanted to view the night sky far from the light pollution of the city. Tanya had said they came to worship the moon.

At least they were united when it came to answering one question. It turned out one deputy had searched the bus for the murder weapon while the women were being interrogated. Of course, he didn't find it, but he did find piles and piles of graying animal fur on the floor. What, the deputies asked, was that all about?

The women's identical answer: The bus had been used as a mobile dog-grooming service for fundraising earlier in the day and hadn't been cleaned yet.

The explanation was just odd enough to be believable. Much more believable than the truth.

When the Werewolf Women's Club finally left the Unger tract and headed home, Kevin was at the wheel but still wiping away tears. Josie's anger at the senseless killing made her heart race. She wanted someone to pay. And she knew, as alpha of the pack, she had to take action or lose the confidence of the others.

She stood up from her front seat and faced the club members.

"Ladies, our club is about friendship, philanthropy and fun. We're good werewolves doing good in the world. But we will not face this tragedy lying on our backs, exposing our throats submissively. No, we're getting revenge."

The women growled in unison.

"We will find out who killed Mary Beth and make them pay. We won't let them get arrested and then get off claiming self-defense. No, we're going full vigilante. Whether the murderer works for the developer or is a crooked cop, we will find them. And tear their throat open."

The women howled in agreement.

⚜

MATT ROSEN WAS a staff writer at *The Jellyfish Beach Journal*, an attendee of boring city commission meetings, an unofficial chronicler of Florida Man stories, and a career-stalled forty-eight-year-old. He immediately took an interest in the murder report. He had been covering the community reaction to the

Unger tract development, which was largely negative except among real estate professionals. A murder on the property really spiced up the story.

According to the police blotter, the murder happened around 9:30 p.m., so the victim probably wasn't protesting at that time. He theorized she was an activist intending to vandalize the property to make a statement. But when he cross-checked the residential address of the victim, he realized she lived at Seaweed Manor.

Where the werewolves lived. Where his friend, Missy Mindle, had patients as a home-health nurse.

Perhaps Mary Beth Godfrey's death had nothing to do with the controversial development. Maybe she was killed because she was a werewolf.

Okay, even if she was a werewolf, that might have had nothing to do with why she was murdered. But what if it did? Since just about everyone who wasn't crazy or a genre-fiction author didn't believe in werewolves, there weren't many people who would intentionally murder one.

He knew such a person. Not long ago, he was in the condo owned by a werewolf drug dealer when the shifter was summarily executed by a cop. A cop who wanted to rid Jellyfish Beach of the supernatural creatures no one believed in.

Detective Fred Affird.

4

## NOT NEIGHBORLY

A lison was a hedge fund manager, and she was filthy rich—a redundant statement for sure. She just moved into a custom-built, multimillion-dollar home on Lake Algae, in the northern part of Jellyfish Beach. The neighborhood had been full of tidy middle-class homes built in the 1950s and '60s. But lately, every time one of those homes went on the market, an investor bought it and promptly flattened it to the ground, replacing it with a giant, modern structure filled with electronics and luxury appointments. A home like Alison's.

Alison was single, in her thirties, and worked long hours so she was rarely home. But her three wiener dogs were. After long days left alone, they were spoiled by their owner who didn't bother to discipline them. She let them roam unsupervised in the backyard facing the lake, and they regularly went to the next-door neighbor's property to urinate and defecate. Alison didn't care.

The neighbor was an elderly woman named Freddie or

Frieda or something like that. Her home, a ranch from the '60s, was neat and the landscaping well maintained, but the woman had a horrible love for kitsch. For tacky decorations and dopey, cutesy lawn ornaments.

There were dumb nautical-themed statues everywhere, from pelicans to leaping fish. What Alison found most offensive were the large taxidermy trophy fish mounted on the side of the house facing hers and around the pool area: sailfish, marlin, and lots of fat bass. Alison couldn't imagine Freddie or Frieda fished anymore at her age, but the monstrous fish were everywhere.

And the worst of the tackiness were the garden gnomes. There were too many for Alison to count. They were in the front yard, the side yards, the backyard. They were in garden beds, next to shrubs, and perched on concrete benches. Some of them had miniature lawn tools and posed as if they were digging or raking or chopping. Quite a few had sagging gnome-pants that revealed their butt cracks. During the holidays, a dozen additional gnomes—Santa gnomes—appeared. Freddie or Frieda's lawn service faced a nightmare to mow and trim in this gnome obstacle course.

Alison deeply regretted moving into a neighborhood without a homeowners association with rules against tackiness like this. She wished the old lady would die or move away. She couldn't wait for the house to be knocked down and the gnomes to be ground to dust by a bulldozer. She chuckled every time Wayne, her male wiener dog, lifted his leg and peed on a gnome.

Freddie or Frieda had been friendly when Alison moved in, but Alison had no time or interest in getting to know this neighbor. Nowadays, the only interactions they had were when the old lady called out from her backyard, asking Alison to keep her dogs from pooping in her petunias.

"Sorry, but your little landscaping guys can clean it up," Alison would say as she let her dogs in the house.

But tonight, things took a terrible turn.

Alison had returned late after dinner and drinks with colleagues. She let the dogs out, and was pouring herself a glass of rare Bordeaux, when a yelp of pain came from the backyard.

She rushed outside.

Her three dogs came running out of the neighbor's yard as fast as their stubby little legs would allow. But Wayne was lagging behind.

Her poor little baby was limping!

She let the dogs in and examined Wayne. He was favoring his left rear leg. There was no visible injury, and the leg didn't appear to be broken. But it clearly hurt poor Wayne.

She stormed next door and rang Freddie or Frieda's doorbell repeatedly and then banged on the door. Finally, it opened. The old woman wore a bathrobe and a sleeping mask hung from her neck.

"What did you do to my dog?" Alison shouted.

"I didn't do anything. I was sleeping."

"My dogs were in your yard and Wayne got hurt. I know you hate my dogs."

"Maybe he stepped on something sharp," the old lady said. "I would never hurt an animal."

"You hate my poor babies."

"I just want them to stop pooping in my yard. If you want them to be safe, build a fence and keep them in your yard. Now let me go back to sleep."

Freddie or Frieda closed the door. Alison considered

banging on it again, but decided not to. She might have to take Wayne to the all-night animal clinic.

Fortunately, when she returned home, Wayne was walking more normally. Alison finished her wine and went to bed.

ALISON AWOKE WITH A START. There must have been a noise. Before she drifted off again, she wondered why her wiener dogs weren't on the bed with her as usual. Maybe they were downstairs drinking water. She began to drift off again.

Wait—why was her bedroom door closed? She always left it open to allow the dogs to come and go. She got out of bed and navigated in the dark to open the door.

*Ow!* She stubbed her toe on something that wasn't supposed to be there. A dog toy?

She limped to the door, opened it, then turned on the light.

A garden gnome was in the middle of her bedroom floor. She recognized it as one of her neighbor's most tasteless: a gnome sitting on a toilet reading a book.

How the heck did this get here? One of the dogs must have dragged it in. The alternative explanation—that her crazy neighbor had invaded her home—was too disturbing to consider.

She picked up the hollow figurine made of some hard, plastic-like material. It was less than a foot tall and didn't weigh much. A dog could easily carry it if it found the right grip for his or her mouth.

Alison carried the gnome down her grandiose staircase. When she arrived in the family room, her dogs were staring at her from outside the sliding-glass door to the lakefront patio. She must have been drunker than she realized to have left them out there when she went to bed. She slid open the door and the three dogs rushed in as if their lives depended on it.

"Mommy is so sorry, my babies," Alison said in a baby-talk voice.

She went outside to the patio and, with all her strength, lobbed the gnome into her neighbor's yard. It collided with something when it landed, hopefully another gnome.

"Come on babies," she said to the dogs. "Let's go to bed."

She crawled into bed and the three wiener dogs jumped on top and curled up. Alison was asleep almost immediately.

She woke up again with a start. Her watch said it was two hours later. How did the door end up closed again? And the dogs were missing.

Moving across the room, her foot collided with something like before and this time she landed on the floor, cursing prolifically. She made it to a light switch and turned it on. Then gasped.

The potty gnome was back in her room. Along with two others: one that was toiling with a pickax and one that just stood there, glaring, with a curved, pointy red hat. She recognized the pickax gnome as one of Wayne's favorite targets for peeing.

How did they get here? She wasn't just confused; she was frightened. Someone was playing a horrible trick on her. It had to be that dreadful woman next door. Should she call the police, or have it out face-to-face with Freddie or Frieda?

The police would think she was nuts. And the old lady would just slam the door in her face and call the police herself. She put on her robe and headed downstairs to look for the dogs.

At the top of the staircase she stopped short. A low moan escaped from her throat.

Her long, magnificent staircase had a gnome standing on every step. Her neighbor's entire menagerie of kitschy figurines snaked up from the foyer. The butt-crack gnomes, the toiling-in-the-garden gnomes. Even the sweet, smiling gnomes. All staring up at her.

This was insane. This was sick. What kind of old nutter would break into someone's home to do this?

Alison ruled out confronting her neighbor. She pulled her phone from her robe to call 911.

A strange, high-pitched chattering came from behind her. It was vaguely human-sounding, almost like a Scandinavian language.

Something hit the back of her calves hard and her knees buckled, the world swayed, and she dropped her phone.

Then she went plunging down the staircase, tumbling head over heels.

THE BARKING of the wiener dogs outside of Alison's home all morning long concerned Freddie, especially since the rude hedge fund manager's Maserati was still in her driveway. Freddie rang the doorbell, knocked on all the doors, and finally called the police. When the medical examiner's van arrived, not long after the patrol cars, Freddie knew her instincts had been correct that something was wrong with Alison.

The good news was that the dogs were fine. Alison's family refused to take them off Freddie's hands, but a friend in Freddie's bridge group was happy to adopt them.

The weird thing was, Freddie's gnomes had all been moved around in her yard. None was in the place it was supposed to be.

# 5

# WHERE DID MY GNOME ROAM?

M issy cast the spell within a chalk-drawn magick circle on her kitchen floor. She didn't have much faith the spell would work, but she brushed that aside for the moment because she had to have absolute confidence in the spell while casting it for it to have any prayer of working.

She chanted:

*The gnome from my garden, so cute and wee*
*I now beseech thee to return to me*
*With power of the earth*
*With power of the sea*
*Each ounce my soul is worth*
*I now commandeth thee*

When she was finished, she broke the circle and went into the living room where she peered past the curtains into the night.

A new gnome sat beneath a palm tree near her driveway. The gnome was actually a used gnome she had stumbled upon at a thrift store. It gave her the idea of using it as bait to lure her enchanted gnome back home. This one was even cheesier than her original. It was beach-themed. Yes, a beach-themed gnome in a pink and green Hawaiian shirt, sunglasses, a straw hat, and a straw coming from its beard into a tropical drink in one hand.

It was guaranteed to dismay her neighbors.

But would it attract an evil gnome?

She had spent the last couple of days using magick to search for her wayward gnome. Her common method was to send waves of tracer spells across the city to look for something that matched the visual image in her mind of the gnome. She sent hundreds of tracers, which were low-powered blips of magick that flew untended like drones. If one pinged her, she would use its general location to focus a more powerful locator spell to nail down the exact location.

The problem was, her memory of her gnome's appearance was fuzzy. And, as she discovered, there were a whole heck of a lot of gnomes in Jellyfish Beach. Who would think gnomes were still so popular? Her tracer spells pinged her with gnomes everywhere from trailer parks to high-end neighborhoods, from apartment complexes to outdoor cafes.

She couldn't be sure if any of these was her gnome. And she needed to find her exact gnome so she could find a way to deactivate the sentinel spell that had gone wrong.

Even more disturbing, Missy was pretty sure her gnome's deadly influence was spreading.

The one time she thought she had located her gnome, she drove to a home in a wealthier part of town, using an aerial image of the home combined with a satellite-view map on the internet. Her gnome wasn't exactly the most unique-looking figure, but her location spell found it in the yard of a home on Lake Algae.

When she drove to the house, an ambulance, firetruck, and police car were in the driveway. Not a good sign. She took a gamble and parked along the curb. She tiptoed to the side of the giant new home and saw a group of four gnomes next to the swimming pool that overlooked a lake. They stood facing each other, as if in conversation, placed where they didn't belong, in a high-traffic area poolside.

A gnome with a curved, red, pointy hat did look a lot like hers. But she was too far away to tell for sure.

"Can I help you, ma'am?"

A young woman cop in uniform was behind her.

"Um, no thanks."

"This is private property. Are you a neighbor?"

"I'm just an acquaintance. Is everything okay with the homeowner?"

"I'm not at liberty to give out information," the cop said. "I have to ask you to move along."

"Sure, sorry."

Before she drove away, she grasped the power charm she always carried in her pocket, closed her eyes, and concentrated. Her astral consciousness probed the scene, feeling for magic.

It hit her almost immediately: black magic. That was interesting, because when she had retrieved her gnome from Old Man Vansetti's lawn, she hadn't sensed magic of any sort in it.

Later in the day, she returned to the house by the lake. The emergency vehicles were gone. She parked in the driveway next to a luxury car and went around the side of the house again.

The four gnomes were no longer by the pool or anywhere in view.

"Excuse me?" a voice called.

It was a woman on the other side of a hedge in the yard next door. She was a senior, dressed in a matching pink sweat suit, holding hedge clippers. Her home was an older ranch style, much different from the two-story modern home where Missy was trespassing.

Missy hadn't noticed when she was here earlier, but the woman's yard was teeming with garden gnomes.

"Hi," Missy said. "My gnome ran away, and I was here to retrieve it."

It was a crazy thing to say, but the woman was unperturbed, as if Missy was talking about a pet.

"What does it look like?" the woman asked. "Male or female? I ask that because they're usually male, but you see female ones sometimes."

"Male. Pointy red hat with a sharp curve, blue coat, wide belt, brown pants, boots with pointy tips. He has its hands on his hips and a grumpy expression," Missy recited, her memory of the gnome refreshed after having seen it beside the swimming pool. "I saw it back here today, but the police chased me away."

"I might have seen your gnome, but what you're describing is pretty much standard-issue gnome. Something's been going on with gnomes lately. All of mine got moved around somehow last night. Why would your gnome run away?"

"Um, I don't know exactly. It just has a habit of doing that."

The woman nodded with understanding.

"Did you remove the gnomes next to the pool?" Missy asked.

"No. There weren't any by the pool. Alison didn't own any gnomes. I don't understand why she didn't. She could have used some personality around this place."

"What happened to Alison?" Missy asked hesitantly.

"She passed on. And she was young, too, though not friendly. Heard she fell down the stairs."

Or was she pushed? Missy wondered.

"I don't want to be a pain, but do you mind checking in your yard to see if my gnome is there now?"

"Come around to the front, then, and we'll look around. My name is Freddie."

"Missy. Pleased to meet you and thank you for your help."

The first gnome they encountered was next to the mailbox, sheltering beneath a large stone toadstool. It wasn't her gnome. Freddie then led the way to a large oak tree. At the base of its trunk was a gnome-sized door and fake window. A chubby blacksmith gnome and a rare female gnome stood beside the door.

Nearby, at the edge of an island of ferns, a gnome with a tiny ax posed next to a miniature woodpile. A walkway of paving stones led to Freddie's front door. Running parallel to this was a walkway of miniature paving stones. Two gnomes in single file appeared to be trudging toward Freddie's home.

On the small concrete front porch was a gnome freak show. A stone bench held three gnomes of varying heights, each with a vertical pointy hat and white beard. On both sides of the door were gnomes brandishing garden hoes as if they were pikes. Behind those guardian gnomes were fake gnome doors, kind of like pet doors but, hopefully, these gnomes weren't allowed inside.

Freddie took Missy around the side of the house where gnomes popped up everywhere along the paver walkway, pushing wheelbarrows and sitting on tiny toilets. In the back-yard where fewer neighbors could see, things got truly out of control.

Freddie had a smaller, more conservative pool compared to Alison's next door. But it was as good as useless with all the gnomes ringing the edge. Beneath taxidermy fish mounted on the outside wall of the house were gnomes holding fishing poles, fighting imaginary fish. And Missy hadn't realized that there were so many bathing-suit-wearing gnomes one could buy. It freaked her out to realize there were enough people willing to buy them to make the products worth making.

Halfway down where the lawn sloped to the shimmering lake was what Freddie called her "gnome village." Gnome cottages, tiny pathways, faux stone bridges, Tudor-style shops and taverns were laid out in a veritable gnome paradise. The size of its population of gnome figurines would put some small human towns to shame.

"Oh, my," Missy said.

"Boats passing by love to stop and take photos," Freddie said.

This woman needed to be involuntarily hospitalized, Missy thought. But she smiled and nodded in appreciation of the world Freddie had created on a third of an acre of land.

"I haven't seen my gnome anywhere," Missy said. "Not that we were all that intimate. But I think I would have recognized it."

"You call him 'it' and not 'he'?"

"Yes. Like I said, I never had the chance to get to know my gnome. And now I'm afraid he's become dangerous. You said that someone moved your gnomes to different locations overnight?"

"Yes," Freddie said. "It was quite odd."

"How do you think it happened?"

"Well, I assumed a bunch of teenagers arrived by boat and played a prank on me."

"And your neighbor fell down the stairs the same night. Was that a coincidence?"

"You mean, did the teenagers kill her?"

"I'm just postulating," Missy said. "What about the gnomes?"

"What *about* the gnomes?"

"Do you think they could move about on their own?"

"Oh, I don't know. There does seem to be something magical about them," Freddie said. "Maybe it's just their cuteness."

Missy remained silent.

"Well, gnomes are like elves and dwarves," Freddie said. "They're fantasy creatures. Of course they're magical."

Missy still was quiet, hoping to allow Freddie to let it all out.

"They have those mischievous grins and twinkles in their eyes. They make you want to escape real life and be in their world, a world of the fairy tales we read as children. A land of forests and pretty villages, of princesses and knights and black-smiths. A land of magic. Right?"

They're made of plastic, Missy wanted to say, but she only smiled and nodded.

"I do sense something special in them sometimes," Freddie said. "Even though I bought them on the internet and at craft stores and garden centers. It's kind of like this cross I wear on my necklace. It's only sterling silver. It's just metal. But it repre-sents something so much greater than itself. It has a kind of power that way. Do you understand?"

"Yes," Missy said. "I believe in magic."

"Good!" Freddie said with excitement. "So you see what I mean? These little poly-resin figurines represent the magic of fairyland and so, in that way, they carry a little spark of it in them. That's what I mean about them being magical."

Missy actually took her seriously. Because somehow her sentinel spell had gone wrong and her gnome was now possessed with something evil. And it appeared to be spreading this perverted magick to other garden gnomes. Which, in turn, turned against their human owners.

Freddie's belief that there was something inherently magical in the gnomes she collected was probably only a human projecting her imagination upon inanimate objects.

But what if it was actually more than that? What if gnomes truly did have a magical essence? That would make it easier for whatever malevolent force her own gnome had to spread to these inanimate objects.

Magic was the art of manifesting the unbelievable. That's what made it so wonderful and worthy of dedicating her life to it.

But it was also what made this world potentially so dangerous.

If silly little garden gnomes from craft stores could come to life and murder human beings, we were in a lot of trouble.

Somehow, she had to find a way to solve this problem.

6

HARD SELL

J osie drove by the Unger Tract the next day with no particular goal in mind other than to see if anything was going on. Two workmen were nailing a large no-trespassing sign onto wooden posts beside the dirt lot where the shuttle van had parked the night before.

"I wonder if one of them did it," Tanya said from the passenger seat of Josie's giant, beloved, white 1977 Lincoln Continental, nicknamed "The Boat."

Josie hadn't wanted Tanya to come with her. Tanya was her biggest critic and was, as Josie put it, a little too "rough around the edges." But Tanya had been a close friend of Mary Beth and had insisted on being part of the amateur sleuthing—an endeavor that Josie now realized, in the cold light of day, wasn't likely to succeed.

On a whim, Josie braked suddenly and pulled into the dirt lot.

"What are you doing?" Tanya asked.

"Testing their defenses."

The two workmen in their yellow safety vests glanced at the car, but kept drilling screws into the sign.

Josie stepped out of the car and swiveled her head as if studying the setting for the first time. She then leisurely strolled toward the abandoned storage shed.

"Excuse me, ma'am," a worker called out. "Ma'am? You're not supposed to be here."

She stopped and looked at the men as if seeing them for the first time. She waved at them. And then continued walking toward the shed.

"Hey!" The man shouted. Josie ignored him.

He jogged over to her. "Ma'am, didn't you hear me?"

"Oh, good morning," Josie said. "No, I didn't hear you. I'm not wearing my hearing aids."

"This is private property. No trespassing," the man said. He was young, dark-haired, handsome. And gave off the air of low IQ. "Didn't you see the sign we're installing."

"Yes, that's a very lovely sign, and you installed it so nicely. I'm just here to check out the land."

"But this is private property. It's a construction site."

"I don't see any construction," Josie said. "I might be interested in buying a home here, so I wanted to check it out."

"They have a sales office for that."

"So what happens if I don't leave here?"

The worker showed his frustration. "We'll call the sheriff to arrest you."

"That seems excessive. Do you have security guards here?"

"Um, not at the moment, but we will."

"With guns?"

"Heck, I don't know. Probably. Are you going to leave now?"

"Yes, I think I will."

Josie got back in her car.

"That was quite a hunk of young manhood," Tanya said.

"Not very bright, though."

When Josie pulled out of the dirt lot onto the main road, she noticed a lone protester standing in front of a gated community across the street. The man held a hand-lettered sign that said, "Greed kills the earth." Josie stopped on the shoulder nearby.

"Don't tell me you're going to talk to that nutcase," Tanya said.

"You bet your booty I'm talking to him. We need leads. Don't you know anything about sleuthing?"

"I read mystery books."

"I'm glad to hear you're literate," Josie said as she stepped out of The Boat. "Excuse me," she said to the protester. "Are you here all the time?"

"Yeah, basically," the man said in a sad voice. "It's futile, though, now that the commission approved the development. But I'll stay. Maybe I'll make potential homebuyers feel guilty."

"Good luck with that," Josie muttered. "You ever see hunters on that land, or anyone with guns?"

"You didn't hear about the shooting last night?" he asked.

"The victim was our friend."

"Oh. I'm so sorry."

He sounded sincere to Josie. He was probably in his late fifties with a graying, bushy beard and a potbelly. He wore a wide-brimmed hat and a T-shirt that said, "Save the Everglades." Aside from willingly standing in the sun holding a sign all day, every day, he seemed fairly normal.

"Are you ever here at night?" Josie asked.

"No, I'm not *that* fanatical."

A car going by honked its horn, and the man brightened. He waved at the car.

"I was wondering if the developer had goons with guns patrolling the property," Josie said.

"I wouldn't be surprised. George Loopi is ruthless as far as I can tell. I've been fighting his developments for years, but he always wins. He has a lot of politicians in his pocket. Do you think someone working for Loopi killed your friend?"

"It's a strong possibility," Josie said.

"Why was your friend on the property at night?"

"Worshipping the moon."

"Well, I got roughed up once when I was protesting one of his developments. He destroyed some fragile wetlands with endangered species to build a golf course community. Some friends and I marched at the opening of the first model home and I got beat up pretty bad."

"By his goons?"

"By a seventy-year-old realtor named Susie. Don't ask."

"Where's the sales center for this development?" she asked.

"Go east about a mile and there's a shopping center at the corner of Avocado Road. It's in there."

"What's your name? I'm Josie."

"Frank."

"Can I have your number in case I need to reach you?"

He handed her a business card. It had a logo of a panther and said, "Frank's Friends of Florida. A non-profit." At the bottom was his name, Frank Fitzwhizzle, and his phone number.

She wrote her number on an old receipt from her purse and gave it to him. "Nice meeting you, Frank. Call me if you see anything suspicious going on."

THE SALES CENTER was in the corner of a new-looking shopping center, in between a supermarket and a sandwich shop. Josie parked nearby and watched the office. No one came in or out.

"Is it even open?" Tanya asked.

"I think so," Josie said. "They probably get most of their business on weekends, though. The people at this shopping center this morning are probably locals who aren't looking for a new home."

"So, Ms. Master Sleuth, what's your plan of attack?"

"I don't know. I'm making it up as I go."

"How is some salesperson going to know who killed Mary Beth?"

"They won't. We just need to learn more about the company, Loopi Communities. Hm, if we were younger, we could apply for a job with them."

"I'm only seventy-one," Tanya said, "and, like everyone tells me, I look much younger. I could easily get hired by this company as an accountant or even as a sales rep. But I have no need or desire to work. When Pete passed, we were set up nicely for retirement. I prefer spending my energies on philanthropic work."

What a crock, Josie thought. Tanya spent her energies gossiping and flirting with single men like Kevin.

"I have an idea," Josie said. "Come inside with me and follow my lead. You're going to be my financial manager."

"Wait, what?"

Josie got out of The Boat and strode across the asphalt to the storefront, Tanya scurrying to keep up with her. The door of the sales center beeped when Josie opened it. The place was not large. There was a desk with chairs facing it, a seating area with a coffee table piled with brochures, and large architectural renderings of the community and its home models covering the walls.

Josie noted a sign that said pre-construction prices started at just over a million bucks. That dwarfed the prices at Seaweed Manor which, although it was on the beach, was built in the 1960s and showed its age. Why would anyone live in a cookie-cutter community for prices like these?

A young man in a blue suit appeared from out of a back room. His skin had an unnatural tanning-salon hue. He had a short hairstyle laden with gel and an expensive smart watch that he glanced at.

"Good morning! Welcome to the future Fox Landing. My name is Chad," he said as he sized up Josie and Tanya. The two ladies wore outfits designed to impress other women like themselves, not a young social-climber like this fellow appeared to be. By his expression, Josie and Tanya did not impress him.

"I saw you pull up in your, um, vintage Lincoln. Are you two ladies thinking of buying at Fox Landing for yourselves?"

"I am," Josie said. "I'm Josie and this is Tanya, my financial manager."

"A pleasure," Tanya said with a dazzling smile, using all her charms to beguile Chad.

He wasn't interested and seemed skeptical that Josie would have a financial manager.

"Good. Please have a seat. Can I get you a beverage?"

Josie and Tanya sat on a leather couch and shook their heads in the negative to the drink offer. Chad sat in a chair opposite with the coffee table in between. He straightened his jacket.

"Fox Landing is the perfect place to spend your golden years," he said, "but there will be families with little children there, as well. Wealthy little children."

"Good. So my grandchildren will feel at home there when thcy visit."

Josie had three grandchildren in their twenties in Dallas. They rarely visited her. And they were not wealthy.

"Fox Landing will have an eighty-thousand-square-foot clubhouse with a media room, game rooms, performance spaces, and more," the sales guy said. "Olympic-size swimming pool. Putting greens. Gym. Jogging trails—"

"What about foxes?"

"Huh?"

"Foxes. It's called Fox Landing. Will any foxes live there? I believe there are some in the area."

"Of course not. Fox Landing will be meticulously land-scaped and safe for all pets."

"Tell me about the homes," Josie said. She enjoyed making this pretentious monkey dance.

"Of course. The entry-level model—"

"I want to see all of them."

"Certainly." He opened a presentation folder and spread five sheets across the top of the coffee table. "This is the Magnolia. Two bedrooms plus den. Now, this next one—"

"I'll take them all," Josie said.

"Take the brochure with you? Of course."

"No, the homes. I'm buying not just for myself, but as an investment. I'll have two of each, please."

Tanya's sudden intake of breath was loud.

"What? You're always harping on me to diversify my portfo-lio," Josie said to her.

The man's brown eyes looked confused, then opened wide as he calculated what his commission could be.

"Would you need financing? We have a partnership with a mortgage company."

"Nope. All cash. But I want to meet Mr. Loopi first, get a feel for his character, you know. I want to understand who's standing behind my investment."

"I'm sure that can be arranged."

Josie grabbed a brochure and stood. Inside the cover was tucked the sales guy's business card. Josie wrote her phone number on the back of it and handed to Chad.

"Tell Mr. Loopi I'll be waiting for his call."

⚜

"I CAN'T BELIEVE he fell for that," Tanya said as they walked toward The Boat.

"I'm not sure he did one hundred percent, but he will pass along my number to his boss, just in case I was legit. I wouldn't be the world's first rich old lady who drove an old car."

Josie unlocked the passenger side door and then walked around and unlocked hers.

Once they were inside and the air conditioning was running, Tanya asked what Josie's plan was.

"If you get him on the phone," she asked, "how in the world would you get him to tell you anything about Mary Beth?"

"I will lie through my teeth and see what happens."

"You're not as smart as you think you are," Tanya said.

"I don't have to be smart, just convincing."

# 7

## SNIFFING AROUND

J osie should have known better, she thought, as she answered the phone call from George Loopi. It had been days since she and Tanya had visited the sales office. Mary Beth's funeral had already come and gone. Josie had given up hope that he would call, and she assumed her subterfuge had failed. Either Chad never forwarded her number, or Loopi had ways of discovering it was impossible for her to afford to invest nearly twenty million dollars in his homes.

Tonight she realized she was wrong. He did call.

And the problem was, she was about to shift into wolf form.

The Werewolf Women's Club had found a temporary hunting ground in a small parcel of land within Jellyfish Beach. It was the Southridge Natural Scrub Reserve, only about twenty acres in size. It was pristine land with a nature trail running through it, but the gate was closed so the shuttle bus couldn't park in the lot and the women had to be dropped off. They also

49

had to be very careful because there were a lot more cops around here than out west by the Unger Tract.

The women couldn't shift inside the bus and had to disembark, squeeze past the locked gate arm, and sneak into the nature trail. They went a ways down the trail before it was safe to disrobe without being seen from the street. They each brought tote bags to hold their clothing after they shifted and hoped no insects would crawl inside.

It was right as the ladies were beginning to shift that Josie's phone rang. She rarely used her cellphone and the only people with her number were club members and her family. She had as yet escaped getting on robocallers' lists. When she saw West Palm Beach on the caller ID, she had a feeling it might be from Loopi Communities. She had to answer it.

There's one thing that every werewolf agrees on: Do not speak on the phone after you've shifted. Claws don't work well with smartphones. And wolf-like muzzles with long, floppy tongues do not enunciate clearly over the phone to human ears. It's just a terrible idea to even try.

But she knew this was her one shot at speaking with the developer. She couldn't let it slip away.

She had to stop her transformation midway through it. She'd never tried to do that before. While her pack whined and growled as they turned into wolf-women, Josie motioned for them to go off hunting without her. She stepped away and tried to answer the phone and stay human at the same time.

"Ruh-roh?"

"What? I'm trying to reach Josephine Denton?"

"Grrrr-yeah."

"Is this the right number?"

This wasn't going well. Josie struggled with trying to turn off the ancient switch that activated the shifting. It wasn't too hard to turn it on before she shifted to wolf and later when she wanted to shift back to human. But midway through the process, her brain couldn't seize on anything.

"I'm, grrrr, Josie."

Thank God she got that out. Her jaws had returned to their human proportions. Her tongue was smaller and more controllable.

"Okay, the connection is better now. I'm George Loopi. I understand you're interested in investing in Fox Landing?" He had an aggressive tone, a deep voice, and a New York accent.

"Yep." That came out a little too much like a bark.

"My rep said you wanted to know more about me? My financials are on file with the state. You want me to send you sales records for my previous two communities? You'll love the numbers. They're beautiful numbers. No other communities around here go up in value like mine." The man sounded like a mob boss from Brooklyn.

"That would be lovely," Josie replied. "I'd like to ask you about something else. Not long ago, a woman was murdered on the property. What was that all about? Are there criminal gangs in the area?"

"Oh, that. Yeah, some crazy old broad was in the woods worshipping the moon goddess in the nude."

"But who shot her?"

"I have no idea. Probably a hunter. Definitely not a gang-banger. There's no crime in that area. It's totally safe. Trust me, there's not a safer area anywhere."

"I know you can't tell me for liability reasons," Josie said, "but I was hoping your security guards shot her. It would make me feel more secure knowing it was a good guy and not a bad guy who did it."

"Don't you worry, I'll have a guard out there once the heavy equipment is on the property. When the community is complete, there will be high-tech monitoring systems. It will be up to the HOA if they want to hire security staff in addition to the gate guards."

"You don't have security there now?" she tried to sound disappointed.

"Intermittently, there is. On account of the protesters. As soon as we have expensive machinery parked out there, you better believe we're gonna protect it around the clock with well-armed personnel."

Josie wasn't getting the admission she'd hoped for. Maybe there had been a guard there and maybe not. But at least she knew for sure he had armed security guards.

"Are the protesters dangerous?" she asked.

Loopi sighed. "We got two kinds. There's the not-in-my-backyard crowd who live around there and don't want to see more traffic on the roads. And then there's the tree-huggers who don't want any development at all. Some of them are wack-a-doodles. They'll vandalize job sites. Or worse."

Josie thought about Frank, the lone protester she had met. Did he seem dangerous?

"Have I answered all your questions?" Loopi asked with an impatient tone.

"Yes, thank you. My realtor will speak with you soon."

She clicked off the call before he could reply. Loopi seemed like the kind of guy who liked to hang up on people, not the other way around.

She put her phone in the tote bag that held her clothes and stood naked in the warm, humid night. She glanced at the sky through the slash pines. There were a decent number of stars, but not as many as you could see out in the Unger Tract, far from the city lights, or even from the beach when the lights were off for sea turtle nesting season.

Cars passed just out of view on the road behind her. It ruined the mood.

She was no longer interested in being a wolf tonight and felt silly standing naked. So she dressed and waited for the rest of the pack to return. Her wait wouldn't be long, because this small gem of preserved land was so pitifully small.

THE NEXT DAY, she was reading an article online about the public resistance against the development of the Unger Tract. The story was from *The Jellyfish Beach Journal,* which she subscribed to for the coupons and the television listings, but rarely read. It was written by a fellow named Matt Rosen. She recognized the name from other articles she'd come across in her research on Loopi and Frank's Friends of Florida.

It occurred to her, why not contact this Rosen fellow and see if he could help her?

No emailing for her. She picked up the phone and called the newspaper office, getting transferred to his extension.

"Rosen," he answered, rather rudely in her opinion.

"Hello, Mr. Rosen. My name is Josie Denton, and I was wondering if you could help me. I'm researching the Unger Tract which, I see, you've written some stories about."

"Yes, I have for some time now," he said. "How can I help you?"

"I was wondering if you know of any violence perpetrated by those protesting the development."

There was a lengthy pause. "Um, why?" he asked.

She wasn't sure how much she should tell him.

"Well," she said, "as you well know—since you wrote a story about it—there was a death there recently."

"Yes, but I haven't seen any evidence at this point suggesting that an environmentalist did it."

He sounded somewhat dismissive of her. Did he think she had a political motive for suspecting environmentalists?

"Who, then, do you think did it?" she asked.

"I don't know, Ms. Denton. It's not my place to suggest theories. I have to be neutral to report the news."

"The thing is, I knew the victim. She was a neighbor."

Another pause, even longer this time. "I see. I'm sorry for your loss."

The way he said, "I see," had an odd weight to it. She had expected him to be more dismissive, as if he thought she was a busybody neighbor trying to do the police's work. But this was different.

"You live at Seaweed Manor?" he asked.

"Yes, I do."

His pause this time made her nervous. Did he know about werewolves?

"Do you know a home-health nurse named Missy Mindle, who visits your community?" he asked.

"I'm one of her patients," Josie said. Where was this going?

"I'm a good friend of hers," the reporter said. "We've worked on some . . . stories."

"Oh, what a small world!" Josie said, feigning delight. She was certain now this fellow knew about werewolves.

"Ms. Denton, can I buy you a cup of coffee? I frequently go to The Sea Urchin Cafe, just down the road from you. How about this morning?"

"Oh, I don't know."

"Would you feel better if Missy came, too?"

"Yes," Josie said. "That would be better."

JOSIE WAS HALF an hour early to her meeting at the cafe. She was always early for appointments. She considered it a virtue in this day and age when people abandoned propriety. She glanced at the menu while she sat at the table on the sidewalk across the street from the beach. Everything here was too expensive for her tastes. Why would anyone go to a restaurant just for coffee, anyway? Her percolator at home worked fine.

She was relieved to see Missy striding down the sidewalk. It would have been awkward if the reporter fellow showed up first, since Josie didn't know what he looked like.

"Good morning," Missy said, kissing Josie on the cheek before sitting down. "I'm so sorry about Mary Beth. I knew her well."

"Then you know how much of a pain in the butt she was, God rest her soul."

"Can't argue with you there," Missy said, lowering her head. "I have to admit I heard about her death secondhand. I didn't realize she was shot while the club was hunting."

"Yes, and the club wants vengeance. Or at least justice."

Missy's eyes fixed on something behind Josie. "Here comes Matt."

"Can I trust him?" Josie asked. "Does he know about our shifting?"

"You can trust him with your life. He knows about the supernaturals living in Jellyfish Beach. Well, some of them at least. He was held captive by Chainsaw and heard him get shot by the police."

"That horrible drug dealer. He gave us werewolves a bad

name."

"And Matt knows about the vampires in Squid Tower. He's a friend of mine and a talented reporter. He'll help you investigate who killed Mary Beth."

When Matt arrived, Missy introduced him. He had a beard which Josie didn't like, but otherwise he was well-kept and polite. His eyes lit up every time he looked at Missy. Josie made a note to learn if anything was going on between the two of them. She knew that Missy had been married previously, and, after she divorced, her ex-husband had died. She was still in her forties and young enough to have another go at it, in Josie's way of thinking.

Josie had lost her husband to a heart attack when she was only in her fifties. She was a middle-school principal and kept working with the desire to marry again but without the energy to pursue dating. Once she retired and entered the busy social world of a senior community, she resisted the flirtations of the few available single men. She realized she was finally happy being single.

But she believed it wasn't too late for Missy to find someone.

After their coffee orders arrived, Matt got down to business.

"The police have labeled this case an accidental shooting," he said. "Their reasoning is that it was a hunter's shot gone awry or maybe a teenager messing around with a gun, shooting it off in the woods."

"I have problems with that. First of all, it was late at night," Josie said. "I thought hunters got up early in the morning. Second, the shot came from a part of the woods where there were no trails, making it really difficult to get in there. I don't think a shot from the road would have made it through all those trees."

"Good point," Matt said, jotting down notes on a narrow pad.

"And the last thing I'd like to mention," Josie said before hesitating. If this young fellow already knew the women were werewolves, there was no reason to hold back. "We were hunting and didn't pick up the scent of anyone else in the area. I don't know the implications of that. Afterwards, I was searching the area and saw a slight disturbance of the leaves on the forest floor. And I caught the strong scent of rubber."

"Like rubber boots?" Matt asked.

"Maybe. The scent was strong and harsh enough to keep me from picking up the scent of whoever was wearing them. I think that was intentional."

"So, back to our phone call, you suspect an environmentalist was behind the shooting?"

"I don't know. At first, I thought someone working for the developer shot Mary Beth. After they bought the property, someone may have seen wolves there and wanted to get rid of them."

"They should have called the Florida Fish and Wildlife Conservation Commission," Missy said.

"Developers don't like the state involved," Matt said. "It's much easier to take care of it quietly on their own."

"I talked to the developer, pretending to be an investor, and he said he doesn't have security guards at the property full time right now. He mentioned environmental extremists have been known to vandalize properties. I saw Frank's Friends of Florida out there protesting. Are they capable of violence?"

"I've covered them before," Matt said. "They seem harmless. I have a hard time believing an environmentalist would shoot what appeared to be a wild animal."

"He could have heard something moving through the woods and shot at it, thinking it was a worker."

"A worker there late at night? I don't know." Matt sipped his coffee. "I think your first hunch about the developer was the strongest one. There is one other direction to look, though. The police."

"Josie, please don't go down that road," Missy said, flashing her eyes angrily at Matt. "The werewolves in Seaweed Manor need to be invisible to them. Don't go sniffing around the police. No pun intended."

"I've heard all the rumors," Josie said. "A few officers know about supernaturals and they kill them. A detective from the Jellyfish Beach Police Department came to the scene and questioned us, even though that area is not in their jurisdiction."

"Oh, my," Missy said. "Was his name Affird?"

"I believe that sounds right."

"But why would Affird know to show up there?" Matt asked. "I don't think the Sheriff's Department informs the city cops about crimes outside the city limits. Even if they share that data, why flag this supposed shooting accident?"

"He must be surveilling us," Josie said. "He must know the werewolves of Seaweed Manor go elsewhere to hunt. And he finally found out where."

"It makes little sense that he would shoot Mary Beth, then return to the scene to question you," Missy said.

"Why not?" Matt asked. "That way, no one would suspect him. Remember, Missy, we were there when he executed a werewolf."

"I know. I'm still troubled by it."

"If it was Affird or another cop, they will pay for this," Josie said.

"No, don't say that," Missy pleaded. "You can't attack a cop."

"He's not above the law."

"No offense, but you seem like the sweet, grandmotherly type to me," Matt said.

"And I could tear out your throat in less than a second," Josie said, smiling.

"I deserved that," Matt said.

"Josie, let us help you find the killer, okay?" Missy asked. "We can't have you tearing out any police throats and endangering your entire community."

"If a cop did it, and it wasn't an accident, I can't promise anything."

"Promise me you won't act before telling me."

"Will do," Josie said. "So how do we get this investigation on the road?"

"Let's talk to some more people," Matt said. "Make sure we cover all bases. I'd like to contact the previous owners of the land, the Unger family."

"Mind if I tag along?" Josie asked. "I've met Mrs. Unger before."

"No problem," Matt said, looking uncomfortable.

"Just let me know when you're planning to go. Thanks for the coffee," Josie said. "I have to head home. I'm playing bridge in twenty minutes."

AFTER SHE LEFT, Matt turned to Missy and shook his head.

"She's quite a firecracker, isn't she?" Missy said.

"Yeah, and I'm worried about her involvement in this. I don't mind seeing if there's a story to report here, but I'm not going to be her tool for pursuing vigilante justice. I'll need your help in handling her."

"I'm a little preoccupied at the moment," Missy said. Her face showed the signs of stress.

"Is anything wrong?"

"I had a minor magick mishap. Something went wrong with a spell."

"Did anyone get hurt?"

"Yes," she said, rubbing her eyes. "Two people have died so far that I know of, though they appear to be accidental deaths."

"Wait, how did your spell cause them?"

"Gnomes caused them. Garden gnomes."

Matt knew his open-mouthed, befuddled look wasn't attractive.

"My spell—actually it was a spell from Don Mateo—made my gnome become animated by a life-force of some sort. Maybe it's possessed by an entity. In any event, this effect appears to be spreading to other garden gnomes, who are taking it out on their human owners."

"My God, that's insane!"

"Welcome to my world."

"Is there any way I can help?"

"You have a police scanner. Let me know if you hear of any fatal accidents."

"I will," Matt said. "Hey, are you free for dinner tonight?"

"Matt, I'm sorry, but I can't go out and enjoy myself when my garden gnome is running amok and people are dying."

There was always an obstacle in his slow-motion pursuit of Missy. But garden gnomes? Really?

"I understand completely," he said. "I would feel the same way if my garden gnome escaped."

"You have a garden gnome?"

"No. And I never, ever will."

## 8

## ROWDY CROWD

F reddie awoke to the faint sound of music and voices. The TV in her bedroom was off, so she must have left one on downstairs. She pulled on her robe and slippers and slowly made her way down the hallway, through the dining room and into the kitchen. The small TV in her breakfast nook that she watched while she ate her solitary meals was off. The rarely used one in the den was off as well.

But the sounds continued. The music came from a fiddle and flute. Tiny, high-pitched voices sang and chattered and broke into roars of laughter.

It sounded like it was coming from her backyard, but that made no sense. Maybe the party was in a boat anchored in the lake just off her property. If the people were actually in her yard, she'd have to call the police. She took a flashlight from the tool drawer.

She walked through the family room with its walls covered with photos of children, grandchildren, and her late husband. French doors opened onto the pool patio where kids once ran (despite being told not to), and later their own children ran. Now, except during the holidays, no one ever enjoyed the beautiful pool and patio overlooking the lake. No one except for her and her gnomes.

She turned on the patio lights and saw what was wrong instantly. The gnomes around the pool were missing. Anger burned in her stomach.

When she opened the French doors, the noise from the party was louder. She could make out the music as some sort of traditional folk music, but nothing she recognized. And the voices—they weren't speaking English. Their words had a vaguely European lilt to them.

The noise came from below, where the lawn sloped down to the lake. The property didn't have any lights past the patio area, so it was too dark to see what was there with the lack of a moon tonight.

She stormed outside, ready to raise hell.

Suddenly, all was silent. She walked past the pool and turned on her flashlight, shining it toward where the sounds had come from. The beam illuminated her gnome village. Her breath caught in her throat.

The village was teeming with a horde of gnomes. All of her gnomes were there, along with some she didn't recognize. The same vandals who had moved them the previous night must have done this.

She reached the village and played her light over it. The additional gnomes were placed to look like they were interacting with the ones that belonged in the village. There were too many gnomes to fit in the village and the overflow crowd spread out on the grass just outside in tiny groups like people at a frat party.

The eyes of the gnomes facing her gleamed as her flashlight's beam passed over them. Her scalp tingled. Those eyes almost seemed alive.

She briefly considered returning the gnomes to their proper places, but that could wait until morning. She walked back to the house, debating if she should call the police tomorrow and report the vandalism.

She tripped on an object and landed on her face in the grass. Before she could get up, her feet were seized by something strong that yanked her backwards toward the lake, her face dragged through the grass.

Panic flooded her chest. The grass muffled her screams as her face bumped across the lawn.

Her feet were released. Hyperventilating with fear, she curled into a ball and looked up.

Dozens of gnomes surrounded her. They were in their normal poses, but somehow their eyes were fixed upon her. Eyes that looked disturbingly alive despite the darkness. And were angry.

"Why would you hurt me? I love you guys," she said. "I treat you like family. I built a village for you."

Something flickered in their eyes. It wasn't sympathy for her; it was a sign of interest, like a cat regarding a mouse.

"I always sensed there was something magical about gnomes. That's why I collect and display you."

It must have been the wrong thing to say. They lifted her from the ground with dozens of tiny unseen hands and carried her toward the house.

"Please don't hurt me," she pleaded in between hyperventilating.

They marched her toward the swimming pool.

Maybe they would only toss her in the pool. Maybe it was

just the gnomes' way of goofing around. After all, she was the biggest fan of gnomes. They had to understand that, right?

They didn't throw her in the pool. Instead, they dropped her on the concrete pool deck. Her knees and hip hurt, but she could live with that.

Until she saw the mounted blue marlin that had been hanging on the wall, the one that Bruce had caught off of Costa Rica, come lunging at her face.

MATT WAS GETTING DRESSED for work when he heard the female voice crackle over his police radio scanner.

"Possible Code Five at 23 Osprey Lane on Lake Algae reported by a passing boater. Nearest unit please respond to the scene."

A Code Five was a homicide, quite rare in Jellyfish Beach. Matt decided to check it out before he went to the newsroom. He finished dressing and drove to the older but upscale neighborhood on the north side of town, not far away. When his GPS app told him he'd arrived at the destination, he was surprised to see only one police vehicle out front.

The officer appeared to have just arrived on the scene. He was leaving his car and walking around the side of the house. Matt parked and chased after the officer through a gate and along a pathway of pavers to a large concrete pool deck.

The officer stopped and glanced around.

"Good morning," Matt said.

The officer jumped and put his hand on his weapon. "Who the heck are you?"

"Matt Rosen with *The Jellyfish Beach Journal*. I heard the call about the homicide on my scanner."

The officer was a young guy, barely old enough to shave. He didn't seem to have dealt with reporters before.

"Don't compromise the crime scene," he said. "Stay right here."

He walked across the pool deck and Matt followed right behind him. He looked at the rear of the house and stopped suddenly. So did Matt. The officer gasped.

An old lady in a purple bathrobe was hanging on the wall of the house like a mounted fish. In fact, she faced a mounted sailfish, both of them curved in a mirror image, as if they were hung together as a pair.

"Wow," the cop said.

"Wow," Matt said. "This is psycho-killer stuff."

"I wonder how he hung her up there. Did he use regular mounting brackets like the sailfish?"

"No doubt. He has a good aesthetic, though, the way he balanced her with the sailfish."

"Man, this sure is an unlucky street."

"What do you mean?" Matt asked.

"The lady next door fell down the stairs and died just yesterday."

"That's quite a coincidence. Hey, did she just move her arm?"

"The dead lady?" The cop reluctantly moved a little closer to her. "I didn't see it."

"Shouldn't you check her to see if she's alive?"

"I'm not touching no stiff," the cop said. "The paramedics should be here any minute. They can touch her."

"Help me down," the old lady croaked.

Both Matt and the officer jumped.

"I guess she's not a stiff," Matt said.

The two walked over to the lady mounted on the wall. She had a bruise on her forehead but looked alive.

"We thought you were dead," Matt said.

"Someone called in about a dead body," the cop explained.

"I was asleep," the lady said. "Now can you help me off of here?"

The cop grabbed her by the shoulders, and Matt held her hips as they lifted her up from three brackets in the wall. She didn't weigh much. They placed her gently on the deck, supporting her in case she fell over.

"These are awfully sturdy brackets," the cop said.

"Do you need to sit down?" Matt asked.

"Please."

Matt pulled a deck chair behind her, and they lowered her into the chair.

The cop pulled a pad and pen from his back pocket. "Can you tell me what happened, ma'am?"

"My gnomes attacked me."

"Your who? Who is Nomes?"

"My garden gnomes. They all ganged up on me and I thought they were going to kill me. But I guess they thought better of it because I'm like a mother to them."

"The little cheesy garden gnomes?" Matt asked.

The lady nodded and wiped away a tear.

"Oh boy," Matt said. He texted Missy that she needed to come here.

"What gnomes?" the officer asked. "I don't see any gnomes around here."

"They left me. After all I've done for them, they up and left me. I had forty-eight of them displayed all over the property. And last night, they were all down at the gnome village by the lake having a party. There were a bunch of other gnomes there too, besides mine. It was an enormous party. Like the beach at Fort Lauderdale during spring break."

The officer walked a few paces away and spoke into his radio. Matt was able to pick up the words, "mental health evaluation."

"My gnomes left me," the woman said sadly. "Even after the love I've shown. Like a bunch of resentful teenagers."

"Maybe they're just going through a phase," Matt said.

"The yard feels so empty without them. I guess I need to find a new hobby."

"Knitting might be a safer bet. By the way, my name is Matt. I'm a reporter with *The Jellyfish Beach Journal*. I'd like to speak with you afterwards if you're feeling okay."

"I'm Freddie. And I'm thirsty."

Matt went inside to get the woman a glass of water. The kitchen was filled with kitschy knickknacks and porcelain figurines which, he guessed, fit the profile of a prolific gnome collector. He felt sorry for the woman, who appeared to live alone in the large house. You can't blame her for wanting to fill her life with cute mythical creatures, he thought.

When he returned to the pool deck, a male and a female paramedic were checking her out, taking her blood pressure and shining a light in her eyes. Eventually, they left, and a plain-clothes police social worker arrived, a young Hispanic woman. She brought Freddie inside to the living room and Matt waited in the kitchen.

After everyone left, Matt felt a little weird hanging out in Freddie's kitchen. But fortunately, the doorbell soon rang.

"I'll get it," Matt said.

It was Missy. "Is Freddie okay?" She asked.

"She seems to be, despite being hung on a wall like a trophy trout."

He led her into the living room where Freddie rested on the couch, and Missy knelt down, taking Freddie's hand.

"I'm so glad you survived. What happened?" Missy asked.

Freddie recounted her ordeal last night, the surrealism of confronting animated garden gnomes sounding minimal compared to the hurt of them turning on her.

"At least they spared you," Missy said. "Your next-door neighbor wasn't so lucky."

"Yeah. Her dog peed on the gnomes. I, on the other hand, glorified them."

"They're angry at humans," Missy said.

"No kidding. I think when I reminded them that I displayed them, the word 'displayed' pushed them over the edge. And they ended up displaying me on the wall."

"Actually, you looked pretty good opposite the sailfish," Matt said.

"Did you see where they went afterwards?" Missy asked.

"No. I think they made me fall asleep. Come to think about it, I never saw them move. They just did, somehow. Whenever I looked at them, they were ordinary gnomes just standing there. But somehow they picked me up and put me on the wall."

"Did you see my gnome among them?"

"I don't know. It was dark. And there were too many of them, including lots of gnomes that weren't mine. But they would look great in my collection."

# 9

# WELCOME GNOME

The crashing of dishes in the kitchen jolted Missy from sleep. As often, she had no idea what time it was since her sleep cycle was so out of kilter. Normally, she kept nighttime hours to make home visits for her vampire patients, but when she had a lot of business with the normal world, she had to adjust and stay awake during the day. Visiting Freddie's home in the morning meant she didn't get to sleep until noon-ish. Her clock read 6:30. That was 6:30 p.m., right?

Great, she had to clean up scattered pieces of porcelain from the floor. She sighed. Either one of the cats had gotten into a cabinet and knocked the dishes out, or a 400-year-old ghost was being a klutz. Her money was on the second possibility.

"Don Mateo?" she called from her bed. "Is that you?"

The reek of strange perfume and ancient body odor struck her. A shimmering figure at the foot of her bed coalesced into a bearded man wearing a purple robe and turban.

"You called, my lady?"

"Yeah. What was all that noise?"

"I lost my bearings and ended up in a cabinet. The platter with the picture of a turkey is no great loss, I assure you. You can surely find a less-ugly replacement in any store selling used items for the needy. The same with the plates with the little birds on them."

"I don't make a lot of money, you know." Missy said. "Being a home-health nurse for cheap vampires and werewolves does not pay well."

"You should monetize your magick. When I was a sorcerer in Grenada, noblemen would pay handsomely for my services. Perhaps I could still fetch a fee."

"Well, I've been waiting forever for you to show up. And I would never pay a ghost who's so difficult to summon."

"My apologies. I am bound to you because you possess my grimoire. But I am not like these mechanical devices you own that you stop or start with a button."

Missy sat up in bed. "I need your help. The malfunctioning spell is spreading among the gnomes in town. So far, I know of two humans killed and one almost killed. There could be many more I don't know about."

"You say one was almost killed?"

"Apparently, the gnomes showed mercy toward this woman who collected dozens of them. She had a gnome fetish. She practically worshipped them."

"Interesting," the ghost of Don Mateo said. "The gnomes have more consciousness and free will that I expected."

"The next-door neighbor of this woman died after falling down her stairs. I'm assuming the gnomes were behind it. The victim's dogs would pee on the gnomes next door."

"Ah, there seems to be a campaign of vengeance here."

"We need to stop it. We need to get my gnome back to see if we can diagnose what went wrong with the sentinel spell. The problem is, my locator spells aren't accurate enough. I think I found my gnome yesterday, but not in time. And I wasn't able to retrieve him before he disappeared again."

"Did you try the summoning spell I suggested?"

"Yes," Missy said. "Nada."

"Did you do it while using the Red Dragon?"

"Um, no. I didn't think of that."

"You have one of the most powerful talismans in the world and you didn't use it?"

The Red Dragon was a small metal figurine once owned by Missy's father, a powerful witch who died when she was too young to remember him. It was modeled after the original one owned by Moses and, later, King Solomon.

"The Red Dragon empowers you to command spirits and demons to obey your will. Surely, a garden gnome would obey you."

"I'm reluctant to use the talisman often," Missy explained. "It's the heavy artillery. It has so much power it takes a toll on me when I've used it. To be honest, I'm a little scared of it."

"By its very nature, great power is frightening. If you want to become a successful witch, you must learn how to control great power."

"Well, what do you suggest I do?"

"Repeat the summoning spell you tried earlier, but hold the talisman while you do it."

"Do you mind giving me some privacy while I get dressed?" Missy said, more rudely than she had intended.

The ghost gave an exaggerated bow and disappeared.

Missy threw on jeans and a T-shirt, slipped into her sandals, and went to her hiding place for the talisman and the grimoire. She had originally hidden it in this spot without a lot of fore-thought, afraid the Arch-Mage Bob would steal it from her. It turned out to be a brilliant hiding place since Bob and his thug weren't able to find it, even after tearing her house apart.

The hiding place? One of her cats' litter boxes. She had improvised a false bottom of sorts and the cat pee along with a simple grounding spell kept away human hands as well as searching spells.

The litter box was in the laundry room. First, she cleaned it, because her cats had been quite prolific since yesterday. Then, from beneath the liner in the bottom, she pulled out a Ziplock bag inside another bag. She took the centuries-old book and talisman out and carried them to the kitchen.

Soon, she had her magick circle drawn on the floor, with a lit candle at each of the five points of a pentagram. She performed her usual mind-clearing and entered a meditative state as she marshaled the energies within her body, and from the earth, air, and ocean.

She chanted the summoning spell she had tried the other day. It was one that Don Mateo had inscribed in the back leaves of the grimoire nearly 400 years ago. Partly, the words of the verse were intended to put her in a hypnotic state to channel her energies into magick. But the words had power of their own.

*The gnome from my garden, so cute and wee*
*I now beseech thee to return to me. . .*

There was the tingle of magick in the air around her, a faint humming in her ears, and the slightest vibration in the floor.

It was time. She grasped the two-and-a-half-inch metal figurine that looked more like a fish than a dragon.

An electric shock hit her palm and ran up her arm and into her heart. Her hair stood on end and she levitated from the floor a few inches.

"Enchanted gnome of mine, I command thee to return to

me. I compel thee, my earth magick compels thee, the power of the Red Dragon compels thee.

"Return to me now! You have no choice but to obey."

All the pent-up energy and tension within her rushed out like a wind.

She dropped the talisman. It clattered on the tile floor. Her body felt like it was crumbling as it relaxed, and her head sagged. She resisted the urge to lie on the floor.

Clapping came from above her. Don Mateo sat on the kitchen island, his ghostly legs dangling a few feet from her. He wore scuffed, black leather boots that, of course, were only an apparition. But they smelled bad anyway.

"Bravo," he said. "I couldn't have done it better myself."

She blinked as she tried to overcome her sleepiness and stretched her arms.

"Be careful not to break your magick circle."

"What now?" she asked.

"We wait."

"How long does it take a plastic gnome to travel across town?"

"I don't know how garden gnomes travel," he said. "What is this thing you call Uber?"

"No, that wouldn't work. I wonder how they walk. I've never seen one move. Does their rigidity vanish, and they move like a normal creature? Or do they just magically appear where they want to go?"

"I would wager they move like gargoyles. Their rigidity disappears and they move naturally, but often faster than the human eye can register."

As if to answer their questions, a loud *BAM* came from the living room. Don Mateo vanished.

"Your front window is shattered, but not broken," he said from behind her.

"Impact-resistant glass," she said. "I got tired of putting up hurricane shutters. These new windows are expensive."

"Now you have to replace one."

The doorbell rang.

"You can break the magick circle now," Don Mateo said.

She wiped away a section of the chalk circle and went to the front door. When she opened it, her gnome stood on her front porch, looking just like he always had, an impish grin on his bearded face.

"Welcome home," Missy said.

SHE HAD PLACED the gnome atop her kitchen island, on spread-out newspapers, because who knows where this gnome had been? She and Don Mateo had been studying it to no avail. She probed it with her mind and immediately sensed that it was still enchanted with the sentinel spell, but couldn't sense any defect in that spell or any traces of an additional, foreign spell.

"Do you have any revealing charms?" Don Mateo asked.

"I can make a potion, but it will take a while," she said, knowing there was no such thing as "a while" for a ghost.

In her garage was a small workbench where she made charms, amulets, and potions. Many of the ingredients could be noxious, so she didn't like doing it in the kitchen. She simmered a small stew of ingredients in a saucepan on an electric burner. Eye of toad and tail of newt were one thing, but heating up corpse flowers really smelled horribly.

One of her cats shrieked. She rushed inside. Brenda, a gray tabby, was dangling from the gnome's right hand that clutched her by the scruff of the neck. His little arm extended straight and unmoving from his body. This was the first time she saw the gnome in another position.

She grasped the Red Dragon talisman in her pocket.

"Drop the cat," she ordered.

Brenda landed on her feet and yowled as she raced from the kitchen.

Don Mateo chuckled from somewhere unseen.

Missy returned to the garage and checked on the potion. It looked ready. She removed it from the burner and let it cool for twenty minutes. Then she poured it into a plastic spray bottle and brought it to the kitchen.

"Don Mateo, are you around?"

He materialized sitting on one of the bar stools at the island.

"Thank you for sticking around," she said. "It's always such a pain to get you to show up when I need you."

"Ghosts do their own thing. In this case, I am eager to see if this potion works."

The revealing potion was one he had developed with the shaman of the Timucuan people he had lived with in northern Florida 400 years ago. Made with Florida plants, herbs, minerals, and other natural ingredients—including some nasty insects—it was activated with a spell designed by the wizard. She had invoked the spell before cooking the smelly stew.

She repeatedly pulled the trigger of the spray bottle, covering the gnome with the slightly brownish liquid from head to toe. The arm that had held Brenda somehow had returned to its normal position while she was out in the garage.

A revealing potion does exactly what it sounds like: It reveals stuff. If a Timucuan leader suspected a rival had poisoned his venison, the potion would light up where it came in contact with the poison. If his spear had been enchanted with a spell, the potion would tell him.

And, yes, if your computer has been infected with a virus, the potion will tell you that, too. Just make sure not to spray too much on your machine or it will fry.

The beauty of the spell that powers the potion is that it ignores any spells you put on the object yourself. Only foreign magic and materials will activate it.

With the gnome now fully covered by the potion, she studied it closely for a reaction. She waited.

And waited.

Nothing. There was no change in color in the liquid whatsoever.

"Darn it. What does this mean?" she asked the ghost sitting on her barstool.

"Assuming you made the potion correctly, it means there is no spell enchanting the gnome aside from the original one."

"Well, duh."

"'Duh'?"

"What does it mean if there's not another spell on this thing?"

"Let us use simple logic," Don Mateo said. "The first possibility is that when you originally cast the sentinel spell, you did it incorrectly and cast quite another spell instead. But I was with you at the time and I can attest to the fact that you did not simply bungle it. Another possibility is that another spell was cast by someone else, or by you, inadvertently, that perverted the workings of your original spell. The potion showed us that is not the case."

"Well?"

"That leaves us with one last possibility: possession by a demon or some other malevolent spirit."

"Wow."

"Yes, that's a problem. A big problem."

"What do we do now?" Missy asked.

"We have to communicate with the demon, find out who it is, and convince it to leave. There are instructions for summoning demons in *The Book of Saint Cyprian*, *The Key of Solomon*, and many other grimoires. But all those books were written for laymen and are full of gibberish. I would instruct you what to do myself, but the last time I summoned a spirit it did not go very well at all."

The last time Don Mateo summoned a spirit, it was the last act of his life. His ghost claimed that the sorcerer had been drinking with a friend and wanted to amuse him by summoning a harmless spirit. Don Mateo mispronounced the spirit's name and inadvertently summoned a demon instead. The demon tore him to pieces, which did not amuse the friend. Or Don Mateo.

"I know someone with experience with demons I could call," Missy said. "He also had a mishap with a demon, but he's still alive."

"Please do not rub it in."

## 10

## TOO MANY POSSESSIONS

"To be honest, I'm not eager to meet another demon," ex-Father Marco Rivera Hernandez said over the phone.

"I understand," Missy said. "It might not be a demon. Maybe just a malevolent spirit."

"That's not much better."

"People are dying, Father. I don't know what else to do."

"Okay. I'll see if I can help. I have a hard time believing you about the gnomes. It sounds like a bunch of accidental deaths. But I'll take a look at your gnome. A garden gnome? For Lord's sake."

"Thank you, Father."

Missy understood why ex-Father Marco would be reluctant to help. He had been one of the few Catholic priests in Florida to perform exorcisms and had earned a reputation as an expert demonologist. Unfortunately, during a difficult ritual with a teenage girl, he rid her of her demon, but it ended up possessing him.

Ex-Father Marco was not at all disabled by this possession. But the problem was, the demon took over at inconvenient times. Defiling the altar during a mass did not go over well with his parishioners. Attacking a caddy and calling down brimstone on a fundraiser golf tournament was equally a black mark on his record.

He was summoned to explain himself to the bishop of the diocese. Since the demon often made ex-Father Marco blurt out offensive comments as if he had Tourette Syndrome, the meeting did not go well. As open-minded as this bishop was, he did not enjoy being called a "two-bit, scum-sucking, hairy-legged, man-breasted scalawag."

Of course, it was the demon calling him that, not the ex-Father. It didn't matter, though. Marco was defrocked and excommunicated. He stooped to making a living as a bingo-caller for crowds of blue-haired old ladies at the local Indian reservation casino. But he continued to be a scholar of demonology.

Missy heard the throaty rumble of his 1965 Ford Mustang pulling up in front of her house. The sun had set, so she grabbed the gnome off the kitchen island to make sure it didn't disappear on her as it was wont to do. Night was when the gnomes were active.

"Hello, Missy," the ex-priest said when Missy opened the front door. "You're holding the gnome like it was your child."

"Well, it turns out they can be just like children. You'd think gnomes would stay wherever you put them in your yard, but it's no longer true. You can't let them out of your sight, or they'll disappear as soon as your back is turned."

She stepped aside for Marco to come in, but he hesitated.

"I felt it right away," he said.

"What?"

"There's something evil in that gnome."

"Will you still examine it?"

"I told you I would."

He followed her into her kitchen. Ex-Father Marco was tall, thin, and elegant, with thinning black hair and a pointy beard. He looked like a Spanish conquistador from Don Mateo's era. His eyes darted frequently in nervousness, as if looking for escape routes.

Missy placed the gnome back on top of the newspapers on the island. To her it looked just as kitschy and insipid as it always had, even though she could now feel the evil energy like the ex-priest did.

"A full exorcism is a very lengthy procedure that could run for days," Marco said.

"I'm not asking that of you. Yet. But please let me know what's inside there and how it's spreading to other gnomes."

"Demons normally possess one host at a time. But there was one case I worked when a child was possessed, and then his three sisters each became possessed in a progression. Then the parents were taken as well. All by the same demon. The original possession resulted after the demon was summoned through black magic by an enemy of the family. I believe something about the black magic allowed the demon to spread its influence over multiple hosts."

"Oh my," Missy said. "That would explain what's going on here. Would we have to do an exorcism on every single gnome that's been affected?"

The ex-priest shook his head. "That would be impossible. I believe that if the exorcism drives the demon from your gnome and sends it back to Hell, it will be driven out of all the other gnomes as well. At least I hope that's the case."

"Okay, well then I guess I *am* asking you for an exorcism after all," Missy said.

"Perhaps there's another way to defeat this demon, but I'm not a witch or wizard. This is the only way I know. Now what I'm going to do will look nothing like your spell casting, so please be patient. First, I have to pray."

He clasped his hands, bowed his head, and closed his eyes. His lips moved soundlessly as he prayed. This went on for a while. Occasionally, he flinched as if in pain.

"Even though I'm excommunicated, I'm still a child of God. But Satan thinks of me as family, so praying can be difficult at times. And painful. Ouch! Stop it, Beelzebub!"

The gnome began vibrating atop the kitchen island. The vibrations were so intense they sent the gnome scooting slowly across the surface, knocking Missy's teacup off. She had enough presence of mind to use her natural telekinesis to stop the cup from smashing on the floor. She moved it to the sink among the other dirty dishes (please don't judge her housekeeping habits).

Ex-Father Hernandez continued praying, mumbling and moving his lips at a more frenetic pace. Missy jumped up to prevent the vibrating gnome from pitching over the edge of the island. She returned it to the center of the surface.

The ex-priest stood and faced the gnome. His face was dark and full of fury. He raised his arms as if he were about to tackle the gnome.

"Dark entity of hell who has invaded this innocent, disarmingly cute lawn ornament, I command you to depart. The power of God commands you! The power of Christ commands you! The power of the Holy Spirit commands you!"

The gnome stopped vibrating. The kitchen was silent. No one moved. Missy realized she'd been holding her breath.

And then a chittering, rodent-like laughter came from the gnome. It didn't move. It just stood there, arms cocked on its hips, its smug little gnomish smile seeming to mock the ex-priest.

Then it flew across the counter and hit the ex-priest squarely in the chest, bowling him over. Marco landed on his back on the floor with the gnome standing atop him like a victorious gladiator.

"Maybe being ex-communicated and defrocked made me lose my juice," Hernandez said. "Maybe demons believe I've lost my authority."

Missy put the gnome back on the island. That was the first time she had seen it move on its own in her presence. She helped the ex-priest to his feet.

"Don't give up, Father Marco. The only thing I know about exorcisms is what I've read in novels or seen in movies, but they're supposed to take a long time, right? Like days or weeks?"

"The last one I performed took weeks. Convincing a demon to leave its host is harder than weaning a rich kid off his allowance. But the gnome is not a living creature, so this process could be super easy or freaking impossible. Who knows?"

Suddenly, the gnome flew across the kitchen and smashed into the window over the sink as if trying to flee. Tiny cracks spread throughout the impact-resistant glass, but the gnome couldn't penetrate it. It dropped onto the dirty dishes in the sink with a loud clatter.

"That's another expensive window I have to replace," Missy said. "I need to cast a quick spell to immobilize this little bugger while you're praying."

This didn't require a magick circle on the floor or the Red Dragon talisman. She merely held the power charm she always kept in her left pocket, chanted the proper words in Medieval Middle-English, and drew an imaginary circle in the air around the gnome with her right hand.

"That should do it, at least for now," she said. "Do you want to try again? He's not going anywhere."

Ex-Father Marco sighed and moved a barstool from the island to the sink. By the defeated expression on his face, he didn't appear to be very motivated.

"Cheer up, Father, I know you can do this."

"From your lips to the demon's ears," he said.

He resumed praying. The kitchen was silent except for the low mumbling from his lips. It was fully dark out now, so Missy mentally probed to make sure the immobilization spell would prevent the gnome from escaping.

The ex-priest stood. He removed a glass vial from his pocket and removed the stopper.

"Time to go nuclear on this chump," he said as he poured the clear liquid onto the gnome in the sink.

"Holy water?" Missy asked.

"Even better. Holy vodka, blessed by Russian Orthodox monks. Like anything else, you can find it on the internet."

Missy drew closer, hoping to see smoke coming from the holy vodka as it landed on the plastic gnome. That's the way it worked in horror movies, but apparently not in her kitchen.

"By the power of God, I command you to leave this adorable garden gnome!" Marco bellowed with convincing authority. "By the power of Christ, I command you! By the power of—"

His voice clenched, as if his throat had seized up. He choked. Missy looked at him with alarm, prepared to use her nursing training to free his airway.

But then a strange voice came out, singing, "By the power of disco, I command you to boogie, boogie, woogie all night long!"

83

Ex-Father Marco sounded like one of the Bee Gees. This could mean only one thing: The demon that possessed him had taken over as it often did at the most inopportune times. Its voice always varied depending on its mood. Sometimes it sounded like a silly cartoon character. Other times it was a deep, monstrous voice of terror. Today, it was an effeminate disco singer from the 1970s.

"Father, are you still there?"

"That clown is on hiatus," the voice said in falsetto. "We gonna party!"

Well, that was that, Missy thought. There was nothing to be done now until the demon grew bored and allowed Father Marco to regain control of his own body.

The possessed ex-priest smiled at her with a vacant expression and swiveled his hips in a dance move.

"Clarence, is that you?" said a voice in a cultured but unidentifiable European accent.

The voice was coming from the sink.

"Caorthannach, baby!" Marco's demon said. "It has been centuries since we last chatted. How have you been, darling?"

"Mostly dormant," the entity said, clearly coming from the gnome's unmoving lips. "Hardly anyone summons me anymore. The demons from Milton's *Paradise Lost* and Dante's *Inferno* have always been the favored ones."

"You sound bitter, girl."

"No one likes to be neglected."

"What are you doing in a garden gnome?" Marco's demon asked. "As charmingly lovable as they might be, it's not like your style."

"Believe me, it was not my choice. It was the summoner's command. I've been dormant too long to have the power to pick and choose whom I want to possess."

"It could be worse. I was once forced to possess a cow. Talk about boring. Even when I made its head twist around, I was out in a field and the only ones I frightened were the other cows. I find it much better possessing this priest. There are so many ways to mortify him and his companions."

Missy decided to interrupt the conversation. She was worried, though. Not about being rude, because what demon would be offended by rudeness? But about becoming possessed herself.

"Excuse me," she said, with as much confidence as she could fake. "I have a question for the demon in my gnome: Who summoned you?"

Silence. Both demons stopped chatting. Ex-Father Marco just stood there, eyes empty, a stupid smile on his face.

"Um, can you answer my question, please?"

"I do not know," said the sophisticated voice coming from the gnome in the sink. "Only that it was a very powerful magician using black magic."

There weren't many powerful magicians in the United States, certainly not in Florida. And who among them would summon such an obscure demon she had never heard of?

The only powerful magician that Missy knew was Bob McGuinn, wizard and Arch-Mage of San Marcos in North Florida. He wasn't supposed to use black magic, as it was forbidden by the guild of magic practitioners that he administered. But she wouldn't be surprised if he did use black magic since he had tortured her when trying to get her to reveal the hiding place of the grimoire she had taken from him. The spells he used were not from the black magic canon, but he used them for evil ends.

The grimoire was rightfully hers, bequeathed to her by her birth father, but Bob had possessed it and now wanted it back.

Worrying about him was why she had attempted the sentinel spell on her gnome in the first place. She had assumed that if he attacked her with magic, it would be to steal back the book, not to mess with the gnomes of Jellyfish Beach. And having a demon possess her gnome? Talk about overkill. Yet it now seemed that Bob was the most likely wizard to suspect of summoning the demon.

"By the power of the Holy Spirit, I command you!" ex-Father Marco said.

He was back. He squinted and looked around the room.

"Something changed," he said. "What happened?"

"Your demon came out."

"Oh, man, that was bad timing. I think I tanked the exorcism."

"Yes," Missy said. "But it wasn't you who tanked it. It was your demon. He happened to know the demon possessing the gnome. It sounded like they go way back. Hell must be a fun place for sociable souls."

"I'm so sorry, Missy. Did the demons say anything revealing?"

"Your demon—"

"It's not my demon," Marco said.

"For all intents and purposes it is. Sorry. As I was saying, he called the other demon by the name Caorthannach."

"Oh, man. Not good. Caorthannach is an ancient Celtic demon, the mother of the devil, who tormented the people of Ireland before the Christian missionaries arrived. Saint Patrick battled her and banished her to the bottom of a lake. Well, until now, I suppose."

"Can you remove her from the gnome?" Missy asked.

"I'll keep trying. Like I said before, exorcisms take a long time."

The dirty dishes in the sink rattled. Missy braced herself for what the gnome would do. Nothing happened. So she pulled the gnome from the sink and placed him back on the newspaper-covered island counter. Water dripped from the gnome onto the newspaper.

"Could you hand me a dish towel?" Missy asked the ex-priest.

The gnome began vibrating again.

And it flew off the counter and hit Marco right between the legs. The ex-priest shouted a bunch of expletives that made Missy wonder, for a moment, whether his demon had taken over again

We don't have the luxury of time to see if an exorcism would work, Missy thought.

Missy thanked ex-Father Marco for his help, apologized for the pain in his family jewels, and ushered him out the door. She didn't have faith that his exorcism procedure would work on the demon in the gnome and didn't look forward to days or weeks of sessions like this one.

She had returned the gnome to the kitchen island, and it was still there, looking like a grumpy old man. She wondered why the gnome hadn't attacked her. Freddie had been shown mercy, probably because she adored gnomes. But Missy had no respect or regard for them at all.

She debated whether her being a witch made the gnome and its recruits unwilling to take her on. Sure, she usually had a protection spell on herself when the gnome was around, but that only saved her from being attacked by a foe. It wouldn't prevent her from tripping over a gnome outside the shower.

Did the demon have any say in this? You would think the demon would have a different agenda than the gnomes. Why would it create a gnome rebellion? Unless whoever had summoned the demon directed it specifically to do that. But why?

The gnome appeared to be looking at her with its beady little eyes. She sensed there was intelligence in there. It freaked her out.

She brought her laptop into the kitchen and searched the internet for hours. She learned that gnome collecting was not just a tacky element of contemporary consumer culture, but had a long heritage dating back to the mid-nineteenth century in England and Europe.

She remembered Freddie saying there was something magical about garden gnomes. That was just Freddie projecting her fantasies onto inanimate objects. But maybe she was on to something.

Missy stared at the gnome. She had to remind herself that this one was dangerous, that the twinkle in its eye was malevolent, not mischievous. But the darn thing was kind of cute.

No, it was not. It was deadly. Even if it didn't kill her, it would enlist someone else's gnomes to rise up and kill their owner.

She moved the gnome to the hallway closet where she kept her vacuum. She cast a quick anchoring spell to keep the gnome from going anywhere. To make it extra secure, she sealed the door with another spell.

The next day, the closet door hung open and the gnome was gone.

## 11

## GET A JOB

Matt asked from the backseat of Josie's giant 1977 Lincoln Continental, "Are you sure you don't want me to take the lead." He sounded miles away from Missy.

She was in the front bench seat while Josie was at the wheel. Josie was the epitome of the cliché of the little old lady driver who could barely see above the steering wheel. Missy herself, at a respectable height of five feet six inches, couldn't see the road anywhere near the front of the car with its hood like the deck of an aircraft carrier. Josie's angle of view must be such that the closest road surface she could see was a quarter mile away.

"How do you park this thing?" Missy asked.

"I'm so used to driving it that parking's not too hard. People honk or scream if I'm running into them."

Missy admired the classic-car touches, from the horizontal sweep of the analogue speedometer to the push buttons for saved stations on the radio.

"Interviewing important people is part of my job," Matt said, from way far away in the state of Georgia. The back seat and its leg room was big enough for a family to live there if Josie wanted some rental income. "I'm good at getting reluctant subjects to open up."

"I've got this, young man," Josie said. "I've done my fair share of fundraising over the years and I've met Mrs. Unger before. The Werewolf Women's Club even got her to sponsor a food bank, though I left the club's name out of it. I told her I was so grateful that I wanted to honor her by getting you to write the story about her."

"But I get to ask the questions," Matt said.

"Nope. I ask the questions. You take the notes. I don't want you to annoy her."

Missy chuckled. "You're getting to know Matt well already."

"But remember, we're here to get clues of who may have shot your friend," Matt said. "We can't just talk about charity. We need to ask if anyone uses the property for hunting. Or, I'm hoping there's some corrupt arrangement between the Unger family and the developer."

"We'll see where the conversation goes," Josie said.

Matt blew out his breath in frustration.

From what Missy had read, the Unger family had been farmers and cattle ranchers in Florida since the pioneer days. The earlier generations worked hard and amassed vast amounts of land throughout the southern and central parts of the state. The latter generations were less interested in working hard. They enjoyed living off the income from the crops and beef, eventually selling land to developers to sustain their income. Lately, the widowed Lydia Unger accelerated the selling as if she wanted to rid herself of a burden.

The home was a sprawling ranch house surrounded by live oaks covered with gray beards of Spanish moss on slightly rolling hills. Long, white wooden fences enclosed grazing horses.

When Josie's car rolled up the crunchy gravel driveway and stopped in front of the house, Missy expected a servant to run out and open their doors. Instead, they got a golden retriever who left slobber on Missy's window.

"Behave," Josie said.

"Are you talking to us or the dog?" Matt asked.

"I'm talking to all of you."

They got out of the car and the spritely Josie beat them to the front door. The bell didn't work, so she pounded on the door.

Cursing came from deep inside the house.

Then, just behind the door, a husky female voice shouted, "I told you to keep an extra key in your truck."

The door burst open. A tall, slender woman in her seventies wearing a bathrobe and holding a lit cigarette, her hair enclosed in a scarf, stood before them.

"Oh, good morning," the woman said, slurring her words slightly. "I thought you were my son."

"I'm Josie Denton. We spoke on the phone yesterday."

"Oh, yes, I remember now." The woman surveyed Missy and Matt suspiciously. "Which one of you is the reporter?"

"I'm the reporter," Matt said.

"And what are you?" The woman asked Missy.

"I'm a nurse."

"You brought a nurse with you?" The woman asked, offended. "I'm not *that* bad off. Not yet, anyway."

"I'm a friend," Missy said, "just along for the ride."

"Well, come in and let's get this over with."

They followed the woman through a giant foyer and down a hall past a drawing room, a dining room, a living room, and, finally, to a study in the rear of the house. It was very masculine, with red leather armchairs, loaded bookshelves, and a fireplace with a painting of a fox hunt hanging above it.

"You folks want anything to drink?"

"I'll have some sparkling water, please," Matt said.

"I got Scotch, bourbon, or gin."

"That's okay," Matt said. "I'm fine."

Mrs. Unger sat behind a large desk covered with printed spreadsheets, an overflowing ashtray, and a tumbler of whiskey.

"What do you want to know about me?" She asked before taking a gulp of her drink.

"Tell us about—" Matt said before Josie cut him off with a deadly glare.

"When did you first become involved in philanthropy?" Josie asked.

"After I married Larry, he was afraid everyone would think he married me just for my family fortune, which was true, so he encouraged me to make large endowments to worthy—"

A crash of several objects falling came from the hallway.

"Jeremy! What the heck are you doing?" The woman yelled. "I told you to be careful."

"Sorry, Ma," a sheepish male voice answered.

"I don't want you bringing your toys into the house."

Something else fell, and a gunshot echoed in the hallway. Missy and Matt dove to the floor.

"You idiot!" Mrs. Unger shouted. "We've got company."

A man in his forties appeared in the doorway. He wore a camouflage military uniform, with night-vision goggles on his head, grenades clipped to his flak vest, and an assault rifle strapped to his torso. He held several handguns.

"Our militia is having a meet-up today and I'm running late. It's my turn to bring the donuts."

"I told you not to bring your toys into the house, especially not loaded."

"They're not toys," the man said resentfully. "They're the exact weapons used by some of the world's top security forces."

"You use them for playing army-man in the woods with your friends. When will you get a job?"

"Ma, I'm preparing for the civil war. That is my job."

"Nonsense," his mother said, taking a swig of her drink.

"What woods do you play—I mean, have exercises—in?" Matt asked.

"That's top secret," the man said, looking defiantly at Matt.

"He plays on our land, so he and his little friends don't get arrested."

"Don't call them that," her son said. "They're deadly warriors. A lot of them are ex-military. When it's time to rise up, we'll be ready!"

"Go and get ready for your play date. I have business here."

The man stormed out of the room.

"Sorry about that," Mrs. Unger said. "I just wish he'd get a job."

Another gun landed on the floor in the hallway. Another gunshot went off, and the bullet ricocheted off the tile floor.

"Ouch!" cried her son.

"So, where were we?" Mrs. Unger said. "Oh yes, charities. The tax write-offs are very useful with all the property taxes I have to pay."

She droned on for quite a while about endowments and charitable foundations while Matt dutifully took notes and recorded it all on his phone.

Josie and Mrs. Unger laughed about a mutual acquaintance, and Missy was beginning to lose patience. And she was sick of breathing cigarette smoke. Maybe it was time for Matt to interrupt with a hard-hitting question.

"I have to say, Lydia, it surprised me that you sold the tract of land west of Jellyfish Beach," Josie said. "And to that horrid man, Loopi."

"Yeah, he's a sleazebag. But the taxes—I couldn't afford them any longer."

"You could have donated the land to the county for a park."

"Yes, but Loopi offered me top dollar. Money is getting tight around here, what with the land we still have, the horses, and my son who won't get a job."

"Did your son ever play in the woods down there?" Josie asked.

Yes, finally! Missy thought.

"I wouldn't know," Mrs. Unger said. "That tract is a long drive from here, but when Jeremy and his friends play armyman, they do like to try different types of terrain, so it's possible."

"Does his group have a name?"

"Why? You're not asking because of that woman who was shot, are you? Remember, we didn't own the land anymore when that happened."

It doesn't mean Jeremy and his friends wouldn't still go there, Missy thought.

"No," Josie said. "I was curious about what he said about a civil war. I wanted to know what side he's on. You know, the name of his team."

"It's all a big fantasy of a bunch of men who still haven't grown up. I think they call themselves the Boogaloo Brigade. Something like that. It's so silly."

Josie giggled. "I guess you're right."

The "interview" went on for another fifteen minutes, but

Mrs. Unger was losing her battle with the whiskey. Her eyes drooped and half-smoked cigarettes were burning to ash.

"I think we have enough," Josie said. She turned to Matt, "do you agree?"

"Yes," he said, pulling himself out of a daze. "Lots of great material here."

"We'll let ourselves out, dear," Josie said, patting Mrs. Unger on the arm.

The three thanked their host profusely and left the room. Loud snoring followed them out.

Once they were in Josie's car, she said, "That turned out well."

"Yeah, I can't believe our luck," Missy said. "We never would have found out about her son otherwise."

"Okay, so he and his buddies run around in the woods with guns," Matt said. "We still have to prove they were there on the night in question. And that they use silver bullets."

"Or," Missy said, "if we can show that they have been there in the past, the police might be interested and can find the proof themselves."

"I'll see if I can come across a trail on social media or the dark web," Matt said. "You never know, I might get lucky."

"If not, you might have to join their militia," Josie said.

"Me?"

"Who else? I'm eighty-seven and a woman. Missy is a woman, too. These boys don't seem like the types who let girls into their club."

"You're looking at a guy who doesn't know which end of a gun the bullets come out of," Matt said. "My dad was a dentist who collected stamps for a hobby, so I didn't grow up with guns. I'm not part of their tribe."

"I know a couple of guys who are very into guns," Missy

said. "The problem is, they're seniors. And they're vampires. They can only take part in nighttime activities."

"I know a bunch of werewolves who own firearms," Josie said, "but they have the same problem with their age. I doubt these militia boys recruit seniors."

"First, we need to learn more about the group," Matt said. "We don't even have a way of contacting them."

## DO YOU BOOGALOO?

hree nights later, Matt strolled into a tavern and scanned the crowd. Jeremy was standing at the end of the bar. This was the only way they could think of contacting Jeremy's group, and, much against his will, Matt was enlisted to do it.

Earlier, he'd found a little information about the militia on the internet. He learned that "boogaloo" did not refer to the Latin music and dance style from the sixties. Nowadays, it was an insider term extremists used for an anti-government, anti-law-enforcement uprising. That's what Jeremy's group, the Boogaloo Brigade, was preparing for.

They didn't have a website, of course. But he found them on watchdog lists of hate groups. Searching the rancid depths of extremist message boards, he came across some postings by or about them. He tried to connect with the users, but they were justifiably suspicious of him.

So, he used the pre-internet, pre-conspiracy-theory way of investigating: Go out into the real world and talk to people.

His tactics included parking near the Unger house and following Jeremy's truck. It wasn't hard to follow, with the giant Nazi flag fluttering from a flagpole on the bed of the truck. Jeremy drove to the tavern on a nearby highway. Matt parked in the dirt lot and waited a short while before he went inside.

Jeremy Unger stood at the end of the bar speaking with a guy with a giant gray beard who looked like an adjutant of Stonewall Jackson. As fat and out of shape as Jeremy was, his friend was lean and muscular. Hopefully that meant they had broad recruitment standards.

"Evening, boys," Matt said as he approached. He realized he was putting on a Southern accent. Exactly why he had no idea.

The two men looked at him suspiciously.

Then Jeremy's eyes flashed in recognition.

"You were at my house the other day," he said.

"My mother was interviewing your mother for some article about charity," Matt said. "Our mothers are friends. I recognized you when I came in here and wanted to say hi."

Jeremy nodded. He looked a little confused, but that might be the way he always looked.

"Can I ask you a question? I was curious when you mentioned the Boogaloo Brigade. I think we share some similar beliefs," Matt said.

"You're not supposed to be talking about our outfit," the bearded guy said angrily to Jeremy.

"He's a family friend," Jeremy said. "He's all right."

"Any way I can help y'all with your cause?" Matt said, appalled at how fake the Southern twang in his voice sounded. "Do you need any extra manpower?"

"How do we know you're not with the FBI?" The bearded one asked belligerently.

"I'm too stupid to pass the entrance exam."

Bearded One smiled, showing stained teeth. "I like this guy."

"What weapons do you own?" Jeremy asked.

Matt had to think quickly. "AR-15s. Handguns. A Samurai sword. Um, and an anti-tank missile launcher."

"Anti-tank missile?" Both militia men asked at the same time.

"Yep. Got it at an auction." Matt instantly regretted his lies.

"Man, I'd love to check that out," Jeremy said. "What kind is it? A Javelin?"

"Sure is," Matt lied.

"Can you take us to see it?"

"Not tonight," Matt said. "It's locked up in a friend's warehouse. Maybe I can bring it by next time you guys have a drill."

"Non-members aren't allowed at our drills," Bearded One said.

"Maybe he can come to our next meeting," Jeremy said. "And bring the anti-tank missile."

Bearded One gave Matt a stern look.

"You must meet three strict requirements to attend a meeting," he said. "First, no phone or recording devices allowed in the room. Second, you must, and I cannot emphasize this enough, you must bring a covered dish. Preferably a dessert. We always come up short with desserts."

"What's the third?"

"No Jell-O."

"Gotcha," Matt said.

"Gluten-free will win you extra points."

"Okay. When can I come?"

"Seven o'clock, the night after tomorrow. At the bunker."

"Where's the bunker?"

"My mom's garage," Jeremy said.

MATT SHOWED up at the bunker filled with trepidation. He didn't have an anti-tank missile. And, even worse, his home-made brownies were not gluten free. He wondered if he would make it through the night alive.

His car rolled slowly along the gravel driveway until his headlights picked up a row of pickups parked along the edge of the drive. He turned around and parked at the beginning of the driveway, nose out, in case he had to make a quick getaway. He walked to the garage from which death-metal music was blaring. He noticed a side door and gave it a knock.

It opened a crack. Jeremy's face peered out at him. A cloud of marijuana smoke billowed out around his head.

"Hey, what's up? Did you bring the anti-tank missile?" Jeremy asked.

"Dude, I'm really sorry but I couldn't bring it tonight. My buddy needed to use it."

"For what?"

"To bring down one of the government's black helicopters."

"Good for your friend."

"I did bring some brownies," Matt added.

Jeremy smiled. "Okay, you can come in, but I'll need to pat you down."

He opened the door and gave Matt a half-hearted patting of his pockets, then signaled for him to come in.

It looked like a high-school party at your friend's house when his parents are out of town. Not counting Matt, there were seven men, including Stonewall Jackson's adjutant on the couch. Matt wasn't a military expert, but he was certain seven men didn't constitute a brigade. The militia men sprawled about on couches and chairs in the garage turned into a man-cave. They ranged in age from early twenties to mid-fifties, a motley crew with nothing in common except T-shirts and ball caps with racist or anti-government slogans. Some caps had a crude logo for the Boogaloo Brigade.

The men all drank from plastic cups of beer. There was a keg fridge in the corner. A bong sat on a side table.

"This dude is Matt Smith," Jeremy said to the group. "He's a potential recruit."

Some men waved to him, but most were too busy talking and drinking to give him much notice. Matt wasn't sure when the meeting would begin, or if the meeting was just a bunch of guys sitting around getting wasted.

"Go get yourself a beer," Jeremy said.

Matt crossed the room and filled a cup from the keg.

"Do you prefer Four-chan or Eight-kun?" Asked a voice behind him. It was a bald guy with a potbelly and a T-shirt that said, "The earth is flat, and you know I'm right."

"I'm an Eight-kun guy," Matt said, referring to the message board filled with hate speech and conspiracy theories.

"Have you seen my posts? I go by the handle of 'Fatcat.'"

"Sure," Matt lied. "Very astute posts. You should be proud."

Fatcat smiled. He had badly botched his most recent attempt at shaving, leaving nicks all over his face.

"I'm a thought leader on contrails," Fatcat said. "I've proven that the government is sending jets to spray chemicals that turn the population gay. It's important to get the word out."

"Thank you for your service," Matt said.

"It's the least I can do for my country. I'm a patriot."

"We all are," Matt said. "That's why we're here. Say, do you guys do a lot of field exercises?"

"Not really," Fatcat said. "We're too busy and rarely have the time."

Matt glanced at the room of guys busy sitting around getting drunk and stoned.

"You ever do night exercises?" Matt asked. "I've got some awesome night-vision goggles that I rarely get the chance to use."

"We have done those. But not during mosquito season."

"With live ammo?"

"Sure."

"I live down in Crab County," Matt said. "Do y'all ever conduct any ops there? That would be mighty convenient for me."

"We did once, not too long ago. There are more cops down that way, though."

Matt was trying to find a non-suspicious way of asking the exact date of this event, when the music turned off.

"Let's get some business out of the way," Jeremy said to the group. Matt wasn't sure if Jeremy was their leader, or if he got to act like it because this was his mom's garage.

"All in favor of an uprising if the government tries to take our guns say 'aye.'"

"Aye!" the group said in unison.

"All in favor of an uprising if the government forces us to become gay?"

The group shouted, "aye!"

"All in favor of an uprising if they don't bring back 'The A Team' to TV?"

"Aye!"

"Okay, meeting adjourned. Let's all make a toast to the Boogaloo. But please drink responsibly. To the Boogaloo!"

"To the Boogaloo!" the men shouted before chugging their beers.

And that was that. Matt faked his way through a discussion

with a couple of members about firearms. He asked them if they or other members ever used silver bullets. They laughed at him. There are some things even conspiracy theorists find impossible to believe, and it seemed lycanthropy was one of them.

He then chatted with an older gentleman with a swastika tattooed on his forehead about recipes for baking bread. Try as he may, he couldn't get anyone to confirm if they had been on the Unger Tract on the night of the murder.

When the first member left for the night, Matt used that as his opportunity to escape. He handed Jeremy a slip of paper with his phone number.

"Thanks so much for having me," Matt said. "Call me when you have another event. And when I can pick up my brownie platter."

"And I still want to see that anti-tank missile," Jeremy said.

"You got it."

AFTER THE LONG DRIVE HOME, Matt called Missy. He knew she'd be up at this late hour. He gave her a synopsis of his evening.

"It's good to know they don't sound like they're on the verge of starting the civil war," Missy said.

"They're not on the verge of doing anything. I don't know if they're our best suspects for the shooting. And I'm not sure if we have enough information to get the police interested."

"And definitely not enough to satisfy Josie," Missy said. "She's out for blood."

"I hope you don't mean blood literally."

"I do."

"I wish we could keep her out of this," Matt said, "but I

promised her a report on the militia. I don't want her werewolves to attack these guys unless there's proof they killed her
friend. To me, they seem dangerous only in their own minds."

"Not if they were shooting werewolves with silver bullets."

"A couple of them denied that anyone used silver bullets."

"It only takes one guy," Missy said.

JOSIE LOPED through the pines and oaks of Ocala National
Forest in wolf form. She hadn't told the other members of the
Werewolf Women's Club about her mission. They weren't good
about following her commands and this mission had to be
stealthy and done right.

Matt had tipped her off about the Boogaloo Brigade's
planned practice operation in a remote part of the forest, far
from where any ranger or other law enforcement would come
across them. Matt didn't want to go himself; he said there was a
problem with a missile launcher or something.

The tricky part for Josie was that the operation was during
daytime. Matt had said these guys didn't enjoy nighttime ops
very much. That gave Josie doubts that one of them was the
killer she sought, but she had to be sure. Werewolves can
voluntarily shift during the day, but she would have to be extra
careful to stay out of sight.

She parked in a space near a remote trailhead deep in the
forest and shifted in the back seat of The Boat. She had memo-
rized the trail map to find her way to where the militia planned
to be, but once she got closer, she would leave the trails and rely
on scent alone to guide her.

As she ran along the trail, she totally freaked out the birds
and small animals along the way. They rarely saw wolves

during the day. This is a nice forest, she thought. The club would have to make a special road trip up here someday to go hunting. They could combine it with shopping in Ocala.

She traveled four miles—easy for a wolf, unlikely for Josie in human form even with sensible shoes. That's when she picked up the first scents: unwashed human males, gun oil, and lots and lots of ammunition. She had to be very careful. Regular bullets couldn't kill her, but they still hurt like you-know-what.

They were just up ahead. Josie crawled through a bed of ferns and looked over the crest of a hill. Down below was a large clearing. Seven humans decked out in military uniforms were setting up wooden targets on posts. The targets were human-shaped.

For the next hour all the humans did was take turns firing at the targets with a huge selection of weaponry. Would any rangers hear this? she wondered. Then they formed a line and ran past the targets while shooting at them. Next, they entered the trees at the edge of the clearing, low-crawled out of the woods, and shot at the targets while lying down. This was getting boring.

By this point, they had shot the wooden targets to pieces. The men, no longer organized, began taking potshots at bottles they placed on fallen logs. Even they soon grew bored with this.

Finally, they called it a day and opened a cooler of beer.

Josie had been sampling scents the entire time, trying to detect if silver bullets were present. She didn't smell any. So with the men's alertness down, she crept closer to them in search of stronger scents. Soon, she was close enough to hear them.

"What do y'all got planned for the rest of the weekend?" a gruff voice asked.

"Wife's got a long list of chores for me."

"I'm going to open-carry with my rifle at the playground," another voice said. "Everywhere else I go, no one pays attention to me."

"I'm gonna bake bread," said another.

She drank in their repulsive man-scents and didn't smell any silver except for a ring and a tiny cross on a chain. It didn't rule them out; perhaps they brought silver bullets with them only when doing their war games at night. But these guys just didn't feel like the killers to her.

She crawled away silently, then raced back to the trailhead.

"I think I saw a wolf!" she heard behind her.

"Don't be an idiot. Ain't no wolves in this forest."

## 13

# FLORIDA MAN VS. GARDEN GNOMES

Kenny was a Florida man. He was also a veritable "Florida Man," as in how the term appeared in news headlines. Kenny wouldn't think of himself in that way, but his arrest record said otherwise. It included the kind of judgement-lacking stunts that end up in the news and go viral.

His most recent stunt, accidentally crashing his truck through the fence of an electrical substation, proved he was also competing for the Darwin Awards. These dishonorable honors go to idiots who die and remove their idiot genes from our gene pool, thus inching our collective intelligence up a fraction of a notch from where it is now: far below where it ought to be. If Kenny's truck had hit the transformer, a few feet to the right, he would have been an award winner.

Only a week after that, how and why Kenny ended up with a chainsaw, a box of rattlesnakes, and a bottle of cheap bourbon was anyone's guess. Oh, and don't forget the bottle of prescription anti-depressants. So far, he only needed to get naked, and he would cover most of the tropes of the Florida Man legend.

The explanation for why he had the cheap bourbon was simple: He always had cheap bourbon on hand, at least until it invariably ran out around 9:30 p.m. That was the case tonight, at 9:45.

The anti-depressants he stole from his mother-in-law. He preferred tranquilizers or painkillers, but these were the only meds left unlocked in the bathroom she used in their house.

The chainsaw he borrowed from his neighbor. A dead tree, long neglected, had finally fallen in their backyard, crushing the storage shed and enraging Vicky. She ordered him to cut the tree into manageable pieces, but he hadn't gotten around to it yet on account of watching NASCAR on TV all afternoon. And because of the liquor. And the medication.

The rattlesnakes? The explanation for those was actually fairly simple. Kenny's brother, Willard, was the pastor at a primitive Baptist church and was planning to introduce the practice of snake handling to his flock. When the Spirit was in you, Willard claimed, the snakes won't bite you. It's a testament of the Lord's love for you and your faith in him.

The box of snakes was sitting on Kenny's porch because Willard couldn't bring them home, because of his dogs, and couldn't leave them at the church, because of some silly town regulations. They would be here only until the morning when Willard picked them up for church.

Kenny had been planning to use the snakes for a practical joke, but could no longer remember what he had planned. That was an entire bottle of bourbon ago. Water under the bridge, as they say. Right now, he had wood to cut.

"Kenny! You moronic mullet-head, what do you think you're doing?" Vicky yelled as she stood in the back doorway.

"What does it look like? I'm cutting this dang tree you've been on my butt about for days on end."

"I asked you to do it this morning. Why the heck are you doing it now after you've been drinking?"

"I've been busy all day. And I just have a slight buzz on. Don't worry, I am legendary for my alcohol tolerance."

"That's what you said when you wrecked the truck at the power substation. It's too late to use the chainsaw. You'll wake up mother and half the neighborhood."

"Leave me alone, woman. I have a job to do."

"One more thing, mullet-head. Why are you naked?"

Kenny looked down. Sure enough, he was naked. Though he was wearing his boots, which were critical. You don't want to use a chainsaw when you're barefoot. He couldn't remember why he was naked, though. He must have been preparing to shower when he got distracted by something. Or the other way around. Didn't matter, he wasn't afraid of sawdust in his chest hair.

"You mind your own business," he said. "Unless you want to head to the liquor store and pick me up another—"

Vicky slammed the door shut.

Okay, let's get this over with, he thought. He checked the chainsaw, and it mercifully had gas in it. He pulled out the choke and yanked the starter cord. Nothing. He yanked again. The motor sputtered in a cloud of oil and gasoline fumes but didn't start. He yanked again, lost his balance, and fell on his butt with the chainsaw falling in his lap.

"Good thing she wasn't running," he said aloud and laughed.

Something caught his eye. The stupid gnome in Vicky's flower garden wasn't where it was supposed to be. And there was a second gnome with it he had never seen before. What was that all about? She didn't need another gnome.

Back to the task at hand, he reminded himself. Before he yanked the cord, he remembered to push the choke back in before the engine flooded. He tried again and this time the dang thing started.

In the faint light of the porch, he went to work on the tree. Cutting two sections of wood from the base of the fallen tree, he paused to rest, wishing he had some more bourbon. The chainsaw rumbled and sputtered as it idled in his hands.

Then he noticed something: The gnomes weren't in the garden anymore. They stood a few yards behind him: Vicky's gnome in the checkered shirt sitting on a mushroom and the new gnome with a crooked red hat. How had they gotten over here? He concluded that he was simply confused, and they had been here all along.

He realized he couldn't cut any more sections from the bottom of the tree because it would collapse further and cause additional damage to the shed. And maybe to him, too. He needed to cut the upper part that was resting on what was left of the shed. He needed a stepladder or something, but he didn't know where the dang ladder was.

Time to improvise. He rolled the two logs he had cut over to the shed, positioned them on end, and stood one foot atop each.

The logs were unsteady. This probably wasn't a good idea, but he was impatient to get the dang job over with.

The chainsaw roared as he pressed the trigger. He leaned toward the tree, tottering on the unsteady logs. Once the saw made contact with the tree and he leaned into it, he felt more balanced. He'd just have to be careful when the blade pushed through.

When it finally did, sawdust flying into his face, he leaned backwards to compensate.

And something kicked the logs from behind. The logs

tipped forward, and he fell backwards. He lost hold of the chainsaw and landed on his back, partly knocking the wind out of him.

He gazed up into the sky to see the chainsaw cartwheeling down toward his head.

He twisted aside just in time. The chainsaw landed right where his head had been. He was both relieved and angry.

High-pitched laughter came from nearby. That made him angrier. He sat up. The two gnomes were right next to him, standing beside the knocked-over logs. More laughter flowed, but the gnomes were absolutely still. There was no sign of their mouths opening.

And why would there be? They were dang garden gnomes. So then why did he suspect they were what knocked the logs over and almost got his head crushed by a fifteen-pound chainsaw?

The laughter continued—squeaky, rodent-like giggling. Those little lawn ornaments made him fall, and they were now mocking him as he sat on his naked ass. Anger surged inside him. It was the worst kind of anger, fueled by liquor and stimulated by whatever was in those perk-me-up pills he had taken.

Kenny got to his feet and grabbed the still-running chainsaw. He revved it and moved menacingly toward the two gnomes.

"You're gonna miss having heads, you little maggots," he said as he staggered toward the gnomes with the chainsaw pointed toward the new gnome.

They disappeared. No, they were a few feet to the right now. How did that happen? He didn't see them move. Maybe they hadn't moved after all. Kenny blinked. Was something wrong with his eyes? Or his brain?

He turned slightly and aimed the chainsaw at the same gnome, the one with the crooked red hat.

"C'mon and take your medicine!"

He stopped in front of the gnome, revved the chainsaw, its chain spinning in a blur, and lowered the saw diagonally onto where the gnome's head met its body.

Except the gnome wasn't there anymore.

And horrible pain flared in his left leg. Dang, when he missed the gnome, he nicked his calf. The blood was making him sick. But it also made him that much angrier. These gnomes would pay if it was the last thing he ever did.

The gnomes were again a few feet away from him, closer to the house now. He staggered after them and swung the chainsaw wildly. But again, they disappeared.

Either these little maggots were magical, or he was having a terrible head trip. And, dang, his leg sure hurt.

"Don't mess with me! I'm gonna turn you into garden mulch."

He followed them across the yard. Every time he lunged with the saw, they disappeared, a fraction of a second before the blade made contact.

Now he had them trapped against the base of the porch. He laughed the low, gloating laugh of a victor. Then attacked with the roaring saw.

The saw buried itself in the porch's edge, and the gnomes were gone. He pried the blade from the wood and checked the tension of the chain.

The rodent-like laughter came from above. The gnomes were on the porch, looking down on him with amusement.

He roared like a bull gator and ran up the porch steps, flinging the screen door open. He revved the chainsaw and gnashed his teeth in anger. A growl escaped his mouth.

"Kenny, get that chainsaw off the porch," Vicky shouted from inside.

He ignored her. He had a score to settle. He didn't care if the deck of the porch got scratched, as long as the gnomes ended up as little pieces of plastic.

"This ends here," he said and attacked.

The blade ended up an inch deep in the floor. Oh, and the tip of his right boot was missing, along with the ends of his toes. Fine. Just fine. He didn't friggin' care anymore. He wasn't stopping until he won.

The gnomes were behind him. He swung the chainsaw like he was teeing off. Now they were on the chaise lounge. He slammed the saw down like an ax. The chaise lounge ended up in two pieces.

Now they were on top of a wooden crate. He chopped at them and the saw cut into the lid. The gnomes appeared in front of the crate. He thrust the chainsaw like a battering ram.

But as he did, a little light went off in a dark, alcohol-pickled part of his brain. Wait a minute, he thought, wasn't this the crate that held the rattlesnakes?

Too late, the saw burrowed into the front of the crate and a big section of wood dropped to the floor. There was a big, gaping opening in the crate. Inside, rattles were going off like machine guns. And rattlesnakes came pouring out,

They were freaked out by the noise and chaos caused by the saw. And they were mad.

Kenny gasped and tried to jump backwards away from the dozen snakes slithering toward him across his porch floor, but he tripped on something behind him. And fell.

Right on the snakes.

After the first bursts of pain, he lost track of how many fangs punctured his skin. He found out that it really sucks to be bitten by a rattler, let alone a dozen of them. And it sucked even more to be naked at the time.

He rolled away and lay on the floor as his body went into shock and his body parts began swelling. One of his parts swelled to such a magnificent size that he had a brief moment of manly pride.

And then he died.

THE HEADLINE of Matt's story in the next day's edition of *The Jellyfish Beach Journal*: "Naked Florida man found dead. Cause of death rattlesnake bites or chainsaw wounds."

No mention, of course, of gnomes. The copyeditor removed that. But Matt saw the gnomes when he arrived on the scene, after he was alerted to the death by his police scanner.

There were two gnomes standing on the porch amid the crawling rattlesnakes. Later, when Matt looked again, there was only one. The other gnome had vanished.

## 14

# THE ARCH-MAGE BOB

Bob was not happy to see Missy. She poked her head in the board-repair room of Bob's surf shop and enjoyed the look of dismay on his face.

Florence, his magically smart African Grey parrot, squawked with alarm from her nearby perch.

"Hi, Bob," Missy said. "How's the surf been?"

Instantly, a sonic force hit her and almost bowled her over. No small talk for Bob; he was going into battle. Fortunately, she had girded herself with a protection spell and amped up its power right before entering the surf shop.

"That's no way to greet someone," she said.

He stood up from the workbench where he'd been sanding a surfboard. He smiled and spread his hands in innocence. His eyes searched behind her to see if she was alone.

"You surprised me, dude," he said. "I didn't expect to see you up here in San Marcos so soon. Especially after you stole my grimoire."

"Do we really have to go through this again? The grimoire

belonged to my father. He bequeathed it to me. You or someone else stole it from him after he died. Just because it ended up in your hands doesn't mean it was yours."

"I paid like big-time money to the city's best vampire thief for it."

Missy was stunned. Did this mean Maurice, who had tried to help her find the grimoire before, actually was involved in stealing it from her father in the first place? She wanted to find out, but that was a matter for a later date.

"And just so you know, I will get the book back," Bob said. He was in his fifties, a little too old and too big in the gut to justify his surfer-dude look with shaggy blond hair, Hawaiian shirt, board shorts and sandals. "I put like hundreds of hours into studying the spells in the addendum. I was sooo close to figuring them out."

"Why haven't you stolen it back already?"

He smiled. His blue eyes appeared earnest. "Because I heard you have the Red Dragon."

The Red Dragon amplified her power enough to be on equal footing with his, even though the Arch-Mage of San Marcos was much more experienced with magic than she was. The Red Dragon was her greatest weapon against Bob, but it also put her at significant risk. He would do anything to steal it from her.

"I didn't come here to bicker about the grimoire," Missy said. "I need some information."

"Oh, sure, dude, you steal my book and you expect me to help you?"

"You tortured me. You remember that? You broke into my home and assaulted me with magic to force me to tell you where the grimoire was. You're a man who committed violence upon a woman. You're human scum."

She tried to control her anger. It wasn't helping with her diplomatic mission.

Bob stared at her without speaking. She tried to read his expression. Then he smirked.

"I used enhanced interrogation techniques, because you were totally lying to me."

She couldn't hold in her anger any longer. She grasped the Red Dragon talisman in her pocket, the heavy, metal figurine carved in a dragon-like shape. The moment she touched it, the sensation of an electric shock hit her hand and passed up her arm, through her chest, and into her head. Her scalp tingled and her heart raced. She recited silently the words of a simple levitation spell that worked in conjunction with her natural ability for telekinesis.

She launched the power at Bob.

An unseen hand grabbed his hair and yanked him into the air, arms flailing and legs kicking.

Florence flapped her wings and squawked, "Knock it off, witch!"

"So, Bob, I could report to the Guild that you used black magic to torture me," Missy said. "You'd be removed as Arch-Mage and banished from the city, forfeiting all your property. Or I could kill you right now, in the most painful way you can imagine, because of what you did to me."

She added a spell that constricted his throat, not enough to strangle him but enough to make breathing more difficult, which causes panic in any creature. It was against her ethos to use her magic to harm. She practiced earth magick. It was white, the polar opposite of black magic. And she was a nurse. So these "enhanced interrogation techniques" she was using were wrong in her heart.

But Bob deserved some payback for what he had done to her. She wanted to wipe that smirk off his face permanently.

"There's another option," she said. "You can answer some questions, none of which should involve any damaging information for you to reveal. Then I'll be on my way."

She released the pressure on his throat.

"Photocopies," he said in a scratchy voice.

"What?"

"Make photocopies or scans of the pages in the grimoire's addendum. That's all I ask, dude."

"But you need the physical book to be present when casting the more powerful spells, don't you?"

"Yes. But many of those spells are for healing, which doesn't interest me. There's other knowledge in those pages I've been trying to decipher. There's more to that book than magic spells. Secrets about life, death, and immortality, dude. It'll blow your mind! This knowledge is nothing that I can use to harm people. It's the kind of revelations that have only been hinted at for millennia. The stuff humans have lusted for since the beginning of time. I had only a taste of it and it's enough to drive you freaking bonkers with the desire to know more. You dig what I'm saying?"

"I do," Missy said.

"Give me copies of those pages and you can keep the grimoire with my blessing. I'll be your ally moving forward. I'll forget about your dragon dropping me in a cesspool."

"He's not my dragon. He's just a friend," she said about Ronnie, the dragon she had once rescued from the Everglades and who answered her call to save her from Bob.

It sounded harmless enough. But could she trust him?

She turned her back to Bob and sent out thought waves to call Don Mateo. He never showed up in a timely fashion when she needed him, but at the moment she grasped the Red Dragon in her hand.

"Don Mateo, I command you to answer me," she whispered. "Is it safe to give Bob copies of your addendum to the grimoire?"

She waited. Silence.

"Answer me, ghost. I command you with the power of the Red Dragon!"

*Yes*, a voice echoed in her head. *It is safe.*

She returned her attention to Bob. "Okay, I'll do it if you promise to cooperate with me."

"I will. Please let me breathe."

She released his throat fully, but kept him hanging by his hair.

"Will you answer my questions?"

"Yes. Please let me down."

"Do you know of a demon called Caorthannach?" Missy asked.

"No."

"From ancient Ireland?"

"No."

"Also known as the mother of the Devil?"

"That sounds vaguely familiar."

"A sorcerer of some sort summoned her and ordered her to possess my garden gnome."

"Your *gnome?*" He chuckled, despite being hung from his hair.

"Yes, my gnome. And my gnome has spread the possession to other gnomes. It's like a gnome uprising."

Bob laughed out loud. She started giggling, too.

"It's not funny. They've been killing people. My neighbor died from a mango shoved into his throat."

Bob laughed uproariously. Her amusement died down, though, when the true gravity of the situation returned to her.

"Do you know who the sorcerer could be?" she asked. "Someone skilled enough to summon not just any demon, but a specific, obscure one. And someone crazy enough to want to possess garden gnomes."

"In case you suspect me, I've never summoned a demon," Bob said. "Can you put me down, please? My scalp is hurting like a bitch."

"You probably have the skills to summon one," she said, releasing him to drop back onto his stool which nearly tipped over.

"I know how it's done. But I've never done it. I've come across true black-magic practitioners before, but we've always run them out of town. A case of possession this weird, though, I don't know. There's only one sorcerer I can think of, but I don't want to make any unfounded accusations. Remember Wendall, who I introduced you to when you came to San Marcos before?"

She nodded.

"Let's go speak to him."

She followed him out the back door of the shop. He climbed into his open jeep on the jacked-up frame with extra-wide tires.

"Are we driving on the beach today?" She asked.

"No. Wendall is fishing the river today."

"Then I'll follow you so I can get on the road back to Jelly-fish Beach afterwards." She had driven northbound in the hours after midnight, timing her arrival for the morning right after Bob opened his store. It was a lengthy trip just to ask questions, and she had to get home to deal with noxious gnomes and vengeful werewolves.

She drove her car behind Bob's Jeep south along Highway

A1A. Dunes covered with sea oats were on the left and wherever the barrier island narrowed, the marshes and oyster bars of Blood River curved inland near the road. Tiny islands dotted the marshes and points of low grass curved near the shore. The oyster bars were dark humps made of jagged oysters cemented together, visible during lower tides.

After a few miles, Bob turned right onto a dirt road that went west. Missy followed. They passed older homes, some of which were on stilts, all of which had boats on trailers in their driveways. One home had a pile of crab traps in the front lawn. The road ended soon at the edge of the marsh.

A sprawling, garage-like building sat by the water's edge. A few canoes and kayaks lay around the sandy lot. A sign on the building read, "Paddling Around."

Bob parked by the building, and Missy did the same.

"A little side venture of mine," Bob said as he hopped out of the Jeep. "Sales, rentals, and lessons. You know how to handle a kayak?"

"Yes." Though to be honest, it had been a while since she had. Working the graveyard shift to provide healthcare for monsters cuts into your daytime recreation opportunities. Her last serious paddling venture had been in the Everglades when she was helping the dragon.

Bob went into the building and came out dragging two kayaks. He tossed her a flotation vest and a paddle. Then they each dragged the craft down a dirt ramp to the water.

"Hopefully, he's not too far from here," Bob said, wading with his kayak into the water and climbing aboard.

Missy did the same, wading up to her calves. The water was on the cool side, but pleasant. She sat in the kayak, pulled her dripping legs aboard, and paddled behind him as they made their way through the shallow marsh. Tiny baitfish scattered out of their path.

They traveled down a wide creek with a maze of smaller ones branching off from it and winding through marsh grass. Soon, the main creek reached the river. A green channel marker to their right indicated it was the Intracoastal Waterway. Bob turned right and paddled past docks that led to waterfront homes.

"Sometimes Wendall fishes the docks around here for sea trout and flounder, but he's not here. Follow me."

He turned left into the primary river channel, looked both ways for boat traffic, then quickly paddled across with Missy right behind. They passed through an inlet between two small islands with narrow, sandy beaches, and then into a wide, marshy area like the one where they had launched. It had meandering creeks, tiny islets of spartina grass, and mangrove trees guarding shallow bays where jagged oyster bars barely broke the surface.

"This is an awesome place to paddle because only the fishing guides would dare bring a boat in here. Too shallow."

They continued west toward a distant line of dark green trees that marked dry land. Missy's kayak ground to a halt in the shallows twice, and she had to push the boat backwards with her paddle to free it.

"There he is," Bob said, pointing to a tiny white shape against the brown of a small islet.

Missy would have mistaken the shape for a wading bird. But as they drew closer, she saw it was a man in a white shirt, sitting in a kayak holding a fishing pole.

"Ah, you're bringing me a witch again," Wendall said with a smile as they drifted up to him. "Missy Lawthorne, correct?"

"Hi Wendall. Actually, it's Missy Mindle. I go by my adoptive family's surname. I didn't use my husband's name when I was married."

"What can I do for you?" Wendall asked. "The redfish don't seem to be biting today, so I'll assume you're here to ask about your father?"

Wendall was a retired wizard who knew Missy's father when he was one of the Southeast's most powerful witches. He died when Missy was only an infant, possibly killed by a rival. Missy had always assumed her mother died at the same time until Wendall revealed that she hadn't and that she had divorced her father prior to his death. Wendall was a genial old fellow with a wide-brimmed hat and a narrow, big-jawed face.

"We're here because you never answer your cellphone when you're fishing, dude," Bob said, "otherwise I would have just called you. We have a question about demon summoning."

"Oh Lord, I'm not going to give you any help with that," Wendall said.

"But you know most of the people in the state who know how to do it, right?"

"They all practice black magic so they're no friends of mine."

"Someone recently summoned a very obscure demon, one named Caorthannach. And whoever did it instructed the demon to possess garden gnomes and to make them rise up against their human owners."

Bob barely finished what he was saying when Wendall broke out laughing.

"Garden gnomes? Rising up against humans? That is too rich."

"It's true," Missy said. "And they have to be stopped. People are dying."

"Really? By golly, that's insane."

"Who do you think could have done this?" Bob asked.

"Nowadays, most witches and wizards who practice black magic are interested in necromancy, bringing the dead back to life. There's not as much interest in demons as there was in earlier centuries. Those who do summon demons choose the well-known ones, such as Agares, Asmodeus, Astaroth. These demons aren't too powerful to control and they're so accustomed to being summoned that they know what's expected of them."

"Which is what?" Missy asked.

"Sometimes to do the things you can do naturally with your earth magick, like protect a person or find something. Usually it's something bad, like kill an enemy. This case of possessing gnomes," he couldn't finish his sentence with his chuckling breaking out.

"Who do you know who has the knowledge and ability to summon a demon that most people have never heard of when there are no known instructions for reaching this particular demon?" Missy asked.

"Bob, you know as well as I do," Wendall said.

"I didn't want to say until I heard your take on it."

They both looked at Missy.

"What? Why are you looking at me?"

"The only person I can think of who could pull this off," Wendall said, "is your mother."

MISSY FELT DIZZY. She was afraid she'd faint and capsize her kayak. She had been shocked a few months ago to learn from Wendall that the mother she had never known, whom she had always thought was dead, was in fact alive. Or at least was alive when Missy was adopted by another family, by her father's cousin and his wife.

But to hear that her mother practiced black magic and summoned demons? That sent her entire world reeling.

"Are you okay, young lady?" Wendall asked.

"I don't know. And I'm not a young lady. I'm forty-six."

"What I would trade to be in my forties again," Wendall said.

"How can you be certain my mother did this?"

"Oh, I never said I was certain, did I? Nope. People practicing the black arts don't keep public records of what they're up to, that's for sure. I was making a reasonable guess based on my knowledge of what it would take to summon a demon like that and who could do it."

"But *why* would she do it?"

"You'd have to ask her yourself."

Even after she had found out that her mother hadn't died alongside her father, Missy didn't know if she was alive today. Searching public records on the internet brought up no information at all. Her mother had probably taken a new name.

So, not knowing if she was alive, Missy had decided to assume she wasn't. Even if she was alive, Missy didn't want to find her. After all, the woman must have given up custody of her when she divorced her father. And after her father was killed, her mother didn't take in her infant daughter. So why would she want to meet this woman?

And the thought of doing so was even more unattractive now that she knew her mother practiced black magic.

Yet the question truly nagged her: Why did she choose Missy's gnome to possess? That meant she knew about Missy and where she lived. She knew she had a gnome in her garage. And she decided to spare Missy's life. So far.

This really freaked her out, the feeling of being lied to, spied upon, and manipulated. She realized, like it or not, she would have to find this supposed mother of hers.

And stop her.

"Do you know where my mother might live?" She asked Wendall.

"I'm sorry, but I don't. All I know is that she was living in Orlando at the time your father died. That was a long time ago."

"Forty-six years ago," Missy said. "A very, very long time."

THE THREE OF them paddled back to the launch together. Missy peppered Wendall and Bob with questions about how to look for her mother.

"If she lived in Northeast Florida, I would know about it," Bob said. "That's why the Guild was established nearly two hundred years ago. We keep track of witches, wizards, and other magicians and make sure they don't use their magic for evil ends."

Missy cut in front of his kayak with hers and gave him a sharp look.

"Okay, sometimes there's a gray line between evil intentions and selfish ones," Bob said.

"There's nothing gray about assault and abuse," she said in a firm voice.

"What are you two talking about?" Wendall asked.

"Something I'm going to spend a long time atoning for," Bob said.

"Black magic sorcerers are hard to find," Wendall said. "They tend to be solitary. Unless they're involved in some satanic religious group, but most of those bozos don't know jack about magic."

"I have someone working for me who could help you," Bob said. "He's an enforcer."

"I don't need a thug," Missy said.

"No, he's not a thug. He's like an internal affairs detective in a police department. He's who the Guild uses to find and bust wrongdoers. He works only in the counties we administer, but I can send him around the state to search for your mother."

"I don't know. It feels weird."

"You said people are dying. That has to be stopped."

"I don't want someone else stopping her. That's my responsibility."

"Then the enforcer will help you find her, and the rest is up to you."

"Okay," Missy said, resigned to following this path. "I accept your offer."

"It's contingent on one thing," Bob said. "That you send me the photocopies or scans of the addendum to the grimoire."

Missy sighed. "Deal."

## 15

## JACK THE OGRE

The white panel van parked in Missy's driveway. It was a generic van with no signage on it, the kind workmen used all over the country. She hadn't called a workman, though. She peered through the curtains and waited to see who got out.

It was a large man. Very large. He wasn't fat, though he had a belly roll. He was Caucasian. Well, actually he had a greenish tint to his skin. His head was shaved and he wore a blue blazer, white dress shirt, and gray slacks. He had hands like oven mitts. His black dress shoes looked much too small for a man of his size and stature. He lumbered toward her front door. Well over six feet tall and probably close to 300 pounds, he could have been an NFL lineman or a villain in professional wrestling.

She got a better look at his face as he reached her front porch steps. Oversized lower jaw, tiny pug nose, giant protruding brow, a slight pointiness to his tiny ears, no neck visible. And there was that green skin tone. She recognized right away what he was.

An ogre.

She had one patient through her home-health nursing agency who was an ogre. The agency, Acceptance Home Care, specialized in customers who couldn't use the regular health system for their needs because they weren't human, or were only partially human. Most of Missy's patients were vampires and werewolves. She cared for a few elves, but elves tended to retire in places other than Florida. And she had her ogre patient who lived near the beach where her other patients lived. Since this was Florida, and these patients needed home care, they were all seniors.

The door shook from the ogre's knocks. Apparently, ogres don't use doorbells.

"Good morning," Missy said upon opening the door.

"You the witch Missy Mindle?" The ogre asked in a rumbling voice tinged with a New Jersey accent.

"That's me."

"I'm Jack. Bob sent me."

"Wow. You got here quickly." She had emailed Bob the scans of the grimoire only the previous day.

"I drove down here overnight. I need to hurry. Powerful witches can sense when they're being hunted, ruining my chances of surprising them."

"Please come in," Missy said. "Can I make you some coffee or tea?"

"Coffee. Lots of sugar."

He followed her to the kitchen. Missy drank tea, so she had to pull an old coffee maker from a cabinet and set it up. She found a bag of coffee in the back of the fridge. She gestured for Jack to take a seat at the kitchen table but was afraid he'd crush the chair. He remained standing beside the island counter.

"So, you're Bob's . . . enforcer?"

"I'm mostly a tracker. It ain't steady work, though. Not many evil witches and wizards in Northeast Florida nowadays. They're usually in Tallahassee or Washington D.C. So mainly I got a moving and storage business."

This guy could probably lift a couch with one hand, Missy thought.

"You know where this witch lives?" he asked.

"Unfortunately, no," she said. That would be too easy.

"Then I need a sample of her magic so I can track her."

"How does that work?" She wished she knew how to do it herself.

"Arch-Mage Bob trained me. The procedure's a kind of magic mixed with religious ritual. It's what the Spanish Inquisition used."

"I thought they didn't go after actual witches. They only accused innocent people of being witches and heretics."

"That, too. But they found plenty of real witches. Most were good ones, though."

"Back to your request, the only sample of her magic I have keeps on escaping from me. He disappeared last night. I'll have to use a spell to get him back. He's a garden gnome."

"A garden gnome?"

"Yes. Little fellow about a foot tall."

The enormous man started laughing. "A garden gnome!" He pounded the island with amusement with a hand the size of a slab of beef. She worried he would crack the counter in half.

"I'll excuse myself and take care of that spell. Back soon."

She didn't want to perform magic in front of this guy and his Inquisition trappings. It would creep her out. So, safely out of his view, she retrieved the Red Dragon from the litter box and carried it into the garage. Like most Floridians, her garage contained everything but a car. Lacking basements because of the high water table, Floridians used their garages to store the junk they couldn't do without and a lot of the junk they should do without. They stuffed yard tools inside as well.

There was very little open floor space, but she found enough room to draw a magic circle with chalk on the concrete floor. She repeated the spell Don Mateo had taught her, grasped the talisman, and called her gnome home.

The garage's side window shattered, the gnome pressed into the impact-resistant glass.

"Oh my, another window bites the dust." She wondered what the total price tag would be.

She went outside and circled the garage. When she came to the window, she was surprised the see the gnome was wearing a purple lei around its neck.

"C'mon," she said, "your partying days are over."

She pried the gnome from the window and carried him into the kitchen. She placed him in his usual spot atop the island.

"He's a cute gnome," Jack said, "with his little lei." Then he started laughing.

"Okay, enough of the gnome mockery." Missy was beginning to sympathize with the indignity the lawn ornaments must feel. What they felt when they were animated demonically, that is.

Jack set his coffee down with his freakishly large hand and picked up the gnome. Then he sniffed it all over.

"What are you doing?" Missy asked.

"What does it look like? I'm picking up the scent of the magic."

"That's what the Spanish Inquisition did? They sniffed people?"

"No. That's what ogres do. We have a better sense of smell than any other creature. I can smell all sorts of magic. Then I use my ritual to locate where it came from."

"Ah, I see. I never knew magic had a scent."

"Wow," he said. "This is some serious stuff."

"It's a demon named Caorthannach. She's possessing other gnomes that this one comes into contact with."

"I smell the demon, but there's also the scent of the spell that binds her to the gnome. It's a doozy of a spell. That's what I'll use to track her."

"How? Sniff around until you find her trail like a hound dog?"

Jack looked offended. "Not like a hound dog. Like an ogre."

"Sorry. But how do you do that?"

"You're asking me for my trade secrets? My tracking skills are what I'm famous for. In my, um, previous career I made good money tracking down humans in the witness protection program."

"You found out where they were living, right? That's all. Right?"

He shifted uncomfortably. "I made sure they wouldn't talk. Ever again."

"Oh, my," Missy said.

"Do you mind if I take your gnome?"

"Jack, you can keep him. Forever. He's yours with my blessings. I bet he'd look great in your garden."

"I need him with me while I track down the black-magic witch. Then I'll bring your gnome home."

"I said that won't be necessary.

JACK PERFORMED the ritual in the parking lot of a home improvement box store. He was at the very far end of the lot, away from any other cars, so no one noticed him kneeling naked beside his car. A cattle egret searching for insects strutted past him and looked at him quizzically. But otherwise, he was alone with his prayers adapted from ones passed down from the Spanish Inquisition.

Shortly after finishing, he caught the scent of the black magic. It wasn't the smell of brimstone or sulfur as you might expect. It was more like bad cabbage. Now he knew which direction to go and he drove the van to the nearest highway. He would need to make adjustments to his route as he progressed, but he felt confident that he could follow the scent to its source.

Two hours later, Jack was hungry, so he stopped at a fast-food chain for a meal. He selected what he called a Happy Meal, a young tourist from Iowa snatched from his car. After Jack tossed the bones in a dumpster, he got back on the two-lane highway that meandered through farm country and small towns in the central part of the state.

The scent was getting stronger, no denying it. He glanced at the gnome standing in the passenger seat, secured by its safety belt.

"You will be free soon, little guy," the ogre said to it.

An hour later, as row after row of citrus trees lined the road, he suddenly felt as if he were being watched. He glanced in the rear-view mirror. Just a beat-up pickup behind him. No one in front of him.

There, he felt it again. Some magic was definitely at work here. A prickling sensation ran through his scalp and down his neck. He swallowed with fear and ran his finger between his collar and neck.

Black magic, he was sure of it.

He shrugged off the feeling and concentrated on the road and the scent he followed. It wasn't a constant smell like driving toward a fertilizer factory. The way it worked was he'd pick up tiny puffs of scent here and there, like tumbleweeds tossed by the wind. And he would simply travel in the direction they came from. The witch who created the magic emitted a certain degree of scent herself, having been permeated with the massive power she'd built to do her magic. But every day she sent out more odors as she cast new spells or used her magic in other ways. Even mundane daily activities emitted odors of magic. If you were a powerful sorcerer, that is.

The scent was getting very strong now. A low humming distracted him. It came from the gnome beside him. It was vibrating compactly, so rapidly it looked blurry.

Again, that prickling in his scalp.

As the unofficial enforcer for the Magic Guild of San Marcos, Jack had dealt with his share of unsavory characters. It was like his years working for the mob, except now his opponents used lightning bolts and concussion spells instead of bullets and bombs. The Guild had other agents who dealt with the normal regulating work of keeping the witches and wizards of Northeast Florida in line and paid-up on their annual dues.

Jack was the one who dealt with the dangerous ones, the magicians gone rogue, the evil sorcerers of black magic. Normally, Jack only had to convince them to leave the area, reminding them he had the power of the Guild behind him if the wrongdoers didn't agree to leave. Sometimes, though, they fought back.

Jack only knew a little magic, not enough to defend himself against a powerful sorceress. If he wasn't able to stop violators the human way—with bullets in their corporeal bodies—he would normally hightail it out of there and let Bob and his troops take care of it. Jack was primarily a tracker. He was an enforcer only to the extent of his limited offensive weapons.

That's why he had no issue with doing as the witch Missy

Mindle had requested: find her mother, convey that information to Ms. Mindle, and then get out of the way.

He imagined the sorceress lived in a creepy, old Victorian mansion on an enormous lot surrounded by moss-draped oak trees. Instead, the scent told him to turn off the highway onto a bumpy dirt road that crossed empty fields and ended at a ditch. There, a narrow dirt driveway snaked parallel to the ditch and disappeared into a forest of pine trees. Just visible through the trees was a small red-brick home.

This was the lair of the sorceress.

A beat-up black mailbox sat precariously atop a wooden post with the number "666" painted on it in silver.

"Really?" Jack said aloud. Was that a joke?

He pulled out his phone. According to his real estate app, 666 Thirteenth Street was truly the address. The house was not for sale and last sold in 1980 for $39,000. With his overly beefy fingers, it took a lot of typos before he pulled up the county property appraiser's website and found that the owner's name was Ruth Bent.

So his supernatural sense of smell and a religious ritual had brought him here. But it was the internet that tied the bow on the package. He texted the information to Ms. Mindle.

Then he pulled partway into the driveway to turn around. And that's when the spell caught him.

MISSY HAD HOPED SENDING her gnome away with Jack would put an end to the gnome-related accidental deaths in Jellyfish Beach. But she was wrong. Her phone rang.

"Hey, Missy, it's Matt. I just heard a call on my police scanner. There's been a fatality in Freddie's neighborhood."

"Oh, my." Missy guessed that Freddie's missing gnomes had returned home and were up to no good.

Matt gave her the address, and they agreed to meet there.

"Is your gnome at home?" he asked.

"Um, no. Someone borrowed him and took him for a road trip."

"Are you serious? You mean that meme where they bring a gnome on their vacation and take pictures of it in front of famous monuments?"

"Not exactly. It's a long story which I promise I'll explain. But I'm pretty sure my gnome was not involved with this fatality."

The address in question was a construction lot about four houses down from Freddie. It looked like an older home had been knocked down and construction on a McMansion had begun. A porta-potty stood near the road and an officer held the door open as he peered inside.

Missy hoped the fatality had been from natural causes while the deceased just happened to be using the john.

Matt parked behind her and they both walked onto the property as if they had every right to. Missy looked past the cop into the shadowy interior of the porta-potty.

A man's legs protruded from the toilet.

"Oh, man," Matt said, "what a crappy way to—"

"Don't even go there," Missy said. "No toilet jokes, please."

The cop turned and saw them. He looked like he was about to puke.

"I think he drowned down there, in the tank that holds all the—"

Turns out the cop truly had been about to puke.

Aside from hers and Matt's, the only other vehicles on the

scene were the patrol car and a Lamborghini. The guy with his head in the sewage was obviously a rich guy.

After the cop finished retching, Missy asked, "is he the property owner?"

"He's the developer," the cop said. "He builds homes on spec and then sells them for millions. That's how good the market is here."

It won't continue to be good if this neighborhood has a gnome problem, Missy thought.

"Who called it in?" Matt asked.

"I did," the cop said. "I was on patrol, saw the developer's car but not the developer. I figured he was in the crapper. But I noticed the door was ajar, so I stopped to see what was up."

"Did you happen to see any—"

"Matt. Come here," Missy said, leading him toward the concrete slab with the plumbing and electrical pipes sticking up like weeds. "Look."

At the rear of the lot, on top of a stack of concrete blocks, stood two gnomes. One of them was the beach-themed gnome in a Hawaiian shirt she had bought hoping it would lure her original gnome home.

"Construction workers normally don't bring gnomes to worksites," Matt said.

"And I don't believe neighborhood kids put them here as a joke."

"I guess the gnome rebellion continues, even without its leader."

"That's not funny," Missy said.

"It wasn't a joke. What are we going to do about this? Notify everyone in Jellyfish Beach to destroy any gnomes they may have?"

"I'm going to try to make the sorceress who started this stop it."

She explained how she determined a demon possessed the gnome and how the demon's influence was spreading to other gnomes. She hesitated, but then told Matt the rest of the story.

"Your *mother* did this? The sweet lady who lives in Tennessee?"

"That's my adoptive mother. I meant my birth mother."

"But I thought she was deceased."

"So did I until recently. I'm not a hundred percent positive it's her who caused all this, but if it was, she's now a sorceress practicing black magic."

"There's a lot you haven't told me," Matt said, sulking. "I thought we were friends."

"You don't have to tell friends everything. Especially not that your mother is an evil sorceress. It's not as if I'd invite you to Thanksgiving at her place."

"So how are you going to get Mom to stop the gnomes?"

"I will try to convince her to release the demon. Hopefully that will erase its influence in the other infected gnomes. Remember Bob the Arch-Mage? His enforcer is tracking down whoever's magic is responsible, whether it's my mother or not."

Her phone vibrated, and she saw the text message.

"Speak of the devil. Oops, sorry," she said. "Poor choice of words."

# 16

## NEW HUNTING GROUNDS

T he Werewolf Women's Club badly needed to find a new hunting ground. The small parcels of land they used temporarily were too dangerous. They could use each only once, in case the police spotted them and started monitoring the area.

The fringes of the Everglades seemed like a decent option at first, but proved to be a horrible choice. First, invasive Burmese pythons had eaten most of the game the women liked to catch. Then, there was all the firm ground suddenly turning into marsh. At their age, they didn't like those kinds of surprises.

The tipping point was the incident with the alligator. Denise, bless her heart, didn't realize how fast gators could be when she stopped to sniff Brenda's butt (as if after all these years she still needed to sniff it). She couldn't have picked a worse place to stop.

Werewolves are strong, even those in their senior years, but no creature alive, supernatural or not, is strong enough to pry open a gator's clenched jaw.

When the gator struck and grabbed her hind leg, Denise yelped in pain. The rest of the pack returned. Josie knew that Denise could regenerate the damage from the bite, but if the gator dragged her underwater, as they do with their prey, even a werewolf wouldn't survive that.

Fortunately, Josie knew one of the few ways to get a gator to open its jaws. As the reptile backed its way toward the water, Denise thrashing as she tried to free her leg, the rest of the pack attacked the beast, trying to tear out chunks of its armored hide. They wounded the gator, but it wasn't enough.

Josie raced up and went right for the creature's eyes. Slashing and poking with her nails, she damaged an eyeball. The gator roared and in that instant of an open mouth, Denise removed her leg. The gator quickly retreated, and the pack did too. As soon as Denise's leg healed, they shifted back to human and headed home.

Tonight, though, they believed they found a promising new candidate for a hunting ground. An electronics plant far west of town had closed, the company bankrupt. They sold all their equipment and left the building vacant. Josie had heard about in the news a while back.

But the best part, which she hadn't realized, was the factory was on a giant parcel of vacant, wooded land. The company had bought it cheaply years ago, planning to expand their plant and lease space to other companies. Josie happened to be having breakfast at the local diner, sitting at the counter, when she saw a newspaper left behind on the seat next to her. It was folded open to the story about how there still wasn't a buyer for the land. Lots and lots of pristine land, no security guards, and a low probability that any human, let alone law enforcement, would go there. The club couldn't wait to explore it.

On Thursday night, Kevin drove them there in the shuttle

bus. This property was farther west than the Unger Tract, so it took a while to get there. The women yelled at Kevin to get off the bus, they were so eager to shed their clothes and shift.

Once their transformation was complete, Josie led them off the bus. That was as far as the leading went. Each member of the pack picked up scents and went off in her own direction. Josie didn't like that. Wolves hunt in packs for a reason, the superiority of numbers and tactical cooperation. It was also dangerous to stray off on one's own, especially in unfamiliar territory. But try telling that to old werewolves set in their ways, not used to hearing what to do anymore. Josie growled and took up the low-ranking position of following behind the pack. At least it helped her keep an eye and nose on her friends.

The bulk of them seemed to have followed a narrow game trail winding north. She knew why: the scent of deer. But she also sensed wolves peeling off to the east and west. Everyone was excited to be exploring fresh territory, and the scents were exhilarating. There was plenty of game here, and it had never been hunted before, so the animals were slow to react.

The scream of a captured rabbit came from her right. Wanda was on it, killing it quickly and beginning to devour it. Josie kept running to keep up with the main body of the pack.

Up ahead, three wolves had treed a raccoon. They used their opposable thumbs and human-like traits to climb the tree in pursuit. The poor raccoon must have been stunned to see that.

A triumphant howl came from several hundred yards ahead. They'd driven their prey to ground. Others joined in the howl. It was a big celebration. They must have killed the deer. Josie left the game trail and raced through the dense woods, instinctively maneuvering in the darkness between trees, under vines, and over the saw palmettos.

Josie smelled blood and deer. And as she approached her

friends, the scent of excitement was strong. Tanya barked in greeting as Josie reached them.

Had this been a Werewolf Women's Club luncheon, her fellow club members would have behaved with decorum, politely dividing the food and sharing with all. Tonight, it was every wolf for herself.

In the midst of the feeding frenzy, the shot rang out.

Oh no, Josie thought. Not again.

After the first shot came two more.

The wolves stopped eating and growled. Josie took off in the direction the shots had come from. She heard the wolves behind her. And sensed that the other pack members who had pursued their own prey were now converging through the forest toward the crime scene.

Teresa lay crumpled at the base of a slash pine tree. She was in human form, naked, face down in dead leaves, legs splayed out at awkward angles. One sniff told Josie that she was dead. Bullet wounds in her right shoulder and upper thigh were visible. Josie whined as the other pack members gathered around their fallen friend.

But Josie had no time for mourning. She circled the area around the body, sampling every scent. Soon, the lingering odor of cordite of the fired weapon was stronger. She saw broken plants here and there. And then a footprint in soft ground. There was that sharp, distinctive smell of rubber. It had to be from boots.

Though there was barely a moon, Josie's sensitive eyes caught the faint glimmer of metal. It was a spent cartridge. It was an inconvenient time not to have pockets, so she picked up the cartridge with her mouth.

Josie followed the trail the human had made back to the abandoned factory. At the edge of the forest she stopped and kept in the shadows, watching for movement. There was nothing. She circled around until she had a view of the side of the building where the shuttle van had been stealthily parked. Where was Kevin? He might be asleep in the van, but the gunshots surely would have awakened him. Perhaps he had entered the woods to investigate.

But then she saw the dark shape lying on the ground at the edge of the forest two hundred feet away from her.

The scent of werewolf blood drifted toward her in the faint breeze. Oh, no, she thought.

She ran to the body. It was Kevin. He lay on his stomach naked. The back of his bald head was covered in blood. Wolf fur lay in clumps around him, so he must have been in wolf form and shifted back when he was killed.

He groaned.

Thank God, he wasn't dead.

She dropped the cartridge from her mouth and licked the blood from his head with her long tongue, revealing the wound. It wasn't too bad, just a grazing, but the surrounding flesh was tender and bruised. She touched his cheek with her muzzle.

"What happened?" he said with a croak.

She took the cartridge into her mouth again and ran around the abandoned factory, looking for signs of the assailant. No one was around.

But the gate of the chain-link fence at the entrance was open. She trotted over. The gate had been locked with a chain and padlocked. When they arrived, Kevin had cut the lock with bolt cutters and, after the bus drove through, closed the gate and arranged the chain to look like it was still attached. Now the chain dangled free and there was a foot-wide gap in the gate the intruder had been too sloppy to close.

Who had done this?

She still had the cartridge in her mouth. It was time to shift back to human form.

After she had dressed in the bus, she put the cartridge in her purse. She found a blanket on the luggage shelf above the seats and stepped out just as the other wolves were returning. They whined and whimpered as they climbed aboard.

Josie found Kevin sitting on the ground where she had left him, hiding his privates with his hands. She covered him with the blanket.

"There were two of them, coming out of the woods," he said. "I had heard the shots, I knew what they had done, and I was furious. I charged them."

"You were in wolf form?"

"Yeah. While you guys were off hunting, I wanted to enjoy the woods a little myself, it being new territory and all."

"You put yourself at much greater risk of getting killed by shifting."

"I know. I couldn't help myself. But they must have run out of silver bullets. One of them shot me with a regular bullet. Trying to recover from that wound must have set me off to shift back. As I did that, the one with the rifle clobbered me in the head. They parked their car over there." He pointed to the side of the building that was out of view of the bus.

"Who were these men?" Josie asked.

"Cops. One of them was that detective in the sunglasses who questioned us after Mary Beth was killed."

Affird. Josie had felt suspicious of him and should have trusted her instincts.

Then she remembered: The man in the diner next to her, the one who had left the newspaper behind, was a cop. She had seen his I.D. card on a lanyard around his neck.

He must have known who she was and deliberately left the

newspaper opened to the article on the factory, hoping that she would see it and read about the abandoned rural land. They were being set up. She was furious.

And scared as hell.

So, what do you do with a dead body and a bus driver with a head injury? You can't call 911 and have the police find you again trespassing on rural land. The honest cops would know something odd was up. The dirty cops like Affird, the executioners, would cackle with glee as you played your role in their evil schemes.

Josie decided quickly. Quickly enough that it made her feel guilty.

Kevin would shift back into werewolf form and allow his head wound to heal supernaturally. Teresa, though, created a dilemma.

They couldn't pretend she had died in her sleep when she had bullet wounds. They couldn't dump her at a hospital like a gang-violence victim. Septuagenarians don't end up that way.

Tanya insisted they needed to involve the police so there would be a record of the murder and eventually Affird could be held accountable. Josie wasn't so sure.

"It's all but admitting what we are," Josie said. "He shot at a creature in wolf form. If we bring her to the hospital as a human, it proves that she and you and me are werewolves."

Josie explained the situation to Missy in her living room before dawn. Missy had just returned home after night visits to her vampire patients.

"I think this is unethical for someone in my profession," Missy said.

"It's the authorities who are unethical," Jose replied. "In the end, we're going to report the death and lay Teresa to rest properly. It's either this or feed her body to the alligators. We have to protect ourselves from Affird and his cronies."

It was a gray area for Missy's ethical concerns. And she knew how toxic and dangerous Affird was. She'd been in the next room when the detective executed a werewolf, just after the shifter had returned to human form. And she'd prevented Affird from staking Leonard Schwartz, her vampire patient.

She nodded at Josie, collected some medical and magickal tools, and followed the elderly werewolf into the shuttle bus parked in Missy's driveway.

"I'm going to move quickly so you can get this bus out of here," Missy said. "We don't want my neighbors seeing it."

Missy nodded grimly to the rows of frightened old ladies whose faces looked sallow in the overhead light. In the rear row of seats lay the body covered with a blanket. Josie removed it.

"We left her lying on her stomach, so you can access the bullet wounds."

One entry point was on Teresa's shoulder blade. The other was on the rear of her thigh. Missy pulled a headlamp onto her head and turned it on. From her satchel she took a pair of forceps. She used her index finger to probe inside each wound, the same technique doctors used until modern medicine. The bullet in the shoulder hadn't traveled far, stopping when it hit bone. The one in the thigh had passed through the muscle and exited in the front of the leg. She then used the forceps to extract the one slug. It was crumpled and no longer resembled a bullet. It definitely looked like silver. She handed it to Josie.

"Now we know for sure the killer uses silver bullets," Josie said. "That rules out Mary Beth being shot in the heart with a normal bullet. I found an empty cartridge at the scene and I'll find an expert to identify it."

Missy's next task was like what an embalmer would do to conceal a wound on a corpse. But rather than using makeup, she was using magick.

Chanting softly so the other women on the bus wouldn't hear, Missy sprinkled a specific mixture of herbs and mineral powders upon each wound. She then placed a few drops of myrrh in the openings. Holding her usual power charm in her left hand, she summoned the energies within her, from the air, from the earth below, from the ocean, and with her right hand traced a circle around Teresa and a star-shaped pentagram within it. She felt the power grow and released it.

Then, before her eyes, the bullet wounds disappeared.

It was only an illusion. The wounds were still there, but the normal human eye could not see them because the spell blocked the light waves. From her bag she withdrew a cloth amulet on a leather cord which she put around Teresa's neck. The pouch was filled with the same herbs and powders she had sprinkled on the wounds.

"Make sure this amulet stays on her at all times, or the spell will be broken," Missy said to Josie.

"I will. Thank you," Josie said, placing her hand on Missy's arm. "You don't know how much I appreciate your help."

"I'm sorry for your loss," Missy said, walking up the aisle of the bus. "That goes for all of you."

She stopped before getting off.

"Is your head okay?" She asked Kevin, noticing a patch of missing hair with pinkish scar tissue.

"Yes, thank you. A cop smashed me on the head with his rifle, but I healed when I was in wolf form."

Missy waved goodbye to the Werewolf Women's Club and exited the bus. She worried about Josie and the others. Werewolves always have a hunger for revenge, and the police were a dangerous target for them to seek it.

## 17

## GROWING THREATS

With all the distractions, Missy hadn't had much time to think about Josie. She worried deeply that the werewolf would do something foolish regarding Detective Affird. Missy called her to gauge her mood.

"How have you been?" Missy asked. "I'm sorry I haven't checked on you since Teresa passed."

"'Passed' sounds like she died in her sleep. She was murdered."

"I know. Sorry. How are you holding up?"

"I'm more consumed by anger than by grief right now," Josie said.

"Yes, it's unfair."

"And it will be redressed."

"No, Josie, don't even think that way. You can't go after a cop. That's crazy."

"I don't want you involved, dear. It's safer if you know nothing about it. Let's change the subject."

"No," Missy said. "I can't allow you to do something so dangerous and reckless."

"I know a thing or two about killing."

"Have you killed a *person* before? Don't answer. I don't want to know."

"That's the right attitude. It's better if you don't know."

"Look, even if you're able to take out Affird, the police won't let it rest. They will do whatever it takes to find his killer. And if they find you, it will endanger all the werewolves in Seaweed Tower."

"Do you think I haven't thought about that? But the Werewolf Women's Club wants vengeance, too."

"Remember, you don't know for sure that Affird did it."

"He was at the murder scene both times. And just to be sure, I'm having someone check the forensics of the bullet and casing."

"Without the police's resources, how will you find the gun?"

"Missy, don't you believe he did it?"

Missy hesitated. She knew what Affird was capable of. He was her most likely suspect.

"See? You, too, think it was him," Josie said.

"It doesn't matter what I think. It's insane to go after him."

"You understand that we can't go to the police and accuse him? This is the only way. Affird went outside of the justice system and we'll have to as well."

"Maybe you'll have to accept not getting justice," Missy said sadly. "In today's world, the most important thing for supernaturals is survival."

"I will not accept injustice."

Missy sighed. "Please promise me you won't do anything yet. Give Matt and me some time to investigate more."

"There's not much time left." Josie said.

After Josie said goodbye, Missy immediately called Matt.

"I'm afraid Josie is going to do something rash. We need to find out who's hunting the werewolves."

"I kind of assumed it was Affird. Didn't you tell me he was seen on the property where the last woman died?"

"That hasn't been confirmed," Missy said. "I don't want Josie taking revenge against Affird. Even if he did do it. Let's keep looking. Maybe we'll find another lead. Maybe we won't. At the very least we can distract Josie until her anger cools down."

MISSY WAS CONCERNED. After Jack had texted her with the address of the person who was allegedly her mother, Missy had tried calling him. She wanted more information. She wasn't going to show up blind and confront the woman. But he never answered her repeated calls and texts. Were all ogres that rude? She tried one more time at dawn. When there was no answer, she went to bed.

The clatter of a lamp falling to the floor woke her at noon. The cats had been known to cause such a thing. Today, it wasn't a cat. It was a ghost.

"What do you want, Don Mateo?" she mumbled into her pillow.

"We had intruders while you slept," the ghost said.

She sat up quickly. "Who? Where?"

"The back porch. I suggest you come see for yourself."

She had gone to bed in a T-shirt and yoga pants, so she jumped out of bed and headed straight through the living room to the sliding glass doors. And stopped, stunned.

The screened porch was filled with gnomes. They stood densely packed in a crowd like tourists outside the studio window of a television morning show, all facing in one direction: at her.

It was an eclectic collection of gnomes, like a catalog photo for a gnome-supply company. They were all bearded, pot-bellied older gentlemen with various pointy hats. But some were dressed in traditional peasant outfits, others in winter garb, still more in Florida-themed bathing suits. She recognized the gnome decoy in the Hawaiian shirt she bought from the thrift store. There were Santa gnomes, gnomes with collegiate logos, gnomes in suits and ties, gnomes in chef's whites, and gnomes representing just about every trade and profession. Some gnomes brandished gardening tools while others held golf clubs and baseball bats—even guitars and saxophones. A surprisingly large number of gnomes bent over with their butt cracks showing or sat on tiny gnome toilets. It was a gnome collection to put Freddie to shame.

"How did they get here?" Missy instinctively asked, realizing it was a stupid question. The gnomes had simply walked here.

The real question was why.

Until now, with the exception of her own gnome, she had been free of gnome trouble. So why all the gnomes now?

Her mother must have discovered that Missy had tracked her down. And it made her mad.

Having an angry, vindictive mother is a heavy load to carry. Having one who was also a black-magic sorceress was a nightmare.

A thud made her jump. A gnome had crashed into a window in the front of the house, shattering it.

The gnome, of course, was her gnome.

Missy cast a warding spell to drive the gnomes from her porch. The screens were all damaged on the gnomes' way in, so she didn't care what they damaged on their way out. After she cast the spell, she didn't turn her back on the gnomes. She wanted to see how, exactly, they moved.

Suddenly, her porch was empty, and the gnomes loitered in her backyard. Missy hadn't seen them move at all. Then, again, in a blink of an eye, half of them disappeared from her property, with only a few lingering along her wood fence.

Finally, her lawn was empty.

They must move too quickly for the human eye to register. She would have to capture them on video and slow it down.

Then again, she realized she really didn't care. She didn't want to see another gnome for the rest of her life.

The question was, would they come after her again, with violence?

It turns out, the gnomes had other assignments to complete before they dealt with her.

※

"GNOMES? WHAT'S A GNOME?" The vampire Leonard Schwartz said while Missy listened to his heartbeat with her stethoscope. It beat six times a minute which was a healthy rate for a vampire.

"You know, those cheesy little statues people put in their lawns? Look like elves or dwarves."

"I never had a garden. I lived in a walk-up condo in Brooklyn. After I was turned, I slept in the building's basement. Do I seem like the kind of guy who gardens?"

His heartbeat increased by one beat per minute. She was stressing him out.

"The gnomes are killing humans and making it look like an accident. They've been possessed by a demon."

"Your magick can't stop this?"

153

"No. I can't stop the demon. I have to convince the sorceress who summoned the demon to stop it. And now, I'm afraid that's going to be impossible."

"Let me give you a little piece of advice," Schwartz said. "I spent three hundred years in New York City. I know how to deal with difficult people. You have to find leverage over this sorceress. It doesn't need to have anything to do with the matter at hand. It just needs to be some way to hurt her more than she wants to hurt you."

Her phone buzzed. It was Matt.

"I'm sorry, I have to take this," she said.

"We've got another gnome incident," he said. "This time it was double duty."

"Okay. I'll be there after I finish this patient visit. Text me the address."

"The gnomes just took out two more humans," she told Schwartz.

"Humans are dumber than I thought," he said. "Makes me feel less guilty feeding on them."

After she finished Schwartz's exam, she went home and changed. It was just after dawn when she drove to the address Matt had sent her.

## 18

# GARDEN GNOMES VS. GARDEN CENTER

The address Matt had given Missy was a nursery and garden center just outside of Jellyfish Beach. She was familiar with it. They sold plants and trees wholesale to landscapers and at retail prices to homeowners. Missy liked the place because they had exotic, hard-to-find tropical varieties.

But what she had forgotten was that they also had garden gnomes. Pathways lined with palms and subtropical plants cut through the nursery's sprawling grounds, connecting greenhouses and gardens. The owner had placed gnomes here and there beneath trees and beside benches. Some had been for sale and others were ornamental. Apparently, the gnomes were done with all that, because many of them were missing.

Missy wandered the paths looking for Matt who had arrived before her. It was early enough that the place wasn't open yet and only Matt's car and a patrol car were in the dirt parking lot. It was quiet and creepy, since Missy knew there were dead bodies here somewhere.

There were still a few gnomes around who hadn't abandoned their posts, like the little fellow pushing a miniature wheelbarrow. Did this guy have blood on his tiny hands, or did he sit out the uprising here? He was a sorry-looking gnome. A bird's droppings had splattered on his head and much of his paint job had been scraped off. He must have endured years of being out in the weather, getting hit by passing carts carrying bags of mulch and being abused by bored children dragged along with their parents.

Missy could empathize if this gnome somehow harbored resentment that had become animated through a demon's powers. She had at first thought this would be a perfect place for the gnomes, but they were just part of the decor here and not cherished like at Freddie's. And even the gnomes Freddie owned rose up against her.

The gravel path twisted around dense areca palms. Missy followed it around a bend and stopped short.

Two legs stuck out behind a palm tree ahead. They were dangling just above the ground, bent at the knee. Someone was sitting there.

She walked forward slowly, and as the path curved, she had a better view. There was, indeed, a person sitting on something next to the path.

The man was dead.

Flies had already found him. He looked like he had been doing his business, dropping some human fertilizer upon the plants. His shorts were down around his ankles, his hands rested on his thighs. His head tilted back with his eyes rolled upwards. He was a heavyset man in a khaki shirt that bore the logo of the business. Missy recognized him as the owner.

There was no toilet there. What was he sitting upon? Reluctantly, Missy moved closer.

156

Despite the heavy rainfall during summer, several species of cacti flourished in this part of Florida. One common species grew in tall, vertical shafts bristling with thorns.

The owner was sitting on one. Really sitting on it. A better way to describe it was that the cactus had become intimate with its owner. The police, who would never in a million years suspect gnomes were behind this, would conclude that the owner had been caught short by intestinal problems, and while he was relieving himself lost his balance and landed on the cactus in a truly unfortunate and improbable way.

It was about as improbable as Mr. Vansetti accidentally getting a mango lodged in his mouth.

Missy cringed. What horrible ways to go. The gnomes were cruel and clever.

She didn't want to stick around with the dead body, and assumed the police officer had already seen it, so she continued onward, hoping to find Matt. She decided not to call out to him. She couldn't bring herself to break this eerie silence.

The path emerged into an open field with irrigated plots covered in dark-gray plastic and topped with rows of potted tomato plants. Next was a greenhouse. She looked inside. Tables of orchids and lilies filled the room. She followed the path to another greenhouse. This one contained rows of large pots holding young citrus trees, each tied to a supporting stake.

Except for one pot. Instead of a trunk protruding from the potting soil, there was an upside-down human torso and legs. The supporting stake ran under the waistband of his shorts and out one leg. The skinny man almost looked at home among the trees, except that he wore the same khaki uniform as the owner.

His head was buried up to his shoulders in the pot.

It was a stretch to say this looked like an accident, but if someone wanted to believe that, they could.

These gnomes had been brutal. To say they must have been angry was an understatement.

Missy quickly exited the greenhouse. So, these were the two fatalities reported on the police radio. Where were Matt and the police officer?

There was no sign of them in the field or the other greenhouses. She found another path leading into the wooded, jungle-like part of the property. Somewhere in here was a building with the office and cashier. She hoped they were hanging out there.

A rattling and crunching of gravel came from ahead of her and grew louder. It was a golf cart, thundering toward her at top speed. She jumped out of the way just in time, landing among a cluster of banana trees.

Her mind was reeling from what she saw in the cart: A gnome perched on the steering wheel. How it kept its balance, she had no idea. And on the floor below, a gnome was wedged atop the accelerator.

The gnomes were driving the golf cart. She didn't bother trying to guess what their destination was. It freaked her out too much just to have seen them doing it.

The gnomes had become remarkably brazen. Instead of doing their dirty deeds only at night, now they were cavorting in the daylight.

They have no more fear of us, Missy realized.

She worried now about Matt and the police officer. They could be in danger or hurt. There was no more time to tiptoe around.

"Matt!" She shouted. "Are you here?"

Silence. Nothing but the buzzing of insects and chirping of birds.

Until those sounds stopped.

Missy's heart raced.

The cart was coming back toward her. She ran along the pathway, hoping to find the building, or at least a place to hide that the golf cart couldn't reach. The path continued to wind. And as she ran past the palms, frangipani, and other trees, as well as the lanterns, benches, pottery, and other human touches, she realized something was missing.

The gnomes. When she first arrived here, she had passed some still displayed in their proper places. Now, she didn't see any at all. Where had they gone?

She rounded a corner and slammed into something with a loud *oomph*. It was a body, wrapped in a vine like a mummy, hanging from a large limb of an oak tree.

The body wasn't dead. It was Matt. He twisted in a vain attempt to free himself.

"Help me," he said in a constrained voice.

"This reminds me of the time you were hanging from my front-porch ceiling in a magical web," Missy said.

"Cut me down. Please."

"I don't have a knife," Missy said.

"Keep going up this path. I saw an open shed with some tools. Get a machete or clippers or anything, please."

"There's a golf cart coming that will smash into us," she said. "I have to stop it somehow."

She forced herself out of the panic mode. Instead of flight, it was time for fight.

The golf cart barreled around a bend and was only yards away. The gnome on the steering wheel looked like a stunt-person balancing atop a wing of a biplane.

A protection spell for Matt and herself would take too long. A better solution popped in her head.

She pointed her hands at the golf cart and released a bolt of energy. The battery fried, the brakes locked, and the cart jolted to a stop. The gnome on the steering wheel catapulted at her. She ducked, and it hit Matt with a thud. It instantly disappeared into the thick foliage, making a chittering sound. The other gnome remained wedged in the cart's footwell.

"I'll be right back," she said as he went around Matt and jogged up the path, looking for the shed.

A few minutes later she found it. It was small, not much bigger than an outhouse, and obviously wasn't the main tool-shed. Inside, she found only a shovel, some rakes, pruning shears, and two machetes. She grabbed the shears and machetes and ran back to Matt.

He was hanging too high for her to reach the vine above him with a machete, but she stood on tiptoes and worked at the vine with the pruning shears.

"Don't cut me," Matt said.

"A minor cut would be much better than what happened to the guys who worked here."

"I guess they didn't kill me because I'm an innocent civilian, a non-combatant, in this war," he said.

"They might change their minds."

She severed the vine in one place, then worked at it in another place to free one of his arms. As she severed it again, suddenly the entire thing unraveled. Matt spun like a drill bit and landed on his butt on the path.

"Thank you," he said. "I was hoping for a softer landing, but I won't complain."

"Where is the police officer?"

"I never saw him or her. I wandered around looking and found the poor guy with the cactus." He shuddered. "Then, the next thing I knew, I was wrapped in that vine and hanging in the air. I never even saw the gnomes do it."

"They shouldn't be active during the day," Missy said. "This is worrying me. There was also a giant crowd of them at my house yesterday morning. I figured my mother knows I've tracked her down and is trying to intimidate me. But seeing what's happening here, I'm afraid the demon is taking this to the next level."

"Or the gnomes are taking it, riding the demon's power."

Missy handed him the machete. "Let's find the cop. Shouldn't the other first responders be here by now?"

"True."

She called 911 on her cell. She explained the situation, leaving out the gnomes. The operator said the other vehicles should have arrived by now.

"The gnomes must have done something to the gate," Matt said. "But I'm not going to check. We need to find the cop now before it's too late."

They jogged down the path and finally came upon a wood building hidden in the trees. Empty garden carts sat out front. They climbed the stairs and went inside the door that hung open. To the left was a crowded office with two desks and several filing cabinets. To the right was a cashier's counter and a small shop filled with gifts and knickknacks.

A tall glass case had a sign that said, "garden gnomes." The case was empty, the glass doors shattered. There were no gnomes to be found. And no cop, either.

There was a door in the back of the building. They went through it, descended stairs, and followed a wide path that led to a much larger building with aluminum walls and garage doors. Those doors were closed, but the door at the end of the path was unlocked. Matt followed Missy inside, each brandishing a machete. Missy had a sinking feeling their search was about to end.

The interior was a single giant space with a tall ceiling and light coming through dirty windows high in the walls. Along one wall, golf carts were parked at charging stations. Another wall had a workbench, storage shelves and dozens of landscaping tools hanging from pegs. The rest of the space was a warehouse filled with stacked bags of fertilizers and mulch, piles of plastic pots, and hundreds of boxes.

"Hello?" Missy called. "Anyone here?"

She looked around as her eyes gradually adjusted to the dim lighting. There were still too many shadows in here. She glanced toward the door and noticed a bank of switches. She switched them all on.

The cavernous space filled with harsh fluorescent light.

"I don't see anyone," Matt said.

"Oh, my. Over there." Missy pointed to the far end of the room and ran over.

An enormous pile of cow manure bags lay on the floor, looking as if one of the orderly stacks had toppled over.

A hand protruded from beneath them. And the sleeve of a police uniform.

Missy knelt and felt the veins in the man's wrist,

"No pulse," she said.

Matt began picking the forty-pound bags off the body and tossing them aside. Missy joined him.

"He was just doing his job," Missy said. "He wasn't a gnome abuser. Like you, he was a non-combatant."

"He didn't deserve this at all. But the gnomes probably saw him as the protector of property owners, the enforcer of the status quo."

"I don't believe anymore they have criteria for whom they kill," Missy said.

They kept moving the bags off him, as if trying to take the

load off their minds as well. But when they were halfway done, movement caught her eye.

Something passed by just outside the door they had come through. Something small.

She was about to return to the task when a gnome appeared inside the doorway. In the blink of an eye, a half dozen more.

"Matt," she said in a terse voice.

Now there were about twenty gnomes, and the group had somehow made it halfway across the floor.

"They've got us cornered," Matt said.

"I hope these machetes are sharp," Missy said. "We'll just have to chop these punks to pieces."

In another blink, there were more gnomes, and they had moved closer and started to spread out, forming a half-circle around Matt and Missy.

"Can't your magick do anything?" Matt asked.

"I'm forming a protection barrier around us if you'll only shut up and let me concentrate."

More gnomes appeared in the group's rear. These were covered in dirt and moss, the oldest ones on the property. The ones that had been mostly forgotten, hidden by foliage and caked with the deposits of time. The painted eyes of these, though faded by age and weather, seemed to glow yellow with evil.

But suddenly, all the gnomes vanished with no sign of movement.

Another cop, a woman, appeared in the doorway.

"Officer down," Matt said.

The cop said something into her radio handset and ran over to help them remove the bags. Seconds later, two paramedics wheeling a stretcher arrived and four firemen followed.

"What took you guys so long?" Matt asked.

"The gate was locked," said an annoyed firefighter. "After we cut the lock we were blocked by a barricade of concrete blocks. Next, there was a barricade of coconuts."

"How did you ever get past the coconuts?" Matt asked, but his sarcastic grin faded when he saw the deadly look the firefighter gave him.

"He's unresponsive," Missy said to the paramedics. "I don't know how long he's been under here."

When the cop was finally freed, and soon after declared dead at the scene, the mood was somber. Missy told the team where to find the other two bodies.

"Did you guys see anyone else around here?" The woman cop asked Matt and Missy.

Matt explained that he arrived shortly after the fallen cop and had looked for him in vain. Missy said she arrived after that and came across the two dead employees but saw no one else.

"I can't believe it," the cop said, her face red from grief. "Three unrelated accidental deaths at the same time? I wonder what the medical examiner will think."

The cop's death looked more like an accident than the other two, Missy thought to herself. The medical examiner will assume some person was behind the other two. And he'll be wrong.

She wanted so badly to blurt out the truth. But being part of the supernatural world means you are obligated to keep it secret from normal humans. If humans got ahold of the slightest thread of truth, the entire shroud of protective secrecy could be unwoven with dire consequences for innocent supernatural creatures. For her, too. Even when evil was involved, it had to be kept secret.

Which put even more pressure on her to make things right again. To stop the killing and the sorceress behind it all.

"I'm sorry for your loss," Missy said to the woman cop. It was the right thing to say, but it didn't seem like enough.

Matt placed his hand on Missy's shoulder. It was an awkward attempt to comfort her, but she was grateful. She put a hand on top of his.

19

# HOW TO HUNT A HUMAN

The problem with The Boat, Josie thought, was that it was totally conspicuous. Even elderly people didn't drive 1977 Lincoln Continentals anymore. Certain retro pimps might. Josie glanced at herself in the rearview mirror. She didn't think she looked like a pimp.

She was parked on the street across from the Jellyfish Beach Police Department's rear parking lot, waiting for Detective Affird to come out. She wanted to see what car he drove so she could follow him.

What did she hope to accomplish by following him? She wasn't quite sure. All she knew was that he was a vigilante of sorts, taking on the self-bestowed role of judge, jury, and executioner of supernaturals—werewolves in particular. She felt strongly that it was he who shot Mary Beth and Teresa. She felt it in her bones. And now they had Kevin as a witness.

So what was she going to do about it? Play detective and find evidence that proves he did it, give it to the police, and expect they would do the right thing? Forget it. Besides, that would be admitting she and her friends were werewolves. No, we're not werewolves, we're just human seniors who like to run through the woods at night and Affird hates old ladies who run? Surely that would fly.

So Josie decided she didn't want to see Affird kicked off the force and prosecuted.

She wanted to kill him.

She felt she had several good justifications. First, there was the eye-for-an-eye law of the wilderness. Second, the pack demanded revenge, and, as its alpha, she had to deliver. Third, eliminating him was crucial for the safety of all the area's werewolves and other supernatural creatures.

Exactly how she would kill him was the nagging question. The easiest way would be in werewolf form with the strength to overpower him. She doubted he had silver bullets in his regular service weapon. The problem with this approach was that the members of the police force who knew werewolves existed would assume a wild animal hadn't killed Affird. They would come after the Werewolf Women's Club in full force.

No, the better way would be to use her little-old-lady persona, so he would let his guard down, and she could shoot him. She still had her ex-husband's pistol. Too bad she had never fired it before.

Affird, exiting the rear of the police department, caught her attention. The tall, lanky man was wearing shades and a short-sleeve white shirt with a maroon tie. She turned on the ignition. The detective's personal vehicle was a black American muscle car. She watched it pull out of the police lot, then shifted The Boat into Drive and followed him at a distance.

She decided she'd answer the question of how to kill him another time. First, she needed to learn his movements.

He stopped suddenly. She slammed on her brakes, almost

hitting him. Did he already know he was being followed? They'd only gone two blocks.

Affird started moving again. He had stopped to avoid hitting an egret strutting across the street.

So, before she learned about Affird's routine, she needed to learn how to tail someone. Killing him would take a little longer than she thought.

※

IT TURNS out that Affird was only out to pick up lunch at a nearby hamburger stand before returning to the police station. Josie then drove to a gun shop that had been recommended to her by one of Missy's patients, a vampire who was really into firearms. The owner of the gun shop was known as an amateur ballistics expert. She left the silver bullet and shell casing with him to see what information he could glean from them.

Then it was back to the police station. She hoped Affird wasn't working a late shift. Fortunately, he strolled out of the building at 5:30 p.m. and she followed him home.

When he turned into an older residential neighborhood, it suddenly occurred to Josie that he probably had a wife and kids. The moral weight of taking him away from them pressed down upon her shoulders. It wasn't their fault that Affird was evil.

He parked in the driveway of a small, older ranch house. It didn't have much personality. There wasn't another car in view and the lawn was free of kids' toys or sports equipment. She hoped he was single. Writing down the address, she planned to return early the next day.

And she did. The Boat followed him on his way to work, when he stopped for coffee, when he arrived at the station. The Boat trailed him to a barber shop at midday and to the same burger joint as the previous day. After he left work, she learned which grocery store he used and where he did his dry cleaning.

Now she had to decide where and when to attack.

AFFIRD WAS GETTING his hair cut when he happened to glance out the window toward the street. There was that crazy old lady again in the Lincoln Continental the size of the USS Iwo Jima. Her white-haired head just made it above the bottom of the passenger seat window as she stared at him through big, round sunglasses that made her look like an owl. Something about her was familiar. She just sat there and stared until the car behind her honked and she finally moved on.

He'd been seeing her wherever he went. She was obviously tailing him. Was she a geriatric private detective? The grandmother of someone he had put behind bars, or killed? Having been on the job as long as he had, he was bound to accumulate a lot of enemies.

On his way to work the next day, he stopped at his usual coffee franchise. He parked instead of going through the drive-through. The giant white car sat only a few spaces away. He walked as if on the way to the entrance, ducked behind a mini-van, then slipped over to the white car.

Its massive V-8 was chugging in idle. The old lady had her neck craned, looking for him to enter the building.

He rapped on her window. She jumped in surprise. He flashed his badge and motioned for her to roll down the window.

"Can I help you, sir?" she asked.

Finally, he recognized her. He had interviewed her with the bunch of other old ladies at the Unger Tract.

She was one of the werewolves from the Seaweed Manor condos.

JOSIE'S HEART, already racing after she was startled by Affird surprising her, beat even faster when his eyes widened in recognition of her.

He remembers me from the night Mary Beth was killed, she thought in horror. Was she in danger?

"I noticed you've been following me around, ma'am," Affird said. "May I ask why?"

"I'm certainly not following you. I'm sorry if I gave that impression. My memory isn't what it used to be, and sometimes I can't remember where I've been or where I'm going. I end up driving all over town. Costs me a fortune in gas." She laughed unconvincingly.

"I could swear I saw you staring at me a few times," Affird said.

"I'm afraid I don't remember. Which is a shame, because you're a nice-looking man."

She couldn't read his eyes behind his dark shades. He wasn't smiling, that was for sure.

"It's almost as if you were playing detective," he said.

"Why would I do that?"

"If I'm not incorrect, I believe a friend of yours was shot recently. Isn't that true?"

"Yes. I lost a friend of mine."

"Now, you wouldn't be following me around because of her, would you?"

"No. Why would I do that?"

"Perhaps you want to keep tabs on me to make sure I'm

doing my job and investigating the shooting. Is that what this is?"

"No, no. I'm sure you're good at your job."

"I should point out that the shooting took place outside of the Jellyfish Beach city limits, therefore it's under the jurisdiction of the county sheriff's office. They're the ones doing the investigation, ma'am. I was there that night only to help them out."

"Good to know, sir," Josephine said, anxious for this conversation to end. "Thank you for helping out."

"Now, the possibility just struck me, strange as it may sound, that you might be following me because you consider me a suspect in the killing. Could that be?"

Josie's stomach plunged. "Of course not, officer. I mean, detective."

"I'm glad to hear you don't believe that. Normally, people of your generation have a positive opinion of law enforcement. It's good to know you're one of them."

"I'm always so grateful for your service, sir."

"Thank you, ma'am." He looked at his watch. "I'm late for work. You have a nice day."

He gave her a smile about as warm as a shark's and walked into the coffee shop. Josie backed The Boat out of its parking spot and drove away before Affird returned.

That was the end of tailing him. At least she had a rough idea of his daily routes so she could ambush him.

Did she have the will to do so?

The problem with being a werewolf was her dual nature. In wolf form, she wouldn't hesitate to rip the man's throat out. But most of the time, she was an eighty-seven-year-old human who cringed at the thought of murder.

The fact was, most werewolves weren't born that way. They

171

were humans who were bitten by werewolves and became infected with the lycanthropy virus. The virus enabled them to shift, but it didn't remake the person they were. Being able to shift, and experiencing the world as a wolf, transformed your outlook and personality to some extent—especially if you were infected at a young age. But it didn't fundamentally change who you were. It didn't put evil into your heart. Though if evil was already there, it was amplified.

In Josie's heart, there was no evil. In times like this, she wished there was. Because she was losing her determination to kill Affird.

She drove The Boat to a big box store. These places often gave her the urge to kill, so maybe she could transfer it to Affird. But the store wasn't crowded and there were few obnoxious customers. She bought a tub of ice cream on sale and drove back to her condo.

In the mornings, Seaweed Manor was usually fairly quiet. The heavy partiers, of whom there were many, were still sleeping off their hangovers. As she approached the garage, she waved to some friends at the pool and to another walking toward the beach. Then, it was up the elevator to the fifth floor and to her two-bedroom facing the beach.

As soon as she had gone inside and closed the door, a gun pushed against her head.

"WHEN YOU TAIL SOMEONE, they're not supposed to know you're doing it." It was Affird's voice.

"How did you get in here?" Josie asked.

"The security in the complex is a joke. And I've dealt with

enough burglars over the years to know how to pick locks pretty well."

"Are you going to kill me?" Josie asked, trying to sound brave.

"That remains to be seen." He pushed the gun more firmly into her scalp. "Why have you been following me?"

"Because you killed Mary Beth."

"Your friend at the Unger Tract? I didn't kill her."

"And you killed Teresa, too."

"I don't know who you're talking about."

"Oh, sure, you're going to kill me, but I'm supposed to believe you didn't kill her?"

"I don't care what you believe," he said, close to losing his temper. "Have you turned into a vigilante? Were you following me because you planned to kill me?"

"You're here to kill me for my believing you killed my friend, and now you're accusing me of wanting to kill you? I'm getting confused here. Who's trying to kill who?"

"Whom. 'Who's trying to kill whom?'"

"I was a middle-school principal. I know the proper use of whom."

"I hated my middle-school principal," he said. Now he was truly angry. "I should kill you just for that."

"Can I sit down now?" Josie asked. "My knees are hurting me."

Affird blew out air in exasperation, picked her up, and dropped her on the living room couch.

"How many werewolves live here?" he asked.

"Werewolves? What are you talking about?"

"Don't give me that bull. I know about you and your friends. How many other werewolves live here?"

"Very few," she lied. "You're killing them off. You killed Chainsaw, too."

"That low-life drug dealer? Yes. Him I did kill. He was going for my gun."

"I don't believe you."

"How many times do I have to remind you I don't care what you believe?"

They were at an impasse, Josie realized. They both knew each other's secret: Affird knew that Josie was a werewolf, and she knew that Affird murdered werewolves. Affird could very well decide to kill her right now. She could tell he wanted to. He wore his service weapon in a belt holster, but it was a second piece that he was threatening her with. It was probably loaded with the silver bullets.

The one thing that could save her was that it would look very bad for Affird to kill a little old lady in her condo with no one to back up a story that it was self-defense.

Affird was looking at her china cabinet. He walked over to it and opened the drawer that held her expensive silver cutlery.

She swallowed hard. Yes, he could kill her and make it appear as if a burglar had done it.

A burglar who used silver bullets?

Affird's second gun was probably a throwaway weapon, a stolen gun with the serial number filed off, the kind crooked cops put in the dead hands of the suspects they shouldn't have shot. That's what he would use to make it appear a burglar shot her.

But that gun would be of no use against a werewolf, only one that was in human form.

On the other hand, if he wanted to defend himself against a werewolf—or to execute one extrajudicially—the gun would be loaded with silver bullets. Silver slugs in Josie's body would look really odd to a medical examiner.

She doubted his service weapon held silver bullets. Using unauthorized ammunition would surely get him in trouble. Or so she hoped.

The reason she was weighing these possibilities was that she was deciding whether to shift right then and there. Assuming that the gun in his hand was loaded with regular ammunition, shifting to wolf form was the only way to avoid dying from those bullets. And then she could kill him, too. Wasn't killing him her mission?

But, then again, she had just put new floors in her condo and had the walls painted. The thought of all the blood on the new hardwood laminate was too horrifying to consider.

"What do you have against us, detective?"

"Against whom? Note my proper use of the pronoun."

"Against supernaturals. It's not as if I decided to become a werewolf. I was bitten by one and became infected by the virus. I was a victim."

"You're a monster," he said with unexpected ferocity. "I've seen people who were killed by werewolves and what was done to their bodies. Unbelievably savage. Sure, some egghead medical examiner always determines the deaths were caused by a pack of dogs or a wild animal somehow in the city. I saw one of those supposed wild animals transform back into human form. The woman that monster killed was the true victim. Not the monster. Monsters like that don't deserve to exist."

"There are good werewolves and bad ones, just like people," Josie said. "Think of all the horrible murders committed by people. Does that make you hate all people and want to eliminate them? I'll have you know that I've never killed a human being. The blood of small animals is all I have on my hands. Are you going to tell me that all the people who hunt for sport are evil, too?"

"Of course not. And yes, serial killers and the like are monsters. But in the metaphorical sense. Werewolves are literally monsters, perversions of nature. Abominations in God's eyes. You are children of Satan!"

Josie felt she had been slapped in the face.

"You'd better tell Reverend Johnson that. He sees me every Sunday at First Episcopal."

Affird started pacing back and forth across the living room.

"I don't care what you do to pretend you're a normal human," he said. "I don't care about all your trappings of a prim and proper lady in your beachfront retirement community. I know that you're evil and I don't want you in my town."

"Why don't you make this public knowledge? Let the citizens decide if they want us or not?"

"Because they won't understand. They'll break into mass panic and they'll blame the police for not protecting them."

"Or they just might decide they don't care if we live here," Josie said. "That's what scares you the most, isn't it?"

Affird stopped pacing and looked at Josie with unbridled anger. His face was dark purple. Josie was afraid he'd get an aneurysm or something.

He pointed his throwaway piece at her, hesitated, glanced at his service weapon in its holster, then back at her. He appeared lost in frustration and indecision.

Josie had a bad feeling about this. Was the throwaway piece loaded with silver bullets after all? She had to make a run for it. As soon as Affird's eyes darted away from her, she sprinted toward the front door as fast as her eighty-seven-year-old legs could take her. Her hand touched the doorknob.

And Affird grabbed her in a bear hug, lifting her off her feet.

He carried her across the living room. She squirmed and tried to escape, but he held her so tightly she thought her bones would snap.

He reached the sliding-glass door to the balcony, slung her over his shoulder, and used his free hand to open the door. He moved onto the balcony.

Josie's eyes were on the interior of her condo as Affird pushed her off his shoulder. She sailed backwards through the air.

And over the balcony railing. His satisfied face looked at her as she began her five-story plunge.

## 20

## MEN ARE THE PROBLEM

F alling backwards off her balcony, Josie was lucky. Panic
didn't overwhelm her right away. Despair and help-
lessness didn't win. Somehow, the fierce desire to
extend her eighty-seven-year run on this earth won out. Some
people would fall frozen in resignation of their doom. Others
would claw at the air like Wile E. Coyote, as if that would keep
them aloft.

Josie did a version of the latter. She instantly forced herself
into shifting mode. Transforming into a wolf normally took
from just under a minute to five minutes or more. But Josie had
to do it in a few seconds.

As she shifted, she turned her body to face the ground that
rushed toward her way too fast. The green grass between the
ground-floor condos' patios and the concrete of the pool deck.
The grass where she would be smashed to death right about —

Suddenly, a wolf with preternatural strength, she flexed
her four legs and absorbed the impact, springing slightly
upward in the transference of force. Still, her chest and

stomach had hit the ground, slightly knocking the wind out of her. Her four legs hurt. But she had survived with nothing broken.

She sprang sideways, almost before the shot rang out above her. A clump of sod exploded inches from her shoulder. She knew what she had to do.

She raced toward her building and leaped to the second-floor balcony. Using her werewolf strength and the opposable thumbs of her hand-paw hybrids, she jumped up and pulled herself onto the third-floor balcony. She pressed her body against the building as she climbed to give Affird less of a target. Now she was on the fourth floor.

The sliding-glass door was open. A werewolf in his early sixties came out onto the balcony in human form with a watering can in his hand. It was Tom Furman.

"Josie, is that you?" He asked. "Did you hear a gunshot? Do we have criminals in our community?"

She growled in the affirmative and leaped to grab the risers of the railing on her own balcony above. This time, it was on the side of the balcony where it met the wall of the building. She had to be careful and quiet to avoid being shot point-blank in the head when she climbed up.

She pulled herself up just enough for a peek over the concrete slab. No shoes were visible. She lowered herself back down to Tom's balcony.

Mangling human speech with her wolf-like mouth, she got Tom's permission to pass through his condo. Once in the hallway, she avoided the elevators (both for tactical reasons and because werewolves in wolf form can't stand the claustrophobia), and ran up the stairwell.

She prepared to use her strength to bust through her condo door, but it was slightly ajar. She sniffed at the crack. Affird's scent was weak and faded. She slipped inside the door to find her condo empty. Affird had fled.

Well, first things first. Josie's outfit, with the matching khaki shorts and top that she had thought perfect for her surveillance work, lay on the ground near where she had landed. It had been split apart when she shifted, but she couldn't leave it there in the grass. People would know it was hers. So she had to shift back to human form, vacuum the shed fur, and run downstairs to retrieve her clothes.

As she gathered the torn outfit from the grass, Doreen from the Werewolf Women's Club approached her.

"Josie, are you all right? I saw what happened. I was doing my laps in the pool."

"What exactly did you see?"

"I heard you scream, so I looked up—"

"I didn't scream."

"You did. I looked up and saw you falling from your balcony, shifting just in time, and landing on all fours. Very impressive! And then I saw the detective shoot at you. I wasn't sure if I should call the police or not."

"Not just yet," Josie said. "Let me think about it. Detective Affird tried to kill me because I'm a werewolf. And because I know he killed our ladies. So it's complicated."

While Josie rode the elevator upstairs, she weighed her options. She had to kill Affird now, not just out of vengeance but because he would kill her as soon as he got the chance. Unfortunately, now it would be hard to catch him by surprise. Where could she ambush him? How could she make sure there were no witnesses?

Maybe Doreen was right. She should report Affird and get him in trouble for using his firearm recklessly. With luck, that would keep him away.

She called Doreen. "It's Josie. Yes, do call the police. Tell them exactly what you saw. Except the part about me being thrown off the balcony. I could never explain why I wasn't killed or injured."

Then Josie called the police herself and asked to make a complaint. She explained that Affird had broken into her condo. He was physically abusive when questioning her. She was afraid for her safety, left the condo, and then was almost killed when he fired a shot at her in a public area. She knew there was at least one witness and possibly more. She emphasized her advanced age and clean record.

Not long afterwards, a male police officer came by, and she repeated her story, playing the role of a sweet grandmother. She even gave him lemonade and cookies.

While he was there, she had ignored her ringing phone. Now the message light was blinking on her answering machine. She still preferred to use a landline over her smartphone. She pushed the play button.

"Hello, Mrs. Denton. This is Jerry from The Shooting Shop. I did some forensics on the bullet and cartridge you brought in. Please give me a call."

She did, and Jerry continued with his report.

"It's an eight-millimeter, and based on the really distinct rifling marks on the bullet, I would guess it was fired from a J.P. Sauer Mauser K98. They were used by the Germans during World War Two and are highly prized by collectors. Coincidentally, I found one at a gun show two years ago and resold it in my store."

"Oh, who did you sell it to?" Josie asked.

"I'm sorry, but I can't divulge that. Except to the police. Does this involve a crime? If so, I should report it."

"No, it doesn't," she lied. "Did the person who bought it work for the police?"

"No. I'll tell you that."

"Thanks for your help, and I'll stop by soon to pick up the bullet."

She hung up, frustrated. This information didn't really help her. Would Jerry have known whether Affird was a cop? Maybe the person who bought the rifle sold it to Affird. Or maybe the rifle Jerry sold wasn't the murder weapon. She drummed her fingers on the kitchen counter while she considered what to do.

If Affird was a rare gun collector, he might belong to a club to which he would have bragged about buying the rifle. Russ, who lived at Seaweed Manor, was a real gun enthusiast. Hopefully, he could point her in the right direction.

She looked him up in the community directory and called him. He answered straight away. After the obligatory small talk, she asked him how she should go about finding the person who bought the J.P. Sauer Mauser. She hoped he wouldn't ask her why she was asking.

"That's funny," Russ said. "One of us here at Seaweed Manor owns a Mauser K98. My buddy, Kevin O'Doodle. He loves historical weaponry, just like me. And his rifle is in excellent condition. He brought me with him to try it out at a gun range. Fantastic craftsmanship, that rifle."

Josie thanked him, her mind reeling. What did this mean? Was this just a bizarre coincidence? But she remembered that Kevin was their driver on both nights when the shootings took place.

It was time to look seriously into Kevin O'Doodle.

Kevin wasn't the kind of guy who stood out in a crowd, but in a retirement community, when women outnumbered men, even a stocky, bald guy like Kevin was a hot commodity. As

Josie had guessed, he had a little thing going with Mary Beth before she was killed. Tanya, soon afterward, filled Mary Beth's shoes by filling Kevin's bed. And there were rumors of other women. Was the slain Teresa one of them?

Josie and Thelma Lou did an exercise walk on the beach every morning at 9:00 a.m., unless an extreme high tide made walking too awkward on the soft sand near the dunes. The following morning, once the conversation slipped into gossip, Josie asked Thelma Lou what she knew about Kevin.

"He's not your type, Josie."

"Of course he isn't! He's also much younger than me. I want to know what kind of secret life he leads. I hear he may own the particular kind of gun used in the shootings. At least the one that killed Teresa."

Thelma Lou stopped dead in her tracks. "Kevin?"

"I know it's hard to believe, but he was there on both nights. He stayed behind with the bus when everyone else went hunting. Who knows what he was up to?"

"He loved Mary Beth."

"Since the beginning of time, men have killed the women they loved," Josie said solemnly.

"But really, Kevin was beaten up the night Teresa died."

"That could have been self-inflicted. So we need to find a motive. That's why I asked if he had a secret life."

"I don't keep up with what those youngsters in their sixties are up to," Thelma Lou said. "I love gossip as much as the next girl, but there's too much Viagra-popping partying going on with that crowd for me to keep it all straight."

Josie agreed. Young people assumed that retired folks were all the same, but Seaweed Manor residents had a wide range of ages. You had to be fifty-five years old to buy there, but a younger spouse could live with you. On the older end of the spectrum, there were Josie and Thelma Lou, plus even a few old birds in their nineties.

"We should speak with Tanya," Thelma Lou said. "She knows more about the party crowd here."

"Tanya is not exactly my biggest fan." In fact, Tanya was the one most likely to challenge Josie's status as their pack's alpha.

"We'll interrogate her after the club meeting tomorrow," Thelma Lou said. "I'll do the talking."

The Wednesday Werewolf Women's Club meetings were fairly brief business affairs in the clubhouse with light refreshments served. Only the five committee chairpersons plus Josie attended. Tanya was chair of the social committee which was why Thelma Lou wanted to speak with her.

"No," Tanya said, "Kevin and I are not an item. We're just good friends."

"You would make a cute couple," Thelma Lou said. "So who is the little rooster dating then?"

"I don't know. I think he's still in mourning over Mary Beth. I really ought to be getting home now. I have a stew simmering." Tanya gave a fake smile and ducked out of the clubhouse.

"She didn't seem very eager to talk," Josie said.

"She knows something."

"You called him a rooster. But Kevin doesn't seem like that type. He makes it no secret that all his parts are in working order, but charisma is not his strong suit. To be a true ladies' man, you have to be good at flirting."

"And dancing," Thelma Lou said.

"And Kevin is good at neither. Maybe we're going at this the wrong way. Instead of speaking to a friend of his, let's find an enemy."

"Does he have enemies?"

"Last month at the Full Moon Social, I was at the bar when he had a very uncomfortable exchange with Wanda Broder."

"Oh, really?" Thelma Lou asked in her catty voice.

"Yes. I'd love to know what that was about."

They caught up with Wanda after she attended a pool aerobics class. The top-heavy blonde in a mauve one-piece was frank.

"Kevin is a creep," she said from her lounge chair. "He was trying to get me to go out with him for months. I told him it was too soon for me to start dating again. But he was so persistent. He turned into a, well, a stalker. He would magically show up wherever I went, whether it was the clubhouse or the Chinese buffet in town. He'd leave phone messages, slip notes under my door. One time, I was walking on the beach and he appeared out of nowhere. And wouldn't leave me alone. He followed me all the way home like it was a date. He even tried to kiss me."

"Gross," Josie said.

"Exactly. So I finally told him—it was at the Full Moon Social—to give me some space. And he didn't take it well. He was pissed."

"I thought he was dating Mary Beth," Thelma Lou said.

"He was. He's just that kind of guy. He sees every woman as a potential conquest. Not that he wants to get to know them. He wants to know he can have them. That he did have them. I wasn't surprised that Mary Beth was trying to get out of their relationship."

"What happened after you brushed him off?" Josie asked.

"He wouldn't speak to me, which was fine with me. But he continued to stalk me. I was worried, frankly, but after Mary Beth died, he left me alone."

"What were you worried about?" Josie asked.

"He has a temper. I was worried he would threaten me like the others."

"Come on, Wanda, tell us what you mean," Thelma Lou said.

"He threatened Teresa."

"Teresa?" Josie and Thelma Lou said at the same time.

"You didn't know about them?"

Both women shook their heads.

"Teresa and Kevin had a little fling after Mary Beth died. Before he had his fling with Tanya. Candidly, I don't know why she would let that creep in her bed, but she confided in me that she was very lonely and just wanted a little intimacy. She broke it off not long afterwards. Kevin was not happy, let me tell you. Teresa said Kevin was taken by surprise and begged her not to break it off. When she did, he stalked her and actually threatened her."

"Threatened to do what?" Josie asked.

"He said he'd make sure she never dated anyone else. Ever."

The women were silent while that sank in.

"Did he threaten Mary Beth?" Josie asked.

"I don't know," Wanda said. "I wasn't a close friend of hers. But Teresa told me the reason Kevin volunteered to drive the bus, and kind of pushed Tony out of it, was to keep a close eye on Mary Beth."

"How creepy," Thelma Lou said.

"Kevin told Teresa that he volunteered because he wanted to be around Mary Beth as much as possible. That was when things were good between them. But when Mary Beth wanted to break up, Keven admitted that he kept driving the bus because he knew it would intimidate her."

"Do you suspect that Kevin killed Mary Beth and Teresa?" Josie asked in a low voice.

Wanda looked at her nails, then glanced around to make sure no one was within earshot.

"I've wondered sometimes," she said. "As horrible as it sounds. But I don't want to believe that anyone I know could do something so evil."

After they left the pool, Thelma Lou asked Josie what she thought now about Kevin.

"I was so certain that Affird killed our friends," Josie said. "He knows we're werewolves, and he's one of the cops believed to take it upon himself to execute supernaturals. He tried to kill me, for Pete's sake." She stopped and stared at the grassy area where she almost met her death. "But you know what they say: Suspect the husband or boyfriend first. I'm feeling strongly that Kevin did this. He's the kind who wants power over women to the point of harming them if they don't submit to him. He guessed correctly that we would first assume a hunter did it and, later, that it was someone targeting werewolves. We would never suspect it was a werewolf who did it."

"He actually used silver to make the bullets," Thelma Lou said. "That's so sick."

"Now, the question is, did he leave his gun at the hunting grounds before we went out there, or did he hide it on the bus? Let's take a look at the bus."

## 21

# THEY'RE COMING FOR YOU

After treating a vampire for a urinary infection, Missy returned home exhausted. The clock by her bed read 3:07 a.m. when she turned off the light and fell promptly to sleep.

The clock read 4:13 a.m. when her eyes shot open after her jewelry box fell off her dresser and scattered its contents across her hardwood floor.

"Was that you, Don Mateo?"

"Yes, it was I. My apologies. I am glad you're awake, however. I have alarming news."

"What is it?" Missy didn't really want to know. There were so many things in her life right now that could be classified as alarming.

"The gnomes are coming," the ghost replied. "They're coming for you."

Missy sat up in bed. "Again? Are you serious?"

"I suggest you get dressed and see for yourself. But first, you need to cast a protection spell."

Missy did the work to establish the protection spell around the entire house. It would be weaker than one around just herself, but she didn't want gnomes coming in the house before she could form a plan. She put on sweatpants and sneakers and went into the living room.

"They're in the back," Don Mateo said.

She turned on the exterior light in her back, screened-in porch. She gasped.

A crowd of gnomes filled her backyard in a semicircle, like a pod of dolphin herding a school of baitfish. She blinked, and they were suddenly closer to the house.

"In the front now, too," said Don Mateo.

She went to the front windows. Sure enough, the gnomes had now formed a circle around her house. A circle that was growing smaller. And each time she blinked, there were more of them joining the mob.

Ambient light glittered off their tiny eyes, making the gnomes appear alive. How could such cute, hokey objects seem so evil?

She cast her warding spell, the same one that had driven them from her yard before.

It didn't work. They kept coming.

"Wait, I have the Red Dragon talisman!" she said to Don Mateo. "I can order them to leave."

"You wish. The talisman compels only sentient beings, not manmade figurines."

"But it worked with my gnome before."

"Yes," Don Mateo said, "because it was your gnome. These others do not belong to you. To complicate matters, you also have the demon to contend with. The talisman can't compel demons you haven't summoned yourself."

"Look, I know I need my mother to call the demon off. But

in the meantime, I just want to get these buggers off my lawn."

When they were just a few feet away from the window, they stopped advancing. They had hit the bubble of the protection spell.

"Perhaps if you hold them off until dawn, they won't attack in daylight," Don Mateo said.

"Nope. I saw them running amok in daylight yesterday. They've grown bolder. Or maybe stronger, too."

"They're so tiny. Perhaps a windstorm will disperse them."

Missy knew a wind spell. The one time she'd used it, though, she only produced a breeze to drive mosquitos away. The windstorm would require a lot more power. The talisman could help with that, at least.

She went into the kitchen and drew a magick circle on the floor with chalk.

"I never needed a circle when I was a wizard," Don Mateo said.

"You know that demon that killed you? If you were inside a magick circle, the demon wouldn't have been able to get to you. Now keep your comments to yourself while I work."

Within the circle, she visualized a five-pointed pentagram and lit a candle on the point corresponding to the element of air. She performed her usual gathering of energies from within herself, from the earth, the ocean, the flame of the candle, and from the air. As she felt the power growing, she recited a simple verse in Old English. Then she directed all the power into the air element, holding the talisman in her pocket for extra effect.

"*Byre!*" she shouted.

A wind immediately picked up outside. Trees bent, palm fronds whipped back and forth, lawn debris blew everywhere.

Finally, one gnome rose from the ground and went flying.

Right into her window, shattering it but not breaking through.

Then another gnome was swept into the air. And smashed into a different window.

Now more gnomes, singly and in small groups, were blown into the air. And always into the exterior of her house. Many smashed into her concrete walls, but most shattered her windows.

She tried focusing on the wind, to change its direction. But invariably, no matter which direction the gnomes were launched, they ended up circling around and hitting her home.

Soon, every single window was shattered. Every single very expensive impact window would have to be replaced. What was it with garden gnomes and her windows?

*"Blinnan!"* she shouted and erased part of the magick circle, ending the spell, leaving the gnomes scattered all over her property.

But when she looked out the window again, they were back in formation: a giant circle growing smaller as if to strangle her home.

"Heat could melt the plastic," Missy thought out loud.

"I don't know what plastic is," said Don Mateo's ghost.

"You're better off not knowing."

She had conjured heat once before, when she had battled a spell that attacked her with extreme cold. She had stopped the cold, but ended up with everything she touched catching fire. It wasn't pretty. So she was a bit leery of once again playing with fire.

"I believe it's too late for your heat magick," the ghost said.

He was correct. Because there was a gnome in her home. A fat little bugger in a chef's uniform, standing just inside the front door. A door she hadn't seen opening.

Make that two gnomes in her home. A woodsman-themed gnome stood just outside the hallway that led to the bedrooms.

Three gnomes now. Four. Soon the kitchen where she stood in a broken magick circle was the only part of her home without a gnome.

"How are you going to get out of this mess?" Don Mateo asked.

"I was hoping you would have suggestions for me."

A gnome appeared in the kitchen doorway. A rustic little guy with an ax molded to his shoulder. He would have been cute if he wasn't intent on killing her.

Scuffling sounds echoed throughout the house as more gnomes entered, and the mass shifted forward toward the kitchen in six-inch intervals, too quickly for the human eye to register.

"How did they get through my protection spell?" Missy asked.

"I am not certain," Don Mateo said, "but I would wager it has something to do with the black magic and the demon."

"What should I do?"

"I will think of a solution. Elsewhere. *Adios, mi amiga*," Don Mateo said as he faded from sight.

Great. Abandoned by a man once again.

She formed a protection spell around herself. It was much stronger and denser than the one around the entire house, but she no longer had much confidence in this spell.

A block of ice formed in her stomach and her heart raced. The doorway to the kitchen was completely blocked now by gnomes, with a crowd pushing up behind them like throngs of kids trying to get into a concert. The shattered kitchen window showed a backyard packed with the possessed lawn ornaments.

She took her largest chopping knife from a drawer and advanced toward the horde, waving the knife menacingly. The gnome with the ax seemed to pause, but then continued its minuscule, unseen slides toward her. Others followed it into the kitchen.

They were not afraid of her. Humans were their prey.

A yowl and hissing came from the other side of the house. There was a great commotion out in the living room with furniture and objects hitting the hardwood flooring.

Suddenly, her gray tabbies, Brenda and Bubba, came bounding into the kitchen, knocking gnomes aside like bowling pins. The two cats jumped up onto the kitchen island. They stared at her like it was her fault that her home was filled with gnomes.

The gnomes, interestingly, had lost their forward momentum. It was as if they were put off by the cats. They weren't scared of humans, their sworn enemy. But the cats seemed to rattle them. But it wasn't as if Missy could enlist her cats to drive out the gnomes.

But maybe something else could.

The gnomes were filling the kitchen as far as the island, leaving her precious little space. But within her last bit of territory was the pantry. And in the bottom was her robot vacuum cleaner.

The robot vacuum was slow and timid, avoiding objects in its way. But with a little magick, and her telekinetic ability to move objects with her mind, she turned the timid robot into a weapon.

A simple spell added speed and power to the motor. Her telekinesis forced it to seek obstacles rather than avoid them. She activated the spell and off it went like a tank into battle.

The rustic gnome with the ax never knew what hit him. He

flew backwards into the air and landed in the throng of gnomes behind him, knocking them over.

The robot vacuum shot forward, battering its way through the gnomes. It pushed and chased the gnomes from the kitchen and then plowed them down in the living room. She directed the robot like she would use her regular, stand-up vacuum, sending it forth and back, radiating from right to left across the room. The gnomes packed her home so tightly that tipping over one gnome did the same to several around it like dominoes.

Of course, she wasn't damaging the resin-composite objects. She was merely sending them into disarray, disrupting their collective consciousness. Rattling them a bit. Anything that weakened them created an opening she could exploit.

As she took a step forward, her leg caught, and she landed on the floor. The evil little eyes of a Santa Claus gnome looked down at her. She swept her arm and set it flying into its comrades. She quickly stood again.

She needed to ramp up her counterattack. The gnomes that filled her home were in retreat, lying on the floor, piled into corners. Some had fled into the yard. But others were back on their little feet, imperceptibly sliding toward her.

An open door showed a tinge of purple in the sky. She hoped the coming daylight would thwart the gnomes, but she wasn't hopeful after seeing them marauding in the garden center during the day.

She yelped in pain as a hard object hit the back of her head. A gnome landed at her feet and she kicked it like a soccer ball. Of course, it hit one of her windows, damaging it further. Another one hit her shoulder.

Dozens of gnomes flew at her like gnome kamikazes. She got hit in the face and tasted blood. The gnomes continued flying at her, pummeling her. She had to keep from falling down or it would be the end of her. But another gnome hit her head, and she felt the world tipping.

Somehow, she ended up in the laundry room and opened the door to the garage. There weren't any gnomes in here. Yet. The robot vacuum had set them back, but now they were on the attack again. She needed another weapon to put them on the defensive. If they became disorganized long enough, she could use a warding spell to drive them from her property.

She scanned the tools in her garage and her eyes lighted on the one thing she knew gnomes in yards and gardens everywhere would fear: their eternal nemesis.

The weed whacker.

"Die you evil buggers!" She screamed as she charged into the house, the weed whacker growling, its deadly cord whirling in a blur.

The first gnome lost his face and half his paint. The gnomes behind it met a similar fate. She swung the weed whacker back and forth like a scythe and worked her way through the house, whacking gnomes. Some were decapitated; others were badly gouged.

And the rest were fleeing.

They piled into the yard in a teeming mass. It was a rout. She quickly closed and locked the doors and returned to the garage. It was time for the *coup de grâce*.

She imagined there was fear in their eyes as she pushed the roaring lawnmower into them. She tilted it onto its rear wheels to expose the spinning blade and pushed it into the crowd.

The yard echoed with the clunking and cracking of shattered plastic and resin, big hunks shooting out to either side. She plowed a path through the field of gnomes and turned to make another pass.

Still, she was battered by flying gnomes. But she sensed the tide of battle was turning.

She made another attack through the backyard, the gnomes pressing against the fence to avoid her. Then she continued around the side, mangling gnomes with every step she took. In the front yard, there was no fence to trap them. She cut a swathe through the gnomes and noticed the numbers were quickly decreasing. She didn't see where they went, but they were definitely fleeing.

She decided to try the warding spell again. Holding her right hand out like a traffic guard signaling someone to stop, she chanted the spell, stepping in a circle to spread the energy throughout her property. Her left hand grasped the talisman and its power surged through her.

"Begone from my land, I command you!" She said. But she didn't shout. She didn't want the neighbors to hear.

Maybe this spell hadn't worked earlier against the demonic influence, but now that the influence was disrupted, the spell worked fine. In a few minutes her lawn was empty, except for chunks and pieces of gnomes scattered about like yard refuse. She needed to rake up the bigger chunks and use the blower on the smaller ones. It looked bad. Her neighbors would complain.

She walked toward the garage and stopped suddenly. A decapitated gnome head caught her eye. Did it move? With a bushy white beard, pointy red hat, and jaundiced eyes, it radiated malevolence.

It rolled over, right in front of her. Then, it began rolling like a grounder, bounced off her foot, and struck her in the jaw.

That's going to leave a nasty bruise, she thought. People will think I'm dating an abuser. Little did they know the kind of evil guys I've got here.

She kicked the gnome head with all her might, and it sailed

down the street, landing in front of her neighbor's house, bouncing three times, and dropping into a recycling bin sitting by the curb. Fortunately, it was the blue bin for plastics and glass.

Missy had beaten the gnomes in this morning's battle, but she hadn't won the war. Not by any stretch. Her life was seriously in danger and she had to end this. The moment she had dreaded, the time to meet and confront her mother, was long overdue.

22

# A COUPON FOR EVIL

Matt was just getting out of the shower when the call came over the police scanner. Something about vandalized construction equipment. As he dressed, another radio call reported a protest. It was at the Unger Tract. Everyone still called it that instead of its new consumer-friendly developer name. Matt remembered the land was where the old werewolf lady was shot and killed. He had to check this out.

He arrived to find a TV news crew had beaten him there. Their van with the station logo and a microwave transmitter sat on the shoulder across the street. The blonde reporter spoke to a cameraman with the protest behind her.

The scene was a chaotic confrontation between a small group of agitated protesters and a much smaller number of bored-looking cops. The protesters didn't look dangerous. They looked goofy.

Frank, of Frank's Friends of Florida, was chained to the front shovel of a large yellow excavator along with two aging hippy women who had flowers in their hair. Near them were about a dozen protesters of a variety of ages waving handmade signs at the news camera. The signs said, "No more sprawl," "Save the earth," "Stop overdevelopment," and sentiments like that.

Matt wondered why they bothered. From what he understood, the development was a done deal. Everything was approved, sales had begun, and the forest along with everything that lived here was being destroyed and scraped away down to the dirt. The only thing that would stop it would be a plunge in the real estate market. As if to hammer this point home, another excavator was in the distance using the claw at the end of its shovel to tear limbs off trees and yank the trees out of the ground. It must have been painful for the protesters to watch.

Two older men in yellow hard hats stood next to a pickup truck sipping coffee and watching the protest with amusement. A fat man in a suit spoke on his phone nearby, gesticulating wildly. He looked like a mafia don. Matt recognized him: He was George Loopi, the developer.

Matt walked over to the two men whom he guessed were construction managers.

"Morning," Matt said.

The men nodded aloofly.

"I'm Matt Rosen with *The Jellyfish Beach Journal*. Did these protesters do any damage?"

"Yeah, they poured something into the gas tank of a dump truck. And now this." The manager made a dismissive gesture toward the group chained to the excavator. "We should have just run them over before the police got here."

"Has this group of protesters given you a lot of trouble?"

"Nah. Mostly they just show up and wave their stupid signs. They come to a lot of projects in this area."

"I'm going to destroy them," said a bellicose voice behind Matt. It was George Loopi.

"That Frank fellow is a fanatic," the developer said. "He's always following me."

"Everyone has their passions," Matt said.

That seemed to further annoy the man.

"He has a vendetta against me. Like he wants to put me out of business. He shows up at every single project. No, I take that back. He doesn't bother me when I demolish historic land-marks. It's only when I build on virgin land. That freaking tree hugger."

"Is he known to commit much vandalism?" Matt asked.

"Mostly petty stuff, not too costly but annoying. Insurance covers most of it."

"What about violence?" Matt asked.

"My guys didn't kick him around too hard," the construction manager said with an evil grin.

"I meant by Frank and his protesters."

"I wish," Loopi said. "That would put him in prison and out of my hair for a long time."

Matt knew that Josie had briefly considered Frank a suspect but had changed her mind. If the man was truly a fanatic, he wouldn't behave logically. But why would he be on this property at night with a gun? Whoever killed the werewolf used a silver bullet because he or she was hunting a werewolf. That had nothing to do with development.

But maybe Frank had a crusade against werewolves. There's no rule he couldn't have more than one hobby.

Matt walked over to the protesters. The police wouldn't let him get close to Frank, so Matt had to shout his questions.

"What are you hoping to accomplish here?"

"Public awareness," Frank shouted, his giant white beard

flecked with sweat. "We have to stop destroying the earth out of greed."

"What do you say to those who claim we need to build more homes because the population of Florida is growing?"

"Higher density," Frank shouted back. "Renovate older neighborhoods. Build multi-family housing in cities closer to jobs and shopping. Stop the mindless sprawl! Stop all the roads clogged with cars connecting all the sprawl."

This wasn't a guy you wanted to be stuck next to at a party, Matt thought.

"Why do you think it's justifiable to vandalize the truck?"

"Because it belongs to a greedy company that vandalizes the earth," Frank shouted.

"Where does it stop?" Matt asked. "How far would you go? Would you harm a person to stop the destruction of the earth?"

"I don't have to. The earth will harm those who harm her."

Matt didn't like the answer. The guy wasn't completely against harming people.

A police officer approached the protesters with bolt cutters and the TV news cameraman pushed into Matt's way to get a good shot of the chain being cut. Soon, Frank and the two women had plastic cable ties around their wrists and were being led away to a police van.

Matt had another question for Loopi, but he decided he'd get a more honest answer if he asked one of the construction managers he had spoken to. He walked back to where they were watching the show.

"Don't you guys have security to protect your property?"

"Yeah. These nuts rushed in when our guy was on the other side of the parcel."

"Can the guard shoot a trespasser?"

The two managers exchanged glances. "The guards would

call the police. But they can defend themselves if they're in danger."

MISSY'S PHONE RANG. It was Matt. He told her about the incident with the protesters at the construction site for the new community.

"That guy Frank—the environmentalist—chained himself with a few followers to an excavator," Matt said. "The police had to cut them free to arrest them. Frank is quite a piece of work. A bit nuts, if you ask me. Maybe you and Josie should take a closer look at him, to distract her from Affird."

"You think he's violent?" Missy asked.

"I don't know if he has it in him to pull the trigger himself. But I get the feeling that he's not against the concept of people getting hurt to protect the planet."

"Like he wouldn't mind if someone in his group pulled the trigger?"

"Exactly. Those women arrested with him seemed brainwashed. We're talking Charles Manson's 'family' brainwashing."

"Sounds intriguing."

"I reported on Frank's group for a story a few years back and I didn't see any red flags. But maybe he's gotten more extreme. I'd look into him myself, but I'm under deadline right now."

"Big story?"

"No." He sounded deflated. "The city council enacted new pooper-scooper laws."

"I'll check it out. Thanks."

This was the second time Missy searched the internet for Frank's Friends of Florida. The fact was, they really weren't very interesting. They didn't lobby legislative bodies for pro-environmental laws or regulations. They didn't raise money to buy endangered lands. They didn't do any direct work to save endangered species. They mostly held meetings and organized protests. In photos on their social media pages, members looked earnest, if a little comical.

She then researched their leader, Frank Fitzwhizzle. Apparently, he had once been an orthodontist, then retired to focus on his passions: the environment and magic mushrooms. Yes, she found a mugshot of a wide-eyed Frank Fitzwhizzle booked in the county jail for trespassing and possessing hallucinogenic mushrooms. That explained a lot.

She also found a news article naming him and several others as being arrested for petty theft of lawn ornaments from several residences.

Lawn ornaments? That was odd, considering what had upended Missy's life lately. Maybe the lawn ornaments had been plastic pink flamingos. Still, this cried out for more investigation.

In the morning, Missy drove out to the development site. Across the street, four forlorn protesters stood in the light rain with their soggy cardboard signs. Their leader wasn't with them. He must not have bonded out of jail yet. Missy parked on the shoulder a short ways past the group and walked back to them. Across the street came a steady roar as the excavator meticulously destroyed the remaining forest and a bulldozer scraped the earth raw. Hopefully, any wildlife living on the land had escaped, though with all the surrounding developments, it wasn't clear where the animals could go.

One protester, a middle-age woman around Missy's age (though more weathered by her years than Missy, thank you very much), glanced over as Missy approached. She flinched a bit, as if she expected Missy to attack her.

"Hi," Missy said. "I just wanted to show my support. It's horrible to see what's happening to the land around here. It used to be nothing but farms and nature."

"It's a sin, it is." the woman said. She looked like she was about to cry.

"It's too late to stop the development, right?" Missy asked.

"Yes. We're here to send a message, that's all."

"A message of what?"

"That destroying the environment is wrong."

"I don't think they," Missy pointed at the men running the heavy equipment destroying the environment across the street, "really care."

"We can't let evil go unchallenged," the woman said.

"Excellent point," Missy said, making the woman smile.

The woman wore a "Friends of Florida" T-shirt, soaked now by the rain. But she also had a campaign-style button bearing the acronym "GLL" in large letters. Missy had never seen that before.

"What's G-L-L stand for?"

"Oh, that? The Gnome Liberation League."

A feeling of disorientation swept over Missy. She almost lost her balance.

"Did you say, 'gnome'?"

"Yeah," the woman giggled. "It's just a fun little group some of us are in. We seek to liberate garden gnomes from unworthy owners and return them to the wild. To places like that," she pointed across the street, "used to be."

The concept sounded vaguely familiar. Missy thought she'd read about groups like that in Europe.

"I do it just for fun," the woman said. "It's like an intellectual joke. But some people take it seriously. Frank is very passionate about it."

"Really? Has he ever stolen gnomes from people's yards?"

The woman checked to make sure the others weren't listening.

"I think so," she said quietly.

There's no way this can be a coincidence, Missy thought. Gnomes have never been a thing before and now they were everywhere.

"Has Frank stolen any gnomes recently?"

"No. The group isn't active now. I wear this button just for the fun of it."

Missy thanked her and stuck around for a while, waving at passing cars along with the protesters to make the woman she had questioned feel comfortable.

Later, on her way home, she called Matt.

"I have to speak with Frank as soon as possible. Can you set up a fake interview with him?"

"Sure. Guys like that love to talk to the press. Are you suspecting him for the werewolf murders?"

"No. For something even more disturbing."

✵

IT TOOK LONGER than expected for Frank to bond out from jail, so the meeting at the beachfront bar was three days later. Missy chose that location because she wanted a noisy, distracting environment. She and Matt sat at a corner table with a view of the ocean. They each sipped beers. The idea was to make Frank as relaxed as possible.

"What if he's not alone?" Matt asked. "Sometimes the heads

of organizations have minders with them to make sure they don't say anything stupid."

"This is not that kind of organization," Missy said. "But if someone else comes, I'll need to enchant both of them."

She knew that her plan to use a spell made Matt nervous.

"Don't worry, this is a very minor spell, and it wears off quickly."

Frank arrived, a little disheveled, and searched the crowded bar. Missy and Matt waved at him.

"Hi, Mr. Fitzwhizzle. Good to see you again. This is my colleague Missy Mindle. Thanks for agreeing to the interview."

"My pleasure," Frank said, shaking their hands. "We need any publicity we can get."

After they sat down, and Frank ordered a water, Matt began with a bunch of softball questions. This allowed Frank to spout off with his talking points and feel at ease. About twenty minutes in, Matt's eyes were drooping, and Missy was seriously bored.

It was time for the spell.

It was a simple truth spell. Missy had learned it early in her witchcraft education. After her divorce, and her husband's subsequent death, she dipped her toe in the dating pool. She found she needed a way to weed out the guys who were interested in only one thing. And the truth spell made them feel compelled to blurt out their genuine feelings. The spell didn't alter their consciousness or force them to do anything. It simply empowered a person's natural urge to unburden oneself of lies and secrets. It made telling the truth feel good.

Frank looked at Matt and rattled off his manifesto of righteousness. Missy recited the words, a short verse in the Middle English of Chaucer's era. Then, out of everyone's view, she opened a small pouch filled with a mixture of herbs, flowers, and essential oils. She sprinkled the mixture under the table upon the floor, tossing some upon Frank's shoes.

Finally, she sent a burst of energy onto the floor to activate the spell.

"Mr. Fitzwhizzle, Do you have anything to do with the uprising of garden gnomes in this area?" she asked in a tone of authority.

He looked at her. "Yes. I do."

Matt's mouth dropped open with surprise.

"Why are you doing it?" Missy asked.

"I believe in real gnomes. And I believe that garden gnomes contain some of the magic of real gnomes. I think they're treated horribly, by classless people who buy them as a joke or because of some tacky sentimentality. I believe the gnomes are mistreated by being used to decorate yards and gardens, by being forced to endure extreme weather, by being urinated upon by dogs, and chopped by weed trimmers. For years I have liberated them and set them free in the wilderness. But now there is so little wilderness left in Florida. And my lawyer says I can't afford any more arrests for petty theft. So I went big. Really big." He smiled.

"Did you summon the demon that possesses them?"

"No, I hired someone to do that."

"You what?" Missy asked.

"There's a sorceress in Central Florida who does black magic for a price. It's just like hiring a lawyer, only cheaper and more satisfying."

Missy's mind was reeling.

"How did you find her?"

"You know those books of coupons you get in the mail? She had one for forty percent off."

"You can't be serious."

"I know it sounds hard to believe, but she really gave me forty percent off."

"No, I mean about the coupon. What kind of magic practitioner would do that?"

"The evil kind. The kind about to have their home foreclosed."

Missy sighed with exasperation. "And what is her name?"

"Ruth Bent." It was the same name that Jack the ogre reported. Her mother, whose real name was Ophelia Lawthorne, was using an alias.

"One more thing. Was it your intention that the gnome owners would be killed?"

"No. Honestly. That's the gnomes' doing. I didn't even know there were deaths until I saw reports of mysterious accidents in the news. I only wanted the gnomes to run away and go somewhere safe. But deadly vengeance is what they want. And it can't help that they're animated by a demon."

"No, that doesn't help. That was a terrible idea to involve a demon."

"It wasn't my idea. I just hired the sorceress. I didn't tell her how to do her job."

"You could have told her to make sure no one died," Missy said.

A look of resistance passed over Frank's face like a cloud obscuring the sun. The spell was wearing off. Missy whispered the words that deactivated it.

"I think I said too much," Frank murmured.

"You were very helpful," Missy said.

"This stuff about the demon and the gnomes—I hope that's not going in the article," he said to Matt.

"Trust me. It won't."

"Well," Frank said. "This has become a little awkward. I

think I should be going." He stood up. "You're still doing the article, right?"

Matt gave him a thumbs up.

Frank walked a few feet, then stopped and turned back to them.

"Can I get in trouble for this?" he asked.

"I don't know," Missy replied.

Frank looked worried, but gave a friendly wave goodbye.

"This is nuts," Matt said. "Every time I help you out, craziness ensues."

"Welcome to my world. But seriously, I need to stop my mother right away. I'm getting no replies to my calls or texts from the guy who tracked her down and I'm worried about him. I'm worried about us all, actually. Can you come with me?"

"You mean to battle a sorceress?"

"Yes."

"I'm not sure I have any vacation days left." Matt's eyes widened after Missy glared at him. "But I'm sure I can find a way to take a little time off to go with you."

"I don't know how I'm supposed to stop this woman. This mother I never knew."

"I see. You don't sound very encouraging."

"What should we do about Frank?" Missy asked.

"We can't exactly report him to the police for this. But he does need to face justice of some kind."

## 23
## MOMMY DEAREST

Missy felt magic in the air as she and Matt drove down the dirt road. No, it wasn't magic between the two of them. She had an extrasensory perception for magic and similar energies, especially when it involved the earth and sea energies she used for the magick she practiced. But this was black magic. She could feel it, not as pure energy, but as if it were radiation. It was dirty, malevolent, dangerous.

And it came from her own mother. What a comforting thought.

"I know I promised you I would stop asking," Matt said, "but have you figured out a plan yet? The GPS says we're arriving."

"I told you not to ask me because I don't have a plan."

"Okay. Good to know."

"Look, I don't want this to be a titanic battle like you'd see in a movie. I've never fought true black magic before, so I don't even know what tactics to use. I'm going to handle this like a normal human would when she's meeting her mother for the first time. The mother she never knew she had until recently. The mother who gave her up as an infant. That's how I'm going to handle it."

"I see. Like a titanic battle."

"Shut up."

"Just so you know," Matt said, "I brought a gun. It's in my bag."

Missy glanced at him. He didn't appear to be joking.

"You? A gun?"

"Yeah. My experience with the Boogaloo Brigade got me thinking I should have one."

"Do you know how to use it?"

"No."

"Well, in case my mother and I get along, please don't shoot her."

"Duly noted."

The dirt road ended at the edge of thick, tangled woods. On their left was a dirt driveway that twisted through the trees, the setting sun giving them a fiery glow. The black mailbox had the address, "666," painted on its sides.

"That's really the address?"

Missy turned into the driveway. Right after it curved, she stopped.

A white van was parked on the side. It was Jack's van.

"You know, I think we should park somewhere else," Missy said, backing the car out of the driveway. "Maybe up the road a bit. I don't like being in a dead end like this."

She reversed onto the dirt road and drove back the way they had come.

"A little walk won't hurt us," she said.

"Was that the enforcer's van?" Matt asked.

"Yep. She must be holding him captive."

"Or maybe they hit it off."

Missy gave him a dirty look.

When she returned her eyes to the road, she slammed on the brakes.

Because the road was gone. Dense woods with vines and thorns blocked their way. Her scalp prickled with fear.

She looked in her rearview mirror. The scene was the same as before: the dirt road ending at the dense forest like the one that blocked them now.

"What happened to the road?" Matt asked. "It's still here on the GPS map."

"Magic. Black magic."

"Is it just an optical illusion?"

She inched the car forward. The grill kissed the trunk of a scrub oak tree. The tree wasn't going anywhere. Neither was the car.

"Not an illusion or apparition," Missy said. "Okay, I'll go talk to her. You stay out here as backup."

"As a backup daughter?"

"As someone who comes running with his gun if I yell for help."

"Uh-oh. I'm hardly the cavalry."

"You're all I've got." Missy handed him the keys and got out of the car. "I'll text you within an hour. If I don't, call the cops."

She left him there in the car and walked the short distance down the dirt and gravel road to the driveway. Now was the time to use a little magick, a basic protection spell that would enclose her in an invisible bubble that shielded her from projectiles and physical attack. It even worked against bullets, the one time she had to try that. Most non-corporeal entities couldn't penetrate it either, but she didn't know if it would protect her from everything, such as black magic. She would just have to find out the hard way. Holding her power charm in her pocket with her left hand, she drew forth the natural energies in the air and earth around her.

She stopped walking. It had never been this difficult before to reach these energies. It was as if she had been weakened. She did the best she could, adding the energies to those that had been born inside her, and recited the brief spell. The formation and closing off of the surrounding bubble gave her some relief.

The protection spell was the only magick she allowed herself for now. It would be foolhardy to unleash blindly a bunch of spells against her mother and the house. She had no idea what the situation was inside. But she did know her mother was likely much more powerful than she was. She had to handle this carefully and improvise along the way.

As she walked along the sandy, rutted driveway, almost tripping on a protruding root, the radioactive feeling of the black magic was nauseating. Her bones ached with it. Sweat trickled down the small of her back. Gray Spanish moss hung from the branches of the twisty oak limbs like the beards of dead men. No birds sang or insects buzzed. It was silent except for the beating of her heart. The protection spell's sense of security wasn't enough to ward off her growing fear.

Jack's van was unlocked. She opened the driver's door. The keys were still in the ignition, but no one was inside. Her gnome, that Jack had borrowed, wasn't visible. Hopefully, it had liberated itself and ran off to live in the forest with dignity and freedom.

The driveway wound through the shadowy woods as the daylight faded. She kept expecting to come across human bones scattered about like in a fairy tale about a witch. Instead, she saw crushed beer cans and used tires like a true-life tale about a redneck.

Was her real mom a redneck? Her father certainly hadn't been, from the little she had learned about him. He had been a well-respected and powerful witch until he was murdered, she'd been told, by a demon.

The driveway twisted left and now she saw the house. It was small and made of red brick with a metal roof. Pine needles covered the roof from the trees that surrounded the house. A rusty old Chevrolet Impala, its red paint faded by the sun, sat in the carport that extended from the side of a one-car garage. The car was surrounded by stacks and stacks of mildewed cardboard boxes, softened by years of humidity and threatening to fall apart and spill their contents.

Missy briefly wondered what was in those boxes. She decided she didn't want to know.

There wasn't much landscaping to speak of. Some scraggly shrubs were planted beneath the windows in the front of the house. The yard had been recently mowed, with chopped-up pinecones scattered about. The home had the feel of neglect. Oh, and of evil, too. Mustn't forget about that.

She hesitated and rang the doorbell. Actually, she just pushed the button, and no sound came from inside. So she knocked. And knocked. Waited politely and knocked again.

The door finally opened, and the loud audio of a TV spilled out. A woman about Missy's height stood there with short hair dyed raven black. She looked vaguely like Missy, with the same high cheekbones and impish nose but with the wrinkles of someone in her seventies. Her eyes were icy steel gray. A cigarette dangled from the corner of her mouth.

"Ah, Elizabeth, took you long enough to get here," said the woman named Ophelia Lawthorne, maiden name Ophelia Finch, who apparently now called herself Ruth Bent. Elizabeth was Missy's name at birth before her adoptive parents called her Missy.

The woman turned away from the door, saying, "Wheel of Fortune is on," as she walked away into the house. Missy didn't know what to do, so she followed her into the smoke-filled living room. Ophelia sat on a wing chair very close to an old television. A small table held a can of beer and an overflowing ashtray.

"There's beer and soda in the fridge," her mother said without taking her eyes off the screen. "Buy a freaking vowel!" she yelled at the contestant.

"I'm good, thanks."

Missy heard a metallic clang coming from behind the house.

"Actually, I'll grab a soda," Missy said and went into the adjacent kitchen. It hadn't been updated since the seventies, with dark paneling and Formica counters. The window over the sink had a view of the backyard. The door of a metal shed opened, and Jack emerged holding a rake. He was shirtless, with lots of chest hair and two nipple rings. He also had bony ridges on the top of his shoulders as ogres do. He began raking the lawn despite the impending darkness.

Missy stood in the doorway to the living room and asked, "Why is Jack doing yard work?"

"Shhh! It's the final round."

Missy watched the woman, who was allegedly her birth mother, fixate on the television while chain smoking. Despite the vague similarity in appearance, how could this woman be her mother?

Finally, when there was a commercial break, Ophelia looked up at Missy.

"I've enslaved the ogre with a spell. This place has really gone to crap lately, so I'm having him do some work for me."

"Is he okay?"

"I'm sure he's not happy about it. But I feed him from time to time."

Missy had feared a cataclysmic battle when she faced her mother for the first time. This was pretty underwhelming.

"So, I'm here about the gnome possessions. Why are you doing this?"

"I was hired to do it. I'm an independent contractor." She pointed her cigarette at Missy. "It's how I make a living. Hiring me is no different from hiring a lobbyist to make things happen for you in Washington. In my case, I use black magic. It's what I do. I'm not a nurse like you."

"How much do you know about me?"

"I've kept an eye on you over the years."

"Why did you pick my gnome to begin this whole thing?"

"I thought it was sweet to reach out to you."

"Reach out? You didn't contact me. You summoned a demon and made it possess my gnome, which is killing my neighbors."

"It didn't kill you. See? I'm looking out for you."

"That's not the case anymore," Missy said. "The gnomes are coming after me now. It's time to call your demon off."

"I can't. My contract was to liberate all the gnomes in Jelly-fish Beach. My cheapskate client couldn't afford a larger geographic area."

"They're not being liberated. They're rising up and killing their owners."

"That's not my problem," her mother said, turning her attention back to the TV.

"You summoned this specific demon. Why?"

"Because she's the mother of the devil. *Mother*. Get it?"

"Okay, I see from whom I inherited my taste for the ironic.

The problem, though, is that the demon is influencing the gnomes to be evil."

"Well, what a surprise."

Missy walked over and got in her mother's face.

"Why are you doing this?"

"I told you. I was paid to."

"I mean, why are you practicing black magic? From what I gather, you were a benevolent witch when you were married to Ted. What made you turn evil?"

"You're not the first daughter who thought her mother was evil."

"You *are* evil. You practice black magic and summon demons."

Ophelia cackled and then broke into coughing. "If you only knew the half of it."

"You didn't answer my question. Why did you turn evil?"

"Power. There's so much more of it when you turn to the black. Your father was getting all the limelight and respect. I was tired of playing second fiddle to him. And I wanted to punish him for making me feel that way."

"Did you have anything to do with his death?" Missy asked.

Ophelia waved the hand with the cigarette dismissively. "Our divorce was well behind us when he died. I had no reason to want him dead."

Missy thought she was too proud to ask her next question, but she couldn't fight the urge.

"Why didn't you take custody of me when Ted died?"

"The Magic Guild of San Marcos wouldn't allow it. They banished me from the area because of my sorcery and they completely ruled out you coming to me."

"But you did ask to have me?"

"Well, sort of. Maybe."

Missy didn't know why she was foolish enough to hope to get an admission of love from this woman.

"I'm not here to litigate our lack of a relationship and the fact I grew up believing I was an orphan," Missy said. "I'm here to convince you to break the spell and free the demon from possessing the gnomes."

"It's not for you to decide. I can't end this prematurely unless my client asks me to."

"I spoke to him and he seems worried about his legal liability for the people who died."

"He doesn't need to worry," Ophelia said. "The criminal code has no mention of deaths or property damage indirectly caused by spells. Now, back in Salem, Massachusetts, in the sixteen hundreds, that was when spells could get you in deep legal doo-doo."

"Please, just break the spell, okay? This has gone too far. They've killed an innocent police officer. And they've started coming after me."

"My client still owes me one third of my fee, payable upon completion."

"Call him. Now."

Ophelia turned her attention back to the television. "Jeopardy's on now."

Missy found Frank's number and called him on her own phone.

"Frank, I'm here with the sorceress you hired for your gnome project. Tell her to end it."

"Well, I'm not sure if it's time," he said.

Missy wasn't having any of this nonsense. "We already spoke about this. The gnomes haven't been 'liberated' to run off and live in the forest. They're marauding through town, killing innocent people. Including a cop. You could go to jail for this."

"I don't think I can," Frank said.

"He can't," Ophelia said.

"You can," Missy said. "I'll make sure of it. Tell her. Now."

She handed her phone to her mother, who listened, then said, "I will when you transfer me the rest of my fee. Yes, send it there. Good."

She returned the phone to Missy and turned her attention to the TV.

Great, Missy thought, now I have to wait how long for Frank to get around to transferring the cash?

"Did he say he would do it right away?" Missy asked.

Her mother nodded.

"Can you check your account?"

"During the next commercial."

Missy sat and watched the game show until a commercial for incontinence panties came on. Her mother reached for her phone, in a garish, black-leather case with evil-looking runes on its cover, and checked her email. She slapped the phone case closed.

"It's there," she said.

"Do you need the original gnome to do this?" Missy asked. "Jack the ogre brought it with him."

"It's not necessary, but it'll make the process easier. The gnome is in his van."

"I didn't see it in there. Are you sure?"

Ophelia nodded. "Look in the back."

"We need to talk about Jack next. He works for the Arch-Mage of San Marcos. You can't keep him enslaved."

Missy went out through the front door. It was dark outside now. She remembered she needed to text Matt before he called the police.

"Things are going okay so far," she typed and sent it.

When she opened the rear doors of the van, the interior light revealed the gnome upside-down on the floor. She placed it on the ground, closed the doors, and—

An explosion of light blinded her. Then a rush of wind tossed her in the air. She landed on the roof of the van.

Through her shock, she realized her mother was attacking her. She probably hadn't taken well to Missy giving her commands. What else should she expect from the mother who had abandoned her?

Another gust of wind blew Missy off the roof of the van. She landed painfully atop a pinecone in the dirt driveway.

Was this attack meant to be a scolding, or something worse? Missy renewed the protection spell around her, just in case.

A fireball arced through the sky and landed on Jack's van, which quickly erupted in flames.

Okay, it's something worse, Missy thought as she scrambled away from the van. Just before the gas tank exploded.

## 24

## WITCH VS. SORCERESS

Missy had never fought true black magic before. And she needed to learn quickly how to do it. Unfortunately, she didn't have much in the way of offensive capabilities.

She had to get face to face with her mother. So she marched toward the front door.

And was met by a thick stream of hot, foul-smelling liquid. She jumped out of the way and took shelter behind an abandoned washing machine. Her skin burned where the liquid had hit it, but it didn't scald her. The liquid smelled like . . . pee? Oh, my, this is awful, she thought. Who or what produced a stream of pee at fire-hose volume?

Another stream hit the washer almost hard enough to knock it over. She darted into the woods and circled around the house to find a better way in.

Something landed on top of her head and slowly slid down over her left ear. It was gooey and smelled like rotten eggs.

More glops rained down upon her, coating her with the thick, slimy, foul-smelling substance.

So this is the arsenal of black magicians? Disgusting stuff? Evil sorcerers want to make you barf before they kill you?

She moved again through the woods and soon escaped the rain of goo. Now she was behind the house. Jack was still raking the lawn even though it was fully dark. She wondered if she could free him from her mother's enslavement. Unfortunately, Missy didn't know what kind of spell bound him.

She crouched in the underbrush and probed Jack for magic. She found a structure of magic, assembled with pieces of hate, fear, envy, and other negative emotions, somehow woven together into a skullcap enclosing Jack's brain. Many of his mental functions seemed to have been shut down. It was as if he had undergone a lobotomy. Her mother must have given him mental commands that made him docile.

Missy plotted how she could disable or destroy this skull cap and free Jack's mind. She could definitely use his help in subduing Ophelia.

She probed Jack's mind, studying the woven cords of misery that entrapped it. She didn't have the power or ability to remove the skull cap. She could tell it was constructed through complicated black magic that she didn't understand and couldn't overcome. But she believed she could weaken it.

She found a cord made from the negative energy of envy. Jack didn't seem like the kind of character who envied others much. He seemed quite the confident, self-satisfied ogre. Sure enough, this cord made of envy felt weak.

It was time to use her secret weapon. In her pocket she had the Red Dragon talisman. It didn't give her superpowers, but it enhanced her natural magick abilities and strengthened her authority when using spells to command sentient beings. Using it took a toll on her and it attracted the attention of powerful magicians, so she used it only rarely, such as now as she grasped it in her left hand.

As if electrocuted, her hand tingled and a current of fire ran up her arm, reached her heart, and warmed her all over. Her face flushed and her hair stood on end.

The talisman alone wouldn't break her mother's spell that enslaved Jack. It could only enhance the spells she knew how to cast. It could only heighten the energies already within her and that she drew from the air, earth, fire, and sea. But it would be enough.

"Banish all envy," she called to Jack as he raked leaves in the dark.

She concentrated on her mental image of the cord made of envy that was part of the magical skull cap that trapped Jack's brain.

The cord strained. With her mind, she pulled on it. And being the weakest of all the cords of negativity, it snapped.

She tugged at a severed end of the cord. And soon the woven skull cap loosened and came apart. The cap that kept Jack enslaved while Ophelia went about her daily life, attentions focused elsewhere, was ruined.

"Jack!" Missy called, as loudly as she dared.

Jack's face had an intelligent expression again. His eyes found her and showed recognition.

Missy left the woods and walked toward him.

"Help me subdue that evil old lady," she said.

A curtain twitched in a rear window of the house. Suddenly, Jack spasmed and dropped to his knees. He looked up at Missy with anger in his eyes.

"Oh, my," Missy said. She stopped walking.

And Jack got to his feet and ran towards her, brandishing his rake.

Missy sprinted back into the woods. Her mother must have sensed the spell over Jack had been broken and was now controlling him directly with another force of black magic.

This, Missy thought, was not good.

She pushed through the underbrush, getting snagged on some thorny vines. The crunching of sticks came right behind her.

She turned and ducked, just as the rake whipped across her inches from her face. It was a heavy-duty rake, with substantial steel tines. Not the kind of rake you wanted to be hit by.

She freed herself from the vine and ran through a cluster of saw palmetto bushes, pushing through their fans of leaves and thick stalks. Yet the rake snagged the back of her blouse and yanked her backwards. She landed on her back among the palmettos.

Jack stood above her, his face the bright green of ogre fury. He thrust the butt of the rake down toward her chest.

She rolled away just in time to miss it. As Jack tried to recover his balance, she kicked with both feet and knocked the rake from his hands.

What was the fastest spell she could cast to slow him down?

She scrambled away, putting an oak tree between her and Jack. Holding the talisman, she frantically recited the words of a sleeping spell. It wouldn't knock him out, but it would make him slow and groggy.

Jack's eyes rolled up in his head, and he dropped to the ground. Wow, it *did* knock him out. He must have been seriously sleep deprived while forced to labor for Ophelia. The spell wouldn't last long, however, especially if her mother tried to rouse him magically.

Time for a binding spell, one of the sharper arrows in

Missy's quiver. To ensure efficacy, she knelt and drew a circle around her in the dirt with her hand. She harnessed her energies, recited the Latin words, and grasped the talisman for maximum effect.

Jack stiffened and lay rigid on the ground.

This spell, too, could probably be broken by Ophelia's black magic, so Missy had to hurry. She ran through the woods toward the house. A loud buzzing came from up ahead. It sounded like a propeller airplane flying right at her, but she kept running.

And was met by a mosquito. A giant mosquito landing in front of her.

Florida is known for mosquitoes. They're all very hungry and many are large. But this was a really, freaking enormous skeeter, towering ten feet above her on legs as thick as tree limbs. Its proboscis was easily six or seven feet long. It beat its wings, making the leaves of the forest rustle. It hovered in the air and moved toward her.

No amount of DEET in the world would stop this mosquito.

This was one of those times that Missy wished her ethics weren't so pure and that she wasn't above using dirty magic now and then. Even a bit of black magic. It would come in handy right now. But at the moment, all she could think to do was run away.

Normally, humans are the lumbering giants swatting ineffectively at the tiny, nimble mosquitos. Now it was the other way around. By squeezing through dense clumps of trees, she kept the giant insect unable to stab her with its spear.

She had to admit she was impressed by her mother's skill and power. It was hard to imagine how she could turn an ordinary mosquito into this colossal monstrosity. Black magic was deadlier than Missy had realized.

Buzzing more loudly than an airboat, the mosquito swooped down on her through a gap in the trees. She had reengaged her protection spell, but somehow the proboscis cut through it like a needle through cloth. She tried to dodge it, but it still sliced through the flesh on the back of her right arm. After the burning pain came the familiar itch of a mosquito bite. But this was a hundred times more intense.

She ran toward another dense grouping of trees. How had it penetrated the bubble of her protection spell? And how had Jack when he attacked her?

It was her mother's black magic. It was too powerful. Missy fought the growing feeling of despair.

And her arm itched so badly she wanted to cut it off.

While the monster mosquito attempted to get to her through the trees that blocked its way, she strengthened her protection spell around her. But she wasn't optimistic it would be powerful enough. She looked at the creature's black-bubble insect eyes, the large, ugly hairs on its face, and the twitching mandibles beneath its deadly spear of a proboscis. She wracked her brain to think of a weapon she could use against it. If it pricked her again, it could drain her of blood in seconds.

Some of her blood was already in the monster's stomach. That gave her an idea.

Blood magick.

Many witches used blood in spell casting. The vital fluid was tied to a person's spirit, giving extra potency to spells. Missy occasionally used drops of her own blood in spells and potions. Black magicians used the blood of others.

The monster mosquito broke the trunks of two saplings, then hovered above them to move closer to her. Though a couple more trees blocked the insect's path, she was almost in reach of its sipping straw. it was close enough that the many discs of its compound eyes were visible, reflecting her image.

Dinner was almost served, the creature was probably thinking.

Missy used her spiritual bond with her own blood to form a psychic link with it as she carefully built the spell. She prayed that there was still enough of her blood in the monster's stomach.

Another tree broke with a loud crack. The mosquito lunged at her and she had to dodge the point of the spear. The insect now used the combined force of its beating wings and its hind legs pushing against the ground to get even closer. Somehow, it had maneuvered her against the trees behind her, so she couldn't back up. She could only escape to the side, making her easy pickings for the proboscis.

Her heart pounding, she finished saying the words and grasped the Red Dragon talisman. Heat built within her torso and she directed it outwards, toward the blood that had been taken from her. She focused it on this blood, in the beast's belly, and unleashed all the power she had generated.

To make her stolen blood boil.

The mosquito stopped its forward motion. It jerked its head from side to side while twitching its lower abdomen. Its wings beat furiously as it tried to escape its agony.

Until goo began pouring from its lower segment in a cloud of steam. The wings stopped beating, the propeller-engine roar ceased. And a tiny cry came from the creature.

Its abdomen broke apart, and the insect fell to the forest floor in two pieces, steam still rising from it. The wings collapsed, and it became yet another husk of a dead insect we barely notice. Except this one was the size of a Winnebago.

Missy crept closer to it, making sure it was dead. She felt the evil magic fade away. Soon, the body itself shrank, slowly and barely perceptibly. Within a few minutes it became the size of a normal mosquito. She could see it only when she shined her phone light upon it, a tiny speck upon a philodendron leaf.

Did her mother know her creation had been destroyed? Missy braced herself for another attack.

She saw by her watch that it was 8:00 p.m. A new television program would be starting. Hopefully Ophelia was engrossed in some must-see TV show.

Missy carefully walked through the woods back to the lawn. She passed Jack, still unconscious and rigid, bound by her spell. She made sure he was breathing. All good.

She reached the edge of the woods and waited. Would she be attacked by a giant firefly? Or a swarm of demonically enhanced no-see-ums? The tiny, biting gnats were hellish under normal conditions. Under black magic they would be the death of her. But they didn't come.

She walked into the yard. The house was ablaze with light. From it came the cranked-up television sounds of studio applause and laughter. This was the calm before the proverbial storm. Missy grasped the Red Dragon and strengthened her protection spell—not that it had helped her much lately.

A door with peeling paint in the house's rear was unlocked. She opened it and went inside.

## 25
## MAKE ME

**M**issy walked through the unlocked door to a mudroom, then into the kitchen. An opened carton from a frozen dinner lay on the counter. The TV blared from the other room. The living room was dimly lit by only one lamp. A talent show of some sort was on the screen. Her mother's chair was empty. The table beside it held the cleaned-out plastic tray from the frozen dinner, crumpled beer cans, and the overflowing ashtray.

Great, Missy thought. Am I going to have to search the house like in a horror movie?

In a dark alcove intended to be the dining area, a table was completely covered with mason jars containing unknown substances. Missy moved past this area to the end of the house with a bathroom and two bedrooms. One room was locked, of course. That would be where Bluebeard hid his dead wives, she thought. The master bedroom was crowded with clothes overflowing from the closet as well as stacks of dusty books and ancient tomes. Many of these were black-magic grimoires.

There was no sign of her mother.

Since it was a small house, the garage was the only space she hadn't searched. Back near the mudroom was the interior door to the garage. Missy opened the door. A small car was stuffed in here among lots of boxes. A workbench at the end held large black burning candles, mason jars, a mortar and pestle, and bags of herbs and powders. Her mother obviously made her potions out here, like Missy did in her own garage. Slight movement caught her eye in a darkened corner.

Her mother hung lifeless from a rope tied to the ceiling.

"Ophelia!" she cried, unable to call her 'mother' even in tragedy. She ran to the corner.

Her mother hung unmoving, her face purple and contorted. A noose bit into her neck, partly hidden by her double chin.

Why did she kill herself? And why did she have to do it when I was here? Missy wondered bitterly.

When she reached for her mother's wrist to check her pulse, her mother disappeared. The body was gone, the rope was gone. Missy stared, shocked, into the empty corner.

"Pretty good, huh?" her mother's voice said behind her.

Missy jumped and turned around. Her mother was sitting on a stool by the workbench.

"Apparitions are a hobby of mine," she said. "Just a hobby, because there's no market for them, except during Halloween, and even then, no one is willing to pay much."

"Why did you do that?" Missy asked.

"Wanted to see how you'd react. I'm glad you didn't clap your hands in joy."

"I should have. You tried to kill me through Jack and the giant mosquito."

"I believed you'd find a way to beat them. And you did. But I

230

got to say your protection spell has lots of flaws. You need to work on that."

"Thanks for your concern."

"I hear you've taken a big leap forward in the magic business," Ophelia said.

"It's not a business for me. I would never hire myself out like you do."

Her mother smiled sarcastically. "We'll see, we'll see. I hear you have your father's grimoire now. Don't play dumb, I know you have it."

"How did you find out?"

"Word gets around. You know, I wanted that book. Not because of the spells—they're all about healing and stupid goody-goody stuff like that—but because it would have fetched a hefty price. But that smug Arch-Mage Bob stole it before I could get there. I'm glad you stole it back."

"It was rightfully mine," Missy said. "Ted left me a letter bequeathing it to me."

"Whatever," her mother waved a hand in dismissal. She lit a cigarette.

"Can you please break the possession spell on the gnomes now? And free Jack?"

"Jack's gonna cost you some ransom money. Maybe Bob will reimburse you to get his hound dog back."

"Let's focus on the gnomes first. I ask you again, please break the spell. Your client released you."

Ophelia stared at her as she took a big drag of her cigarette. What was the evil sorceress plotting? She was clearly reluctant to give up her bargaining chip.

"Make me," she said.

"What do you mean?" Missy asked.

"Make me. I'll break the spell straight away after you force me to. Let's see if your stupid white magick can do anything useful. You don't summon demons; you don't like inflicting pain and suffering. How could you possibly force me to do what you want?"

Actually, it was a good question. How could her magick force a person to do something against their will?

She had the Red Dragon talisman, which had the power to compel obedience, but she didn't want her mother to know she possessed it. That would be damaging to her health, to say the least. So what else did she have?

*Smother them with sweetness* popped into her head. Yeah, right.

Yeah, maybe?

Maybe not sweetness exactly. But something innocent and playful—something that her mother might have done to her when she was a baby if her mother had only stuck around.

Sweet, but cruel enough to get her way. She built the spell from scratch, using her natural telekinesis mixed with the energy that dwelled within her and the elemental energy she harvested from the world around her. She didn't even need the Red Dragon.

She released the spell, using her telekinesis to control what she could only describe as the "magic fingers."

Ophelia suddenly doubled over on the stool.

"What are you doing?" She began giggling. "Stop!"

She thrashed about, trying to fend off Missy's invisible attack. The stool fell over and clattered on the garage floor. Ophelia sat on the concrete beside it.

She giggled hysterically without ceasing.

"Stop, please!" She barely had the breath to utter the words in between giggles.

The giggles turned into painful laughter.

"What are you doing to me?"

"It's a tickle spell. What did you think it was?"

"It's cruel. Stop!"

"It's not hurting you, is it? It's not black magic, I'm sure of that."

Ophelia rolled on the ground, giggling, laughing, crying.

"I won't stop tickling you until you command your demon to leave the gnomes now and forever. You were the summoner. You're the only one who can do it."

Her mother thrashed about on the floor, convulsing with laughter. Missy couldn't deny it gave her pleasure to watch the mother who had abandoned her, the supposedly fearsome black-magic sorceress, behaving like a two-year-old.

Missy sniffed. "Oh, my, I think you peed yourself."

"I-I-I can't summon the demon while you're tickling me."

Missy paused the spell. "Do it now, or the tickling continues."

"I hate you," her mother said.

"I know. Now do what you have to do."

Ophelia, still on the floor, struggled to regain her breath. She motioned for Missy to back off.

"Give me plenty of room. This is dangerous." She coughed violently. "Got to cut down on the cigarettes."

Ophelia took chalk from the workbench and drew a large circle around herself, like Missy often did. Only the pentagram she drew within it was upside down, its top point facing the sorceress. She placed small, black tea candles, one at each point of the pentagram, and lit them. Then she brought various materials and implements into the circle with her.

She lit a butane stove and heated a small pot which she filled with various herbs and a liquid from a mason jar, chanting all the while. Missy gasped when her mother drew a long, ceremonial dagger from its sheath, its blade curvy like a snake, and sliced into her inner forearm. Her blood dripped into the pot.

The chanting grew louder as she rocked back and forth on her knees. Oddly, she seemed younger and more muscular while she was fully engaged in her magic.

The temperature dropped several degrees in the garage. Missy wrapped her arms around herself and shivered. Strange noises, moans and shrieks, appeared just at the boundaries of her hearing. Something ancient and primitive in her brain told her to get the heck out of there, to get far, far from the dangerous entity that lurked just beyond this world.

"O Caorthannach, I command thee to abandon the inanimate beings you are possessing. I release you from the garden gnomes." Ophelia suppressed a snicker, "I release you from the terrestrial plane. Return now to Hell."

The ground vibrated with a rumbling as if a freight train were passing in the backyard. Wind somehow swept through the garage, extinguishing the candles on the floor and workbench.

A piercing shriek passed through the garage like a projectile. And then it was gone.

And all was quiet.

"Is it, is it done?" Missy asked in a whisper.

"Yes. The garden gnomes are free to be garden gnomes again. Caorthannach passed through here on her way to Hell, which should be the state motto for Florida. Anyway, I don't sense her presence on earth anymore, so let's hope she stays in Hell."

"Thank you. Mother."

"Awww, sweet of you to say that." She erupted into phlegmy coughs. "Now about that ransom for Jack. I was thinking a modest fifty grand would do the trick."

"I'm a home health nurse. I don't have that kind of money."

"Like I said, I'm sure Bob would reimburse you."

"You don't know Bob. He would say Jack was enslaved while working for me, so I'm responsible for his ransom. Once again, I don't have fifty grand and the bank wouldn't loan me fifty grand."

"Forty grand."

"I can't pay you anything. Can't you stop being evil for once?"

"No," Ophelia said, "I can't. Twenty grand. You know you're good for it."

"Look, keep the ogre. I don't need him anymore and you obviously do, based on the condition of your lawn and landscaping. Goodbye, mother, hopefully we won't meet again."

Missy went inside and headed for the front door.

"I could enslave you, too," her mother called after her.

Missy stopped next to the TV. She turned it off, allowing it to cool down for the first time in years.

"I can crank up the power of that tickling spell to the point of death," Missy said. "You don't have a defense against it. Ready to die from tickling?"

"Okay. Take the dang ogre. Just make sure he puts the rake back in the shed."

MISSY WAS surprised how late it was when she and Jack finally trudged down the driveway to the dirt road and walked toward her car.

Matt appeared out of the darkness.

"Finally!" he said. "I was worried about you. You sent me the text that everything was fine, but then hours went by and I haven't heard from you."

"Things turned out not to be so fine," Missy said. "But now they are. Matt, this is Jack. He needs a ride to a rental car office. His van was burned to a crisp."

"I saw the fire through the trees," Matt said.

"And you didn't call 911?"

"No. If you said things were fine, I wasn't supposed to call."

Missy shook her head. "It was probably for the best. The firefighters would have just ended up as collateral damage."

"Did you take care of the gnome thing?" Matt asked.

"I think so. Jack had my gnome in his van. I ended up tossing him into the woods. He should be happy here. Let's hope I never see him again."

## 26

## UNDER THE BUS

Josie picked up the keys to the bus from the property management office in Building A, then she and Thelma Lou found the bus parked in the far end of the parking garage. It had last been used to ferry werewolves to a production of *Cats* in a nearby city. The Werewolf Women's Club hadn't ridden in it since their last fateful hunting trip.

"Search the interior for secret compartments," Josie said, handing the keys to Thelma Lou. "Under the floor, under the seats, in the luggage compartments. I'll check outside and under the bus."

"You'll get your outfit dirty."

"It's okay. It will be my second ruined outfit in two days."

Thelma Lou climbed aboard, and Josie walked around the vehicle looking for compartments. Sometimes small buses like these had additional luggage storage below, but that didn't seem to be the case here.

Wait—there was a panel in the lower rear. She squatted and looked for a latch. She slipped her fingers into a small gap and pulled. The panel opened. The compartment held a fire extinguisher. Nothing else.

Now came the messy part. She lay upon the oil-stained concrete floor and slid beneath the bus. Surveying the underside of the vehicle revealed nothing obvious, like a rifle strapped to the suspension. There were no box-like objects that didn't belong. That didn't mean it wasn't here. Someone mechanically minded could easily have hidden it among these strange pipes and axles and struts.

A scuffling sound to her left. A pair of men's shoes—sensible walking shoes—and the cuffs of white trousers were visible on the side of the bus. The door of the bus opened. The vehicle swayed slightly from the weight of someone climbing aboard.

Thelma Lou screamed inside.

Josie struggled to slide out from underneath the bus, bonking her head on the drive shaft. Finally, she was back on her feet. She rushed to the door.

But it was locked. And Thelma Lou had the keys. Inside came the muffled screams and grunts of a struggle. She couldn't see anyone through the door's glass panels or the windows of the bus—the man must have pulled Thelma Lou down into the aisle or below a seat. What was he doing to her?

The man roared in pain and bewilderment, the kind of sound associated with family jewels being damaged.

And then the terrified shriek of a woman fearing she was about to lose her life.

Josie stripped off her outfit and shifted. As soon as the transformation was complete and adrenaline flooded her wolf body, she flung herself at the door. It bulged inward and cracks spider-webbed across the glass, but it still held.

Another lunge against it and the door snapped open. She

flew up the steps and saw the man atop Thelma Lou in the aisle. The man turned his head toward her.

It was Kevin. And just past them in the middle of the aisle was an open compartment. The black metal of a rifle barrel was visible inside, as were rubber waders, the kind fishermen and duck hunters wear.

"Why can't you girls mind your own business?" Kevin asked.

And then he shifted. Josie dove into her attack before his transformation was complete.

Where his trousers split open, revealing a human leg sprouting fur and a knee in the middle of changing its shape, she sank her teeth. She chewed and tendons snapped against her tongue. She shook her head, tearing flesh, trying to separate his femur from his knee.

Kevin yelped and punched her in the back of her head. Then the jaws of a wolf clamped down on her neck.

The man in his sixties surpassed the eighty-seven-year-old woman in size and strength. In werewolf form, she was much more formidable than a human. But so was he. If she didn't get free of his jaws, she would be finished.

She turned, exposing her belly, signaling submission. He released his hold on the back of her neck and held his jaws just above her throat, saliva dripping upon her.

Josie twisted to the side, just before his jaws came down, and grabbed his family jewels in her human-like claw. Kevin yelped and Josie skittered beneath a seat without letting go of his valuables.

Kevin raked her arm with his claws, sending blood droplets flying. He grabbed her hand-paw and tried to force it to let go.

But a snarl came from behind him. Thelma Lou had shifted. And she was very angry.

Kevin tried to face her, but Josie still had a death grip on his begonias. He snarled and sank his fangs into Josie's arm. The pain was intense and searing. She pulled her arms from his jaws and hoped her werewolf healing powers worked quickly. Often, bites from other werewolves didn't mend as well as normal wounds. It was something about the werewolf saliva.

Meanwhile, Thelma Lou charged into Kevin, trying to go for his throat. He managed to block her jaws with his forepaw, but his knee that Josie had damaged hadn't yet healed. It buckled beneath him and he lost his balance, falling on the seat above Josie.

Thelma Lou dove atop him. He kicked her with his hind legs, blocking her momentum, but she still managed to gouge his chest with her front claws. Blood spattered on the seat and windows.

Josie carefully slipped from beneath the seat, pressing against the wall of the bus to stay out of Kevin's view. She grabbed each of his pointy ears with her hand-paws, held his head steady, and chomped down on his face where his muzzle met his eyes. She arched her back and tore fur and flesh from his face, then clamped down upon him again, her fangs next to his eye sockets.

Kevin yelped and whined, struggling to free himself from Josie's grip. But Thelma Lou had got past his flailing legs. While Josie held his head, Thelma Lou found an opening and her jaws locked onto Kevin's throat. Was she going to tear it out?

Josie barked a command to wait.

Kevin's struggles ceased. He knew they had beaten him.

"Don't kill me," he said in speech thickened by his werewolf mouth, but werewolf brains have a way of compensating enough to understand the human words.

"Why shouldn't we?" Josie asked. "You're a murderer."

The word "murderer" merged into an ominous growl.

Kevin had to know that intra-pack justice was swift, brutal, and absolute.

"I'll confess to the police," he said.

"You won't survive in jail," Thelma Lou said. "On the full moon you'll be forced to shift. They'll kill you."

"I've been a werewolf long enough to fight the change on full moons so that I shift only partially. I can pretend I'm sick and hide under the covers of my cot."

Josie didn't fully trust him, but if he confessed it would close the cases and keep the police from sniffing around Seaweed Manor.

"You will shift back to human and call the police with your confession," Josie said. "We'll stay in wolf form to make sure you obey."

Kevin shifted to his human form, some of his wounds still unhealed. Josie tossed him his clothes, which were split at the seams and weren't going to do the job, so she found a blanket on the luggage rack and handed it to him.

Kevin looked at Thelma Lou, and she growled at him, baring her teeth. Josie studied her friend, who hung her head as if traumatized. Josie feared that Kevin had done more to her than rough her up.

"Call the police now," Josie ordered Kevin.

He removed his phone from the pocket of his split trousers, then hesitated.

Josie growled at him.

"Call Jellyfish Beach Police Department main number," Kevin spoke into the phone.

"Put it on speaker," Josie said.

Kevin complied. The phone rang until a chipper female voice answered.

"Jellyfish Beach Police Department. We hope you're having a sunny day."

"No, I'm not," Kevin said. "I'm calling to confess to two murders."

"Thank you for entrusting us with your murder case," the chipper woman said. "Please hold while I transfer you to a detective and please don't murder anyone else."

"Gotcha."

The line buzzed. "Homicide. Detective Ramirez. I hope you're having a sunny day in beautiful Jellyfish Beach."

"I murdered two people," Kevin said.

"Today?"

"No, but recently."

Josie poked him with her claw and motioned for him to elaborate.

"It was Mary Beth Godfrey and Teresa Brunel. They're the ones I shot. They dishonored me, if you really want to know."

"Were they friends or lovers?" the detective asked.

"Lovers. Until they betrayed me."

"I see. Can you come down to the department and turn yourself in?"

Josie growled.

"What was that?" the detective asked.

"I said no, I can't drive right now," Kevin said. "Will you come pick me up? I'm in the parking garage at Seaweed Manor on Ocean Road."

"Okay, we'll dispatch a unit to get you. And please don't murder anyone else in the meantime."

"I'll try not to."

Josie took the phone from Kevin. "Detective Ramirez, you're not bringing Affird with you, I hope."

"Affird? He's on vacation."

"Good." She hung up. She suspected Affird's vacation was mandatory.

Josie exited the bus so she could shift back to human form and get dressed out of Kevin's view. When she returned, Kevin was cowering in the corner of his seat while Thelma Lou, still in wolf form, snarled at him viciously.

"Why did you do it, Kevin?" Josie asked. "Why did you kill them?"

He didn't answer. He pouted. The section of flesh that Josie had bitten off beneath his eyes hadn't fully healed and it made him look like he was crying.

"Was it because they were rejecting you? Your fragile male ego couldn't handle that, could it?"

Still no answer.

"Why would you use silver bullets to kill fellow were-wolves?" Josie asked. "In my mind, that makes the murders even worse."

"That's why," he said. "Because no one would suspect me. I knew everyone would think vigilante monster hunters, or a rogue cop, did it. When I heard that you thought that detective did it, I came up with the story of him and a partner attacking me the night Teresa was shot. It wasn't fun wounding my own head, but it was pretty convincing, wasn't it?"

The creep appeared proud of himself. Josie didn't answer him. Thelma Lou emitted a low growl that chilled Josie's blood. She considered whether it would have been better just to kill him. It would have felt so satisfying to tear him into shreds. But it was too late now. It was up to the human justice system to give him what he deserved. He would probably be killed in the county jail before trial or afterwards in the state prison. She couldn't imagine he could keep his lycanthropy secret for very long. Hopefully now, with his confession on record and

Affird sidelined, the authorities would leave the werewolves alone.

"I'm going to stand at the entrance to the garage so I can see when the police arrive. Is your phone on? Okay, when you hear it ring, you'll know it's time to shift," Josie said to Thelma Lou. "You," she looked at Kevin, "are staying on this bus so you don't get any crazy ideas about running away. And if you act up, Thelma Lou will rip your intestines out. Understand?"

Kevin nodded. But he had a smirk as his cockiness returned.

"Let me get his gun out of here," Josie said.

Thelma Lou growled and shook her head. She made some noises that Josie understood as about fingerprints and not disturbing evidence.

"Okay, then," Josie said, walking toward the rear of the bus and closing the compartment in the floor that held the rifle. "Don't let him anywhere near that."

Josie exited the bus and used a lever to close the door behind her, although it was severely damaged from her forced entrance. She walked toward the sunshine outside of the garage. Her joints ached as they normally did, compounded by lingering pain from the wounds she received in the fight with Kevin.

Shifting to wolf form always made her feel decades younger, but, still, she was getting old for this. She couldn't keep her role as alpha much longer—the ability to fight and win was a requirement. At least she wouldn't insist on being killed before giving up that role. She would gladly give it up to a worthy protege. Although she had to admit it would be difficult to live with her fallen status.

The bus was parked in a dead-end at the far end of the garage. As she neared the entrance and the ramp to the upper levels, two cars passed her. Mary, and then Stan and Edith.

They all waved to her, which made her feel good despite all the recent tragedy. Part of the anger she felt toward Kevin was from knowing the murderer was one of their own.

She stood by the entrance, with a good view of the main gate to the complex off A1A, Ocean Road. It was hot and humid, the breeze from the ocean not finding its way to this side of the garage. She wished there was a place to sit down.

Finally, two police cars and an unmarked car between them arrived at the gate. The attendant opened the gate arm and the small convoy drove toward the garage.

She called Thelma Lou's number and listened to it ring until it went to voicemail. Did she hear it ring so she could shift in time?

The first police car arrived at the entrance to the garage. The officer lowered his window.

"Hello officer," Josie said. "We trapped the murderer in that bus up there at the end of the first level."

The cop, a fat, older guy, smiled patronizingly. "Oh, you captured him, did you?"

"Yes, officer. My friend is watching over him, but I want you to know in advance that the murder weapon, a rifle, is also on the bus, in a hidden compartment."

The cop's face turned serious. He said something into the radio handset attached to his vest at his shoulder. He drove slowly into the garage followed by the other cars. Josie walked at a fast pace behind them.

The cars slowed down at a moderate distance from the bus and parked across the lane to prevent the bus from escaping. Two uniformed officers and one in plainclothes got out of the cars with guns drawn. One of them had a shotgun.

"Police," the first cop shouted. "Remain where you are. We're coming into the bus. Do not move."

The first officer approached the door of the bus, covered by the one with the shotgun. The detective, the only one not wearing an armored vest, took up the rear.

Suddenly, the door of the bus flew open, and Kevin stumbled out.

"He has the gun!" Thelma Lou shouted from inside the bus.

And, yes, Josie had a glimpse of the rifle in the blur of movement as Kevin practically fell from the bus.

And all three cops opened fire.

Innumerable gunshots echoed in the concrete cavern so loudly they hurt Josie's ears.

Kevin flew backwards, hitting a support column, and crumpled to the floor in a spreading pool of blood.

In human form, he's as vulnerable as anyone, Josie thought.

The rifle lay beside him in the lake of blood. But Josie hadn't actually seen him holding it.

As the police surrounded Kevin's body, making sure he wasn't a threat, Thelma Lou stepped out of the bus in human form. She met Josie's eyes. Hers spoke of defiance. And vengeance.

## 2 7

## GNOME JUSTICE

It was the Werewolf Women's Club's first hunting excursion in weeks. To celebrate the end of their communal nightmare, Josie took them to the Ocala National Forest. They traveled north in a brand-new bus, purchased with funds raised in bake sales and a charity fashion show, and they stayed overnight in a lodge just outside of the park's border. The trip did wonders for the group's morale.

Plunging through the forest with its tall oaks and longleaf pines bisected with shafts of silver moonlight was invigorating. Catching the scents of the abundant game was electrifying. There were many more deer here than around Jellyfish Beach, and the pack feasted on a buck they caught. At one point, they caught the scent of an endangered Florida panther, but it wisely kept its distance from the pack.

Just after midnight, Josie, Thelma Lou, and Tanya came upon a black bear. They had it surrounded, and it reared on its hind legs, roaring in challenge. It was a large, muscular beast with paws the size of dinner plates, but the three of them could have taken it down with the wolf technique of attacking from multiple fronts, distracting, and wearing it down with quick thrusts and retreats.

But they didn't want to attack it. The predators, comprised of three different species if you included the human sides, regarded each other with respect. Josie knew the bear had a tough existence. It didn't have charity fashion shows or potluck dinners. It had to fight and forage for every meal, survive the elements, and avoid human hunters. She felt as if it looked at them with an understanding that they were not typical wolves, and as apex predators they had much in common. There was wisdom in those dark eyes.

They turned away and now were onto the scent of raccoons.

Until the shots rang out.

The three wolves looked at each other, sharing the sentiment, "oh no, not again."

The main body of the pack was up ahead, in the direction of the gunshots. Josie and her two companions raced through the trees to catch up to them.

More gunshots splintered the night. Thelma Lou whimpered with concern. Then came the sound of a human screaming. It was a man shrieking like an infant.

With Josie in the lead, the three women werewolves followed a narrow game trail. Josie caught the scent of a panicked human nearby. They rounded a slight hill and suddenly the human was in front of them.

He sprinted toward them in blind terror. He wore night-vision goggles and a dark T-shirt with large white lettering that said, "Boogaloo Brigade." It was one of the guys who had played army-man in the forest when Josie surveilled them.

As soon as he saw the three werewolves loping toward him, he shrieked and ran from the trail. A loud, painful-sounding *crack* of a skull hitting wood echoed as he slammed into a tree and went down.

Josie stopped and sniffed him. He was alive but unconscious. The moron had two handguns strapped to his body but had made no attempt to use them. The problem was, one or more of his comrades had, and Josie worried about her fellow were-wolves. They should be able to survive being shot with a normal bullet, but no one knew if that was one hundred percent guaranteed.

A little farther along the trail they came upon a large clearing. The rest of the pack was there, a few lying on the grass in the center gnawing on bones while the others were gathered around the trunks of two live oaks. Five Boogaloo Brigade members clung to the branches, looking like very depressed chimpanzees.

"Are any of you hurt?" Josie asked Wanda, who sat on her haunches below the nearest tree.

"I got nicked, but I'm healing fast," Wanda said. "The human who shot me is not doing well."

Now Josie knew what bones the girls were gnawing on.

"These jokers had a captive, a woman park ranger. They were abusing her. After we tore into them, the ranger escaped. I think they got the message not to mess with women anymore," Wanda said.

"They need to stay healthy for the civil war they want to start," Josie said.

"Are them wolves talkin'?" asked a voice from the tree.

"Shhh, you idiot. Be quiet so they'll go away."

If they only knew that werewolves could climb trees, Josie thought with a smile.

She gave an abrupt bark and all the wolves stood at attention. It was time to end the hunt and return to the bus, shift, and head to the lodge for a good night's sleep.

Josie's lead in identifying Kevin as the murderer helped make the pack more loyal to her as alpha. Josie's show of strength swayed even Tanya, who was an ally of Kevin. Despite the old tart not liking Josie very much.

They returned to the bus. Their new driver was Cookie, a younger member of the Women's club and pack. From now on, their hunt excursions would be women-only.

"To the Werewolf Women's Club!" Josie toasted after they had shifted back to human on the bus and pulled the wine from the coolers.

"May we be forever strong," the members said.

No one seemed to mind that the piles of discarded wolf fur still needed to be vacuumed.

MISSY WAS on her way to meet Matt for breakfast early in the morning, two days after they returned from Central Florida. It was the day of the week when bulk trash was picked up, and Missy was surprised to see piles of discarded garden gnomes at several homes, piled at the curb with the broken furniture and unwanted toys.

Had everyone in Jellyfish Beach realized that their gnomes were potential threats? No, it was more likely that the demon, as it departed, dumped the gnomes there in a fit of pique. At least they were inanimate again.

Sipping her hot tea at the ocean-side cafe, Missy watched the joggers stream past the sand dunes and told Matt what she had seen.

"I hope there will be no more trouble from gnomes," Matt

said. "There haven't been any reports of freak accidental deaths in town since your mother took care of the demon."

"I'm pretty sure it's finished. I can feel the void in the spiritual realm since the black magic left."

"I can't argue with that."

"But I don't feel this story has ended," Missy said.

"What do you mean?"

"Justice has not been fully served. Innocent people died, and no one payed a price for it."

"Technically, the demon killed them," Matt said. "How do you punish a demon?"

"I guess you have to ask Satan to do that."

"No thanks."

"Then there's my mother, who summoned the demon. She knew that a demon means trouble. But she didn't order it to kill anyone. The actual culprit here is Frank. He's the one who started it all when he hired my mother."

"Did he ask her to make the gnomes kill their owners?"

"You know he didn't," Missy said. "But he asked for an uprising and it killed people, as often happens in uprisings. So it's like murder in the third degree or manslaughter."

They went silent when the server dropped off their food: banana crepes for Missy and an omelet for Matt.

"Are you implying Frank should be criminally charged?" Matt asked with his mouth full.

Missy sighed. "Not really. You know I can't bring law enforcement into the supernatural world."

"You can get the survivors of the victims to sue him."

"The supernatural doesn't belong in a human court of law, period. But still, I just don't feel right letting Frank wash his hands of what he caused."

"Maybe you can curse him or something," Matt said while

shoving toast in his mouth.

"I don't do curses. That's a black magic thing."

Matt shrugged and shoveled copious amounts of egg into his face. She didn't understand why men felt they had to break speed records every time they ate. No one was timing him. He wouldn't get a medal for finishing his breakfast before Missy had her third bite.

"I wish I understood *why* Frank did this," she said. "I thought most of the gnome-liberation groups did it with a sense of irony, as performance art. But Frank seemed so serious about it."

"Yeah, like he believed the lawn ornaments had some real gnome in them."

Missy had an idea. "I think he needs a beatdown from a real gnome. Real gnomes aren't the adorable characters these figurines represent. They dislike humans."

"You know gnomes?" Matt asked, finally wiping the detritus of his feeding frenzy from his face with his napkin.

"I treated one once for gnome toe."

"For what?"

"A fungal infection. Do you want details?"

"No thanks. I didn't know there were gnomes in Florida."

"There aren't many. They prefer to live underground, in mines and such, guarding gemstones and precious metals. And Florida doesn't have much of an underground with its high water table. But there are some gnomes upstate guarding the pure water of the natural springs."

"How do you contact a gnome?" Matt asked. "Do you summon them?"

"No. They're not spirits. They're living creatures. Supernatural ones, of course. I'll need to reach out with my magick."

"What kind of beatdown do you want this gnome to give to

Frank?"

"I'll explain the situation and let the gnome decide."

"Reaching out" to a gnome proved to be more complicated than Missy realized. She had no idea how to do it. Don Mateo didn't know either. She had to go through several books of spells and magical lore before she came across a spell to request an audience with a gnome.

She had to wait two days for a quarter moon. Then, atop a flat rock facing east, she placed a clump of rosemary, a pound of salt, a coin of silver, and a coin of gold. That wasn't all. The spell also called for a cup of ale, a small cake, and a can of Cheese Wiz—why, she didn't know. Then she attempted to recite a short verse in a language she didn't recognize. When this was completed, she was supposed to close her eyes and "clear her thoughts of all things impure." That's what the spell instructions said. Really.

She sat in her front yard in the dark beside the stone paver she'd placed there with all the offerings. She kept her eyes closed for what seemed like hours.

Until she heard the high-pitched belch.

She opened her eyes, and a gnome stood before her.

He was a little shorter than the average garden gnome and rather slim, not of the chubby, cartoonish proportions of the lawn ornaments. Despite his diminutive size, he had managed to finish off the ale and the cake and was squirting the can of cheese into his mouth.

"Thank you for coming," Missy said.

"Yeah, what do you want?" He had a high, nasal voice that matched his stature. But she didn't understand why he had a Brooklyn accent.

"I'm asking you to serve justice in the name of gnomes everywhere."

"Huh?"

Missy explained the complicated story. Simply mentioning garden gnomes made the real gnome furious. He said they were a tremendous insult to his people and that even hinting that garden gnomes were spiritually connected to the real creatures was incredibly offensive.

"Okay, I'll help you. This guy needs some tutoring," the gnome said. "When I'm done with him, he'll see the error of his ways. Trust me. Now give me a ride to his place."

"It's in the middle of the night."

"And I'm his worst nightmare. Let's go."

Missy opened the passenger door of her car and the gnome took a running leap and landed on the seat.

"Maybe we should use a child seat—um, never mind," Missy said, receiving a deadly glare from the gnome.

She got in the car and backed out of the driveway. The silence during the ride was awkward.

"I'm Missy, by the way."

"We don't give our names out," the gnome said, sitting on the armrest so he could see out the windshield. "Your name gives someone else power over you."

Missy understood. The power of your name was a well-known law of magic and the supernatural. What she didn't know was how this little guy would teach Frank a lesson. Was he just going to trip him like a plastic garden gnome?

Missy turned off her headlights before pulling up in front of Frank's house in a neighborhood that had large lots but drab homes. The gnome pushed the button to lower the window.

"How are you going to get in?" Missy whispered.

The gnome looked at her like she was an idiot and jumped out of the car. He scurried away so quickly she didn't see where he went.

Gnomes were born with a small amount of natural magic, but Missy didn't know what they could do with it. Breaking into homes was apparently an example.

She sat in the car for a while, getting more worried about what the gnome was doing to Frank. What if he killed him? Someone might have taken note of her license plate. She drummed her thumbs nervously on the steering wheel.

"Let's go."

She jumped. The gnome was in the car again, sitting on the armrest.

"What did you do to him?" she asked after the gnome closed the window.

"I can't divulge that," the gnome said. "Let's just say that I disabused him of his stupid romantic notions about plastic lawn ornaments. And I encouraged him to understand—and I mean the kind of encouragement that comes with a big doctor's bill—that he needs to make restitution to the victims of his cockamamie scheme. He assured me he's gonna set up a generous victims' fund anonymously."

"That's awesome," Missy said. "I guess." She still worried about her license plate number.

When they returned to her house, the gnome hopped out and climbed on top of the rock with the offerings.

"Your request for my visit has been fulfilled," he said. "Now I'm gonna take my leave. Consider your problem fixed."

He disappeared. The salt and the coins disappeared with him.

No more gnomes. Those were words to live by.

## THE END

# AFTERWORD

**GET A FREE E-BOOK**

Sign up for my newsletter and get *Hangry as Hell*, a Freaky Florida novella, for free. It's available exclusively for members of my mailing list. If you join, you'll get news, fun articles, and lots of free book promotions, delivered only a couple of times a month. No spam at all, and you can unsubscribe at any time.

Sign up at wardparker.com

**ENJOY THIS BOOK? PLEASE LEAVE A REVIEW**

In the Amazon universe, the number of reviews readers leave can make or break a book. I would be very grateful if you could spend just a few minutes and write a fair and honest review. It can be as short or long as you wish. Just go to amazon.com, search for "gnome coming ward parker," and click the link for leaving reviews. Thanks!

**COMING NEXT IN FREAKY FLORIDA**

Book 5: *Going Batty*
**A vampire tale even a caveman would love.**

The retired vampires at Squid Tower in Jellyfish Beach, Florida, have it good. Until some ancient vampires show up. These strange bloodsuckers can turn into bats, unlike modern vampires. And they're also a bunch of Neanderthals. No, really. Not all Neanderthals went extinct. Some went undead. And now they want to rule all the vampires of Florida.

Missy Mindle, midlife witch and nurse to elderly supernaturals, uses her magick to help her vampire patients fight back. But when the Neanderthals start taking vampire hostages, and kidnap the daughter of Missy's cousin, get ready for a conflict of prehistoric proportions. Find *Going Batty* at Amazon or wardparker.com

**OTHER BOOKS IN FREAKY FLORIDA**

Have you read Book 1, *Snowbirds of Prey?*
**Retirement is deadly.**
Centuries-old vampires who play pickleball. Aging were-wolves who surf naked beneath the full moon. To survive, they must keep their identities secret, but all the dead humans popping up may spell their doom. Can Missy Mindle, midlife amateur witch, save them? Get *Snowbirds of Prey* at Amazon or wardparker.com

Or Book 2, *Invasive Species?*
**Gators. Pythons. Iguanas.**
**Dragons?**
**Why not? It's Florida.**

Missy, midlife amateur witch and nurse to elderly supernaturals, has two problems. First, she found a young, injured dragon in the Everglades with a price on its head. Second, her vampire patient Schwartz has disappeared after getting caught by Customs with werewolf blood. (It's like Viagra for vampires. Don't ask.) Order *Invasive Species* today at Amazon or wardparker.com

Or Book 3, *Fate Is a Witch*?

**Embrace your destiny. Even if it kills you.**

Missy Mindle has two mysteries to solve. First, who is making a series of dangerous magick attacks against her that appear to be tests of her growing witchy abilities? And who is stealing corpses from funeral homes in Jellyfish Beach? When an embalmer is murdered, one of Missy's patients, a werewolf, is arrested. Can she exonerate him? Oh, and don't forget the hordes of ghouls and Hemingway lookalikes. Who will stop them? Find out by ordering the book at Amazon or wardparker.com

# ABOUT THE AUTHOR

Ward is a Florida native and author of the Freaky Florida series, a romp through the Sunshine State with witches, vampires, werewolves, dragons, and other bizarre, mythical creatures such as #FloridaMan. He also pens the Zeke Adams Series of Florida-noir mysteries and The Teratologist Series of historical supernatural thrillers. Connect with him on social media: Twitter (@wardparker), Facebook (wardparkerauthor), Goodreads, or wardparker.com.

## ALSO BY WARD PARKER

The Zeke Adams Florida-noir mystery series. You can buy *Pariah* at Amazon or wardparker.com

The Teratologist series of historical paranormal thrillers. Buy the first novel at Amazon or wardparker.com

"Gods and Reptiles," a Lovecraftian short story. Buy it at Amazon.com

"The Power Doctor," a historical witchcraft short story. Get it at Amazon.com

Made in United States
North Haven, CT
25 September 2023

41960806R00161